GREEN IS FOR GREED

BC COWLING

BC Cowling

ISBN 978-1-7362884-2-9
eBook ISBN 978-1-7362884-0-5

Edited by Kate Seger
Interior Design by Eli Neff-Akridge
Cover Design by NappyHead Studios

PROLOGUE

I n previous lifetimes he had been a she and often
had pushed the then acceptable limits of behavior
in various directions. She had enjoyed a few periods of
rest and harmony, had railed at freedoms lost, but
mostly had slugged out the slow, small steps of Soul in
the human consciousness torn between love and power,
reaching for a glimmer of Its true self.

In this lifetime...

...his parents named him Zither. Zither P. Blevins.
The Blevins had agreed the baby's gender would deter-
mine which parent chose its name. Mrs. Blevins
yearned for a daughter and thought "Marion" would be
both a fine name for a boy, only a vowel away from
"Marian," her choice if the baby was a girl. Mr. Blevins
loved nothing more in life than playing his hand-made
Bavarian Zither. When the baby was born male, Mr.
Blevins was adamant they stick to the arrangement,

saying to his wife, "A deal is a deal," and immortalizing his musical passion through his son.

Little Zither would not tell anyone what curious middle name lay quietly behind the "P." He was not enthralled by his first name either, but lived with it for eleven years. During the summer of Zither's eleventh year, his father bought a small sailboat from a friend and a Navy Commander's cap from the Army-Navy Surplus store in Indianapolis. Zither claimed the hat. Sporting the Commander's cap stuffed half full of wadded newspaper to keep it on his head, Zither and his father set sail in the boat on a nearby lake. Zither was named honorary Commander. The day was windy and raw. Experienced sailors stayed home during March in Indiana, listening to the state high school basketball championships, but Mr. Blevins did not follow basketball or weather reports.

Zither, then his cap, got wet. By the time Mr. Blevins was soaked through to his skin and shivering, the newspaper in Zither's hat had wilted. They turned back toward the dock. Zither struggled with the mainsail rope, and Mr. Blevins manned the tiller, guiding them toward the safety of the shore. On what should have been their last tack downwind, wind and spray caused Zither's cap to shift over his eyes. He was blinded, just as Mr. Blevins was nearly bounced off the back of the boat by a large swell. Mr. Blevins yelled. Zither heard him, tightened his grip on the rope, and grabbed for his cap. He felt the rope slip through his fingers and clutched it harder. Mr. Blevins righted himself. Zither hit his cap with stiff fingers, knocking it farther over his eyes. His father yelled for him to let some slack into the rope. Holding onto the rope and regaining his vision consumed all of Zither's attention, so he did not understand his father. The rope began to hurt his hand. Mr. Blevins yelled again as the boat pitched.

Zither's fingers were numb, but finally, they found the front of his cap and pushed it back. He looked down into the water, not out over it. His other hand, frozen around the rope, burned. Then Zither was in the water. Mr. Blevins, too, was thrown overboard as the sailboat overturned. The spill happened near the shore, so Mr. Blevins and Zither saved themselves and dragged the boat on its side through the water to the dock. After loading the boat onto the trailer, they drove home, dripping, freezing, and silent. After Mr. Blevins thawed out, he regained his sense of humor. They compared notes and discovered that by holding fast to the rope in a strong gust, when Zither needed to let it play out so less wind would catch the sail, he had caused the wind to push the boat over into the water.

Zither had managed to keep a hold of the Commander's cap as he had swum ashore. He was soon hounded by his family and friends with the now-teasing name of Commander, which he secretly loved. When the joke tarnished, he kept the name going. By the time he was an adult, only his family knew his true name.

By the time he was an adult, Zither—Commander— had also developed a unique ability to leave his physical body and explore the Invisible Worlds consciously. Eventually, he crossed paths with a group of people who shared his interest and, to some degree, his talents.

A combination of Inner World Travel and Outer World marauding left Commander Blevins wide open for Psychic Parasites. These Parasites are beings who have become so out of balance in their physical body that, when they leave it, they are unable to move into their next reincarnation. Trapped in the physical realm, the Parasites have needs but no physical body to satisfy their desires.

These beings lose their gender and become "Its." The overriding passion that keeps a Psychic Parasite in the physical world past its physical body's life often determines what It craves after dropping the body. The only way a Parasite can satisfy Its craving is to attach to a Host being who still has his or her physical body.

A Host being makes himself available—or not—to these Parasites by choices made. After many decisions in a particular direction, the Host being's aura develops a small rupture; even more choices of a similar nature and fractures become fissures. When this fissure is large enough, a Parasite can sprout a small tube from part of Its no-longer-physical body and attach it to the Host being who has been abusing himself or herself.

When this attachment takes place, a relationship begins. What the Parasite wants, the Host being now begins to desire. What the Host being experiences, the Parasite starts to experience. The relationship continues—usually without the Host being becoming aware of the Parasite—for a short while, occasionally lasting throughout the remainder of the Host being's current lifetime in his or her physical body.

Commander Blevins, rarely satisfied with the mundane, compressed several lifetimes of risk-taking into a mere score of years. The result of this mania for life on the edge, without the clarity of wisdom, was an intimate relationship with Psychic Parasites. Awareness only sometimes follows Blevins' experience, however, and he now struggles blindly with his own webs of Cause and Effect, occupied with simple survival, spiritual growth, and hazy apparition.

ONE

FROM WHENCE HE CAME

"I'm so excited I could just molt," Ember said.

"Molt? That's a real talent," said Pins.

"Well, hanging around this Bozo's is dead-end stuff."

"I want to watch a Wire-Sitter molt."

"Oh, can it, Charcoal Butt."

"Gripe, Gripe, Gripe," Pins said.

"Am not."

"Are too."

Pins had been named by a gnarly old acquaintance who thought the youngster's pin-striping was hilarious. Pins had continued the custom of naming new arrivals and had dubbed Its new, uninvited company, Ember.

"Lookeyloo! There's an invitation if I ever saw one." Ember said and pointed It's stumpy little arm down and across the street toward a skinny fellow walking and shaking at the same time. Small tremors ran up and down the man's body.

"That's a piece of work, all right. Probably gonna last another month at best. But be my guest, but unhook first."

"Nah, I think I'll just snake a line over to Ol' Graceful, there, and still keep a hold of the Slug, too."

"Not on anybody's life," said Pins. "I'm not going to be party to that kind of blowout. Two hooks are guaranteed chaos. Not in my backyard, Jose."

"Oh, this is childish. I'm not talking anymore," Ember huffed.

The Two sat in silence on the drooping high wire that ran from the pole in the middle of the block to the pole at the end of the block. Cars drove by. Buses threw soot into the air at Their feet. People walked by in varying states of consciousness and lucidity: climbing or descending the hill beneath them. No one minded or noticed the two Wire Sitters, but then people usually do not react to what they cannot see. Special people can see the unseen. These people are rare, though, and do not come along often, especially on sunny afternoons on Fillmore Avenue in the Lower Lower Haight of San Francisco.

The Two Wire Sitters loved to bicker, but for now were locked in Their funk, short-circuiting Their warped little imaginations and making conversation difficult.

A dirty grey line of fuzzy light ran from Pins diagonally across the street and through the intersection on the uphill side of where It sat. The beam of light hung like a cord stretched over half a block, pulsated slightly, and emanated a feeling of small-time evil. Had one of the special people who can see unseen things seen this cord of light and stood on a tall ladder to smell it, they would have wrinkled their nose and climbed down from the ladder quickly. The light cord smelled rotten.

The light cord swayed in the breeze, even when there was no breeze, which was seldom on Fillmore in the Lower Lower Haight. The current that blew the light cord back and forth, though, was not the same breeze that stirred newspapers and played havoc with Commander Blevins' state of health.

Blevins was directly involved with this light cord, which at the moment stretched across the intersection of Fillmore and Page Streets. It ran above the buildings' tops, down the roof above apartment number 307 at 600 Page. The cord passed through the apartment's ceiling and ended by implanting in the middle of Blevins' back. He did not know this: Blevins was not one of those special people who could see things most people could not see. Had he been able to see this dirty grey line of fuzzy light, he would have reached around and jerked it out. Commander Blevins was, after all, at times, a sensible fellow, not without talents.

At this particular juncture of Time and Space—ruling as they do in the Lower Spiritual Worlds—Commander Blevins sat in the kitchen patiently disassembling an old Burroughs Adding Machine. It was eleven o'clock. The oven was on low; its door was open, and the dirty grey light cord passed through the back of the white kitchen chair in which sat Commander Blevins. The light cord quivered slightly.

In previous days, after one of Commander Blevins' more memorable forays into worlds unseen, Pins' light cord had been a lustrous, shiny black and had glowed brilliantly. Pins thought Its cord was majestic. Soon after Ember arrived, everything changed. Ember craved only warmth. That Ember had picked Commander Blevins as Its host was a combination of fortune and karma: good fortune for Ember, short-run bad karma for Commander Blevins. At some point in Its evolution, the Soul that was today known as Commander Blevins in the Physical World would learn the particular lesson underlying Its relationship with Ember. Then Ember would get to face Its next test. So it went.

Today what tied them together was another light cord: a well-defined, dull-red line of warm light. It looked much like the electric oven's heating element when Commander Blevins turned the thermostat knob to high and left the door open.

This well-defined, dull-red light cord was fastened to Blevins' back. It ran through the chair, up into the ceiling, out the roof, across Filmore and Page's intersection, directly into the yahooney of Ember. Pins had a yahooney, too. Yahooneys enable Misplaced Entities to generate light cords and attach to people, animals, and other life forms. This attachment process keeps a Misplaced Entity—or ME, as They are called by those who call them anything—misplaced. Had these two Beings that were now MEs not been so attached to one passion or another when They left the Physical World, They would have been able to transit in a normal way and get on with their development. Instead, They became stranded in an in-between level that is not usually a rest stop in Soul's evolution.

The MEs lived the result of a lifetime spent in the Physical World, presuming that life was a singular occurrence fully perceivable by the five senses. Contrary to that limited viewpoint, life does not stop after death. Death and birth are different ends of any single loop in an ongoing spiral. Birth on one level follows death on the same or another level.

There were both differences and similarities between these two MEs. Ember was fat, dumb, and happy, a condition It could—with the cooperation of Commander Blevins—occupy for an embarrassingly long time. Pins was whithered, dense, and wretched. The arrival of Ember had a direct impact on Pins' unfortunate state of affairs.

They shared a basic trait of all MEs: Their focus. The MEs were wholly consumed with themselves, with ME... the striking characteristic of a Monomoron, a name of a species that also describes the species. Some MEs could not even say the word "you" in polite conversation with other MEs. MEs did, however, revel in slandering Their host whenever They did not draw up enough juice through Their light cords to satiate Their tunnel-visioned little minds.

"Here he comes now," said Ember. It fluttered Its energy around and through Pins' aura.

"Hey, cut that out, Emberhead." Pins moved away a little. "Where's he coming from?"

"He's coming from his apartment, oh Winsome Apparition of Bratwurst."

And that's precisely what Commander Blevins did. He opened the front door to 600 Page Street, squeezed through it with his two bags of laundry, wearing a good portion of the rest of his wardrobe, and walked across Page Street. Two light cords followed him, whipping in an unseen breeze and trailing back up to the MEs sitting on the telephone wire.

TWO
ANOTHER DAY OF SHIVERING

A barely audible tap-tap-tap came from the front door. Commander Blevins had just returned home from putting his laundry and many dimes into the dryer. He got up from the white kitchen table and bumped the corner with his hip. Several hundred small metal parts rattled. They used to be a Burroughs Model 17B Adding Machine.

"Rats," he said. The yogurt tub, which held a quart of undiluted household cleaner, sloshed and spilled onto the towel spread over half the table. There was nothing to be done about the spill except to let it soak into the towel. He made a mental note to wash the towel before using it in the bathroom again, put the lid on the yogurt tub, and clicked it shut.

Commander Blevins shuffled across the hardwood floor in his yellow and orange "Goofy" slippers as he made his way to the front door. Two light cords brought up the rear. Pressing one eye to the peephole, he jumped back suddenly. Staring back at him through the peephole had been another eye, a big eye. A muted squeak from the hallway accompanied the eye. Blevins took a deep breath, reached for the doorknob, and open the door. He shivered as the cold air from the hall whirled in around him. Standing in the hall was a middle-aged woman wearing a purple hat and a star-tled expression. "Oh, hello," she blurted.

"Good day to you," Commander Blevins said. "In what way might I be of assistance."

"Is this the office...er home of Commander Blevins?" She kneaded her handbag.

He pointed to a small card pinned to the door just below the peephole, "Read that."

"Oh, dear, I shall have to get my glasses."

Blevins waited patiently while the woman rummaged through her purse. Finally, she pulled out a burgundy and lavender striped glasses' case, opened it, and put on an old fashioned pair of spectacles. Squint-ing, she read the card out loud:

COMMANDER Z. P. BLEVINS
Purveyor of The Akashic Records
Occult Debunking

She removed her glasses and said, "Did I get it right?"

Commander Blevins nodded.

"Is Commander Blevins in?"

"Barely. One more step and I will be out. Is that all you wish to know?" Commander Blevins had a very dry sense of humor, especially when he was interrupted in the middle of a project.

"Oh, gracious no," she said, "There is so much I wish to know. May I come in, please? I can pay you."

Blevins' eyes brightened. "Of course you can, dear lady. But I warn you that payment is rarely necessary." She slipped her glasses into their case, tucked it into her purse, and permitted Commander Blevins to guide her by the arm into the flat's foyer. The main room was off to the left, and he accompanied her across it and to a deep green velvet love seat near the window. Other than the kitchen, bath, one large walk-in closet, and a connecting hallway-foyer, this room was the apartment: living room, bedroom, study, and consultation room. Commander Blevins prepared for a consultation.

"My it is warm in here," she said, noticing there were three heaters in the room.

"Here, let me turn that down." Commander Blevins reached down to the heater next to the old Victorian love seat and turned the thermostat from 9 to 4. The little fan stopped its whirring.

"Thank you," she said.

"May I get you some tea," he asked, "I've just made a fresh pot."

"Why yes, that would be so nice." She wasn't thirsty and was already overheated, but thought a little tea would be refreshing. She was also chronically polite. Commander Blevins padded off to the kitchen, wrapped warmly in his floor-length terry cloth robe, light cords following.

Moments later, he reappeared with two steaming mugs of tea. He handed one to her and then sat down across the room in his overstuffed reading chair. The light cords blended into the back of the chair on their way up to and through the ceiling.

"Now tell me...what was your name?"

"Gladys. Gladys Frumpwooler." Gladys Frump-wooler looked around frantically for somewhere to set the steaming cup of tea.

"I see. And tell me Mrs...? Miss...?"

"It's Mrs. Mrs. Frumpwooler. But I'm a widow. Malvandian passed on three years ago this August, bless his heart." She sniffled a moment and started to reach for her hankie. The mug of tea was too hot to be held by a single hand, though, so she quickly abandoned the idea. She was too polite to set the cup on the floor.

"Well, Mrs. Frumpwooler, what is it that brings you to my doorstep." Blevins took a deep swallow of his tea.

"Commander Blevins, I don't quite know how to begin." She paused. Her mind focused on the reason for her visit Mrs. Frumpwooler relaxed her vigil with the hot mug. She took a long sip of tea. Her glasses steamed up. Molten lava flowed down her throat. Her eyes bulged, she opened her mouth wide, and sweat beaded on many parts of her body.

"I can see that this is something that affects you

deeply, Mrs. Frumpwooler. Please take your time and begin anywhere you like."

She did take her time. She had to. Slowly her breath returned, then her voice. The shock of the tea had washed away all reserve. "Thank you for your patience," she said with a slight rasp in her voice. "I was walking around the Palace of Fine Arts Tuesday afternoon. It was a pleasant day, sunny, and a crisp breeze was blowing off the Bay. I passed a large tree and felt something pop." She paused for a minute and took another sip of her tea. Gasping moderately, she continued, "As I walked on wondering what this pop was all about, nothing felt akimbo, you understand," she fluttered her eyelashes. "I slowly became aware that where I was wasn't where I had been. If you follow."

Commander Blevins nodded his head, careful to do nothing to interrupt his new Client. She resumed her monologue, "I stopped, stood still, and listened. Sounds were echoing from where I couldn't tell, and the breeze had died completely. These were sounds I had never heard before, and yet they were as familiar as...as Malvandian's snoring was for nearly thirty-four years. I decided to walk on a bit further and did so. Then I stopped again and turned around. You know, I just don't know why I did that, but I did. That's when I got the shock of my life. Standing right behind me...was myself! And I had my back to myself. Can you imagine!"

Commander Blevins could imagine and did. He put himself in Mrs. Frumpwooler's picture and looked around at the grounds of The Palace of Fine Arts. There was nothing unusual about what he saw or heard: just a run of the mill sub-Astral transmitigation. He shifted back to listening to Mrs. Frumpwooler talk as she sat in his apartment, while simultaneously watching her scene unfold in the Inner Worlds.

"...everything I did. It was so fascinating. And a bit unnerving, I must say. Anyway, I finally decided just to run after myself. I was starting to get alarmed, not knowing how long I might be stuck where I was."

Commander Blevins watched as Mrs. Frumpwooler hurled herself at her physical body in the Inner World replay.

"That's when I saw this silvery-looking cord. It was coming straight out of my stomach! And it curved around in front of my...other...self. Oh, this is all so difficult to get a hold of." She paused, drank some more tea without noticeable effect, then continued. "So was I surprised when, as I took the first step—thinking, 'what is this silver thing coming out of my stomach'—I felt a rushing sensation and heard a volcano or tornado or something rumble in the distance. Just as quickly as that, I was back with myself." Mrs. Frumpwooler looked up from the area rug in front of the love seat and directly into Commander Blevins' eyes, and said, "Now, isn't that the darndest thing you have ever heard?"

Commander Blevins shook his head gently and withdrew his attention from the shimmering ground around The Palace of Fine Arts.

"No," he said.

"Oh, yes. Later that day, I told my neighbor, Mrs. Glockenspiel, about it, and she told me about you. She said to give you her very warmest. She said you were always catching a chill. 'Poor dear man, he's always catching a chill.' she said. She said she used to bump into you at the strangest places. And that you knew about the 'other worlds,' as she called them."

"Thank you for the kind message." He vaguely remembered a woman who might have been this Mrs. Glockenspiel. For a couple of months, when he was researching the Fall of Lemuria from the Inner Worlds, he had run into an extremely tall, thin woman several times a week in the Physical World. They had met in odd places, like the unisex bathroom at a little coffee shop in the Mission, or coming out of a thicket of bushes in Golden Gate Park. Once, he had been speared in the back with a loaf of bread while laboring up a hill in North Beach. When he had turned around, he had come face to face with this same woman. She was holding a slightly blunted loaf of sourdough bread as though it were a battering ram. She had smiled. He had smiled. Then he had hurried on his way.

"Well, I now understand what brought you here." Commander Blevins was silent for a moment. "Do you have any idea what you would like to do, now that you have arrived?"

Mrs. Frumpwooler looked utterly blank. Finally, she said, "Why I thought you would know what to do next, Commander Blevins. Don't you?"

"Well, I know many things that can be done next."

"Is it a matter of money? I have several hundred..."

"Oh, don't profane your experience with talk of money. What needs to be determined is why this happened to you. And why it happened at this particular point in time. It could be, for example, a significant zoidation which represents deeds left undone in the past. It could be a whirling dervish out to have some fun who picked you at random. Or it could be something you planned long ago to wake you up at this point in time and space to accomplish something preordained."

"Do you really think so, Commander Blevins? This is so exciting. How do we find out?"

"There is only one way, Mrs. Frumpwooler. Only one way." He hesitated while anticipation grew in the room, emanating from Mrs. Frumpwooler. "We must Journey back to the root. To the fundament of your existence."

"Where is that?"

"The Akashic Records."

"Your card on the door said something about that, didn't it?"

"Yes, of course. Do you want to go?"

"Yes!"

"Some people come back changed. You can never tell what will happen when you open your past. You must be completely sure you wish to know."

"I am completely sure. Can we go there now?"

"Yes, we can." Commander Blevins relaxed into his chair for a moment. The light cords quivered.

Outside, a half a block away, the Ember and Pins also quivered. Ember quivered with anticipation and fear. At the end of Commander Blevins' last foray to the Akashic Records, Pins had attached to Their host during Commander Blevins' 're-entry' into the Physical Worlds. Pins might drop off next time; They might have more company; the Slug might return even more drained, or he might not return at all. It was like rolling the dice. Pins quivered without knowing why: It was generally excitable, and although It had experienced plenty of opportunities to figure out the process, this newest member of the club was solidly in the dark about many of the fundamental laws governing life as an ME.

Mrs. Frumpwooler interrupted Commander Blevins' reverie. "What do we do first?"

Commander Blevins bolted to his feet, empty teacup in one hand, and said, "We shall have some more tea." He marched over to where Mrs. Frumpwooler sat, picked up her cup, and strode into the kitchen. Mrs. Frumpwooler sighed.

THREE

UP, UP AND AWAY

After several minutes of clanking, groaning, and off-key humming, Commander Blevins reappeared with the two refilled mugs of steaming tea. Thrusting the full cup back into Mrs. Frumpwooler's pink hands, Blevins began pacing the room: three paces one way, three paces back. Mrs. Frumpwooler watched him cross the room in each direction as though she was a spectator at a slow-motion tennis match played on an extraordinarily small court. Partially mesmerized, she began sipping the tea again.

"Is there a problem, Commander Blevins?" She finally asked, rasping. Her stomach was just beginning to turn sour as dizziness settled upon her.

"What? Oh, Mrs. Frumpwooler. I was just...reviewing possible...approaches. He sat down, slightly winded, and regained his focus. "Well, now, where shall we begin?" He took a large gulp of tea and was silent for another minute. Mrs. Frumpwooler felt it was her duty to respond, but had no idea what to say.

"That's it. We shall jump off near the Casual and...no. I think not. Mrs. Frumpwooler, are you stout of heart? Ready for some derring-do adventure? I can personally guarantee you that whatever we run across, no matter how it may seem, nothing will be able to affect you adversely. Unless you choose to be adversely affected, that is."

Mrs. Frumpwooler nodded wide-eyed, sipping her tea.

"I need to hear words, Mrs. Frumpwooler. It is imperative that we are both prepared for our little Journey."

"Well, then, in that case, yes, I am ready for an adventure. And if you say nothing will harm me, then I believe you. What are we going to find out?"

"That is the big question, isn't it?" Commander Blevins stood up and walked over to the edge of the loveseat, near Mrs. Frumpwooler. Taking the cup of tea from her very red hands, he placed it on a narrow little shelf that he pulled out of the love seat's arm. Mrs. Frumpwooler looked at him with admiration and relief.

He walked around behind her. "Now, if you will relax and allow me to remove this stunning purple hat of yours," he did so and tossed it casually on his desk behind him."I will open your upper chakras. Please close your eyes." He placed one hand on the top of her head, mashing her well-lacquered hair, and the other across her forehead. "Now, I want you to relax and gently let your attention rest on a place in the middle of your forehead, just above your eyebrows." He gently massaged that area of her forehead with the ball of his hand. "Let a calm sea take shape in your mind's eye. Let yourself feel the rocking of the waves and smell the fresh sea air. A seagull caws in the distance." He stopped massaging her forehead for a long minute then began rubbing the very center of her head with his other hand. "Now, I want you to feel a gentle breeze blowing across the sea toward you from all directions. Feel it brush across your face and turn upwards, so it is flowing straight up around your head." He paused again, then slowly removed both hands and said, "Hold the image of the sea and feel the breeze flowing up around you. Gradually, as I tell you, the wind will increase and exert a stronger pull upon you."

Quietly Commander Blevins walked around the love seat over to his overstuffed chair. Draining his tea, he settled down into the cushions, put a pillow behind his back, drew his robe tight, pulled the elastic cuffs of his sweat pants down snugly upon the tops of his slippers, sighed deeply, and closed his eyes, then opened them again. He quietly reached over to the table next to the chair. Two electric digital clocks sat behind a pile of books. One read "1:47," the other "1:51." He carefully picked-up the fast one, reset it to noon, and noted that the slow one was the Journey record this time. He sat the clock down and closed his eyes again.

"Mrs. Frumpwooler, I can now see the same sea that you see. The waves are rocking us, a stiff breeze is blowing, the sun is shining, and we see no one else on this sea but us today. The wind is blowing stronger. It now feels like it will surely suck us right up with it. Do not be afraid. I will prepare you for each step of our Journey today. In a moment, I will reach out and take your hand, and we will step up into the wind. Extend your arm and open your hands. There I have you now. Let's—on the count of three—take one big step. One...two...three."

Several things happened at once. Commander Blevins neatly stepped out of his physical body. The telephone rang. The neighbor dropped a bottle of milk in the hall and cursed. And Mrs. Frumpwooler raised one arm and stood straight-up so fast she caught the front edge of the love seat with her calf and dumped it over on its back. She then floated gently out of her physical body with a serene expression on her face.

Commander Blevins and Mrs. Frumpwooler hovered in the room, near the ceiling. He watched her closely. They each looked nearly the same as their two physical bodies, which were unmoved from a moment earlier: he sitting comfortably in the easy-chair, she standing at erect attention with her right arm sticking out and up. Blevins considered re-entering the physical and repeating the process, hoping his Client would smoothly exit her physical body on the second try. He quickly vetoed the idea. The door was locked, Mrs. Frumpwooler would soon forget a few sore muscles, and a transmitigation was a transmitigation.

Several moments passed, and Mrs. Frumpwooler

tuned in, "Commander Blevins! This is quite amazing. I feel the same way I did on Tuesday when I was outside myself." She paused. Little lights twinkled throughout her. "Is that the correct way to put it?"

"Close enough."

"Oh, and look, there's the silver cord coming out of my stomach. I wish I had a necklace that was as pretty a silver as this is."

"There's something..."

"Commander Blevins, you have one, too. Only your silver cord is coming out of the back of your head."

"Yes, yes. We all have one that connects our Astral body to our Physical body. It's the natural order of things and means nothing. Unless you choose to break the cord."

"Break the..."

"Now, there is something significant we need to work on before we go any further, Mrs. Frumpwooler," Commander Blevins said. She nodded. He had her complete attention. "Please look to your right. Put your attention on the far corner where the wall meets the ceiling above the window." Mrs. Frumpwooler followed his instructions. "Now think about being there," Blevins said.

Mrs. Frumpwooler was suddenly there, though she did not appear to move. One moment she was next to Commander Blevins hovering in the middle of the room; the next moment, she was hovering just below the ceiling near the wall over the window.

Mrs. Frumpwooler looked at Commander Blevins

with awe. Her mouth was open and moving slightly, but no sound came out. "You are a quick student Mrs. Frumpwooler. I commend you. Lesson number two you are currently practicing, though I imagine it is by accident. The Law of Silence is critical to understand. Its basic principle is that you can wreak all kinds of havoc by talking about things that need to be kept as they are...in the Inner. When the Inner Secrets are brought to the Outer Worlds, we unleash forces we can not control. Also, if you have a good thing going in some respect and talk about it, it will often go kaputt. Instantly. So please keep this in mind during our adventures, and especially after we return."

Commander Blevins floated around the room a bit, peering at unseen things. A silver cord did spiral out of the back of his head, shimmering and pulsating. This cord wound its way down to his physical body, connecting to the back of his physical head. The two light cords attached to the back of his physical body also pulsated and in an identical rhythm to his silver cord's pulsing. They did not, however, make the leap to his hovering Astral body.

"In case you are wondering. I am looking for a Blip-spule." He was quiet as he looked further.

"Can I ask what a 'Blipspule' is?" Mrs. Frumpwooler asked.

"Of course, Mrs. Frumpwooler. Asking is how any of us learn. Asking a question is much different than talking about something you already know. A 'Blip-spule' is one of those little wonders of the Inner Worlds that we often overlook. If you look down at yourself, you will notice thousands of tiny sparkles sparkling about on and in yourself. We are, by the way, in our Astral bodies. If someone were to walk into the room right now, other than your physical body's unusual posture, they would see nothing out of the ordinary and would presume that you and I were probably asleep."

"Oh, dear," Mrs. Frumpwooler said.

"Not to worry!" Commander Blevins said. "No one shall walk into the room while we are gone. We shall not be gone long by Physical World standards, anyway. We aren't going to leave the time track in today's little Journey completely, but time does move differently in the Inner Worlds. It's not hard to bend time to one's wishes, so long as the wishes do not affect another person in an ill way. No, that's not entirely true. It could be bent to—Oh, that's not important." He stopped for a moment, lost in his muttering.

"Oh, hello. Yes, now, as I was saying, we are looking for a Blipspule. It will look very much like one of the little sparkles that are dancing. Oh, I know what I was going to say! Darn, but there's a lot to keep track of sometimes. If someone ELSE walked into the room now, someone with the ability to see unseen things, that person would see two clouds of little sparkles dancing about and floating here and there. That is if we choose to float around. If that person were uninformed or weak constitutioned, they would probably run out of the room screaming. But if they had been able to see unseen things for a while, then they would either be naturally a sound person, having strengthened themselves, or be in an institution by now. This, my dear Mrs. Frumpwooler, is where all this bunk about ghosts comes from...from the uninformed or weak constitutioned people who stumble onto things they should not... Well, enough about that for now."

From the area above the door to the large walk-in closet, he continued his inspection in silence.

Bravely, Mrs. Frumpwooler asked again, "I would still like to know, Commander Blevins, what a Blipspule is and how you know if you find it. There seems to be a cluster of little sparkles hovering over here by the window."

"Really!" Commander Blevins joined Mrs. Frumpwooler by the window in a blink. "Mrs. Frumpwooler, I must commend you again! You have found a veritable bevy of Blipspules!" He peered at them closely. "Eureka! Great Fortnoy! Grab my hand, Mrs. Frumpwooler." Commander Blevins extended his sparkly arm. Mrs. Frumpwooler grasped his hand firmly with hers, though it did not feel firm. Nothing felt firm to her at that moment. Before she could think, focus her attention on any other spot in the room, or even consider violating the Law of Silence, she was speeding down a bright blue tunnel. Commander Blevins stood in front of her, legs apart, a frozen smile on his face, one hand reaching back to hers, and the other pointed ahead, his forefinger leading the way. Although they seemed to be speeding toward whatever was ahead of them at a breakneck pace, Mrs. Frumpwooler did not feel any wind racing by her. Commander Blevins was certainly not leaning in the direction of their travel any instinctive aerodynamic fashion, as might be expected. Perhaps they were standing still, and the bright blue tunnel was rushing by them. It was this curious thought that occupied Mrs. Frumpwooler until everything around her changed.

FOUR
WELCOME TO MY WORLD

The bright blue tunnel disappeared slowly. Commander Blevins and Mrs. Frumpwooler found themselves standing on a white path, still holding hands. Their bodies looked a little less substantial than a moment before but still twinkled with many little sparkly sparkles. Some birds chirped in the distance as they began moving again. Mrs. Frumpwooler looked down. The path whisked them along at the pace of a brisk walk. It seemed to be made of thousands of small pebbles that moved closer to each other, then farther away. Underneath the surface of the path ran a swift stream, or so it looked to Mrs. Frumpwooler. Waves were rolling down the stream at regular intervals, pulling the top layers of small pebbles along with them. This much made some sense. However, Missing was the sensation of rising and falling with the waves as they moved beneath the gravel. Mrs. Frumpwooler suddenly had a vision of riding on the belly of an infinitely long white snake. She looked up quickly, unsure just where she was being taken.

Commander Blevins stood in front of her, legs still apart, taking deep breaths and facing forward, his hands clasped behind his back. "What a grand tour, Mrs. Frumpwooler, wouldn't you say?" Hearing no response, he looked back just as she looked up. "Chin-up stout heart. Our adventure's just begun." He looked again in the direction of their travel—a grove of scarlet trees passed by on the left, outlined against a pale yellow sky. The trees were tossing bouquets of flowers back and forth to each other, catching them in long tendrils at the ends of their branches. "It's true we are taking the long way to our destination. But what's the hurry when time is an ally," he said, turning and winking at her.

"W-W-Where are we, Commander Blevins?" Mrs. Frumpwooler stammered slightly.

He turned back, looking ahead. "We are in a sub-Astral World, Mrs. Frumpwooler. It is the most immediate Inner World to the physical. Called the Moondog World, it's a thin veneer between the Physical and the beginning of the Astral Worlds. From that point on, each world has many sub-worlds within it. Don't take this too literally, though. Inner World borders are tough to pin down. Usually I can jump the Moondog. This time we didn't. Oh, well. Perhaps it was because of the little commotion we had getting you out of your body. You're a trooper, though I must say. Imagine you won't even flinch next time."

'Next time' echoed through Mrs. Frumpwooler's mind. She was puzzled with Commander Blevins' voice. His mouth moved, but she heard him before he spoke. As she was about to break the Law of Silence to voice concern, a hot breath blasted the back of her neck. This diverted her attention. She turned around and found herself staring directly into the open mouth of an enormous white dog. It bared its teeth. Its ears pointed straight-up and were higher than Mrs. Frump-wooler could reach, even on tippy toes. The colossal dog was running full tilt, but not moving any closer to her. She screamed. Commander Blevins turned around and laughed. The large dog continued running, breathing hot with hard eyes fixed on a point far in the distance.

Commander Blevins took Mrs. Frumpwooler by the shoulders and gently pulled her over to one side of the pathway. "It's only the Moondog, Mrs. Frumpwooler. I told you we were in the Moondog World, remember?"

She nodded numbly. The huge white dog began to move past them. They were standing still on the pathway and moving past the countryside at a pleasant clip. The Moondog was running at full stride on the path and yet moved past them slowly.

Commander Blevins put out his hand to touch the Moondog, and Mrs. Frumpwooler eeked. "Don't fret, Mrs. Frumpwooler. Watch this." He put his hand into the side of the Dog as it passed, legs churning hard.

Sparks showered them, coming from where Commander Blevins' hand entered the Dog's side. Commander Blevins laughed. Mrs. Frumpwooler giggled. "See, wasn't that fun, Mrs. Frumpwooler?" She nodded in silence. "That's his way of welcoming us to his world."

FIVE

THE JUMPING OFF POINT

They continued for what seemed like an eternity to Mrs. Frumpwooler. She was grappling with Commander Blevins' statement that time was now at their mercy.

The scenery was pleasant; nothing much out of the ordinary happened. The white path of rippling motion pushed them along. Commander Blevins commented on passing items of note, most of which Mrs. Frumpwooler did not hear, caught as she was in her mind. A steep hillside faced them. Beyond it, the sky was now midnight blue. The white path wound straight up the hill, though pulsing strangely at times. Mrs. Frumpwooler wondered if the path was coughing or trembling in fear of something. She thought this until she realized what she was thinking. Before she could chastise herself for such absurd thoughts, the path came to an abrupt end. Beyond it lay only the deep midnight blue sky.

"Well, here we are," Commander Blevins said.

"Where is here?" Mrs. Frumpwooler asked. "And when will we be wherever we are going?"

"Why the Jumping Off Point, of course." Ignoring her second question, he took her by the arm, leading her to the end of the path. His fingers glowed where he touched her. The little white pebbles undulated right up to the end of the path, then turned back upon themselves, blending in with the steady march of white stones coming up from behind, and heading into an unseen reservoir of white pebbles to be used again when needed. The irregular pulsing that Mrs. Frumpwooler had noticed earlier was more pronounced now.

"What's out there?" she asked tentatively, not sure she wanted to know.

"Why, the Astral Worlds, of course."

Mrs. Frumpwooler thought Commander Blevins was beginning to sound like a stuck record. "How do we get there?" she asked.

"We jump. That's why it's called the Jumping Off Point. Are things really that difficult to understand? You should be letting go of that chokehold on your mind by now."

She looked at him like he was crazy, which is precisely what she thought.

"Now, I didn't mean 'you' in particular," Commander Blevins said. "It's common for Soul in the human consciousness to be so afraid of losing what it thinks is control over itself and its world that it gloms onto its mind as though its life depended on it. A mind is a wonderful tool and a lousy master. By holding on so tightly to the mental machinery, people inadvertently buy into a gross illusion. Most of the Physical World is an illusion, my dear.

"So as we wind our way into the Inner Worlds in this Journey, you will have the opportunity to slowly relax your death grip on your mind and experience a somewhat more direct connection with your true self. Were we to go far enough, which we won't today, we would go beyond the mind altogether. That's the only time when someone can truly say they have gone out of their mind," he said, chuckling to himself at the joke.

Mrs. Frumpwooler stared at Commander Blevins, trying to digest what he said. "It" kept running through her mind.

"Lighten up, my dear. I know you have it in you." He gave her a little squeeze around the waist and said, "Here we go now..."

"Go wheeerrreee..." she said, suddenly pulled along.

"Jumping oooooooooffff..." he said.

And jump off they did. Well, Commander Blevins did. Since he was holding tightly to Mrs. Frumpwooler, she went too.

Descend, though, they did not. The deep midnight blue swallowed them, along with Commander Blevins' parting "Wheeeee," and then, almost immediately, deposited them gently into a large field of purple flowers shaped like little drums. There was a pink cast to the light all around them.

Mrs. Frumpwooler was beyond shock and amazement. Commander Blevins was as happy as a duck in mud, looking around, drinking in the meadow, and the pinkish-red sky. Yellow clouds shot overhead in formations, zig-zagging the sky like an Astral precision flying squadron. Which they might have been. The Astral differs little from the physical in most ways. Many beings can run their bodies on more than one Inner World, while at the same time living "fully" in the material. "Time" here was, of course, a different matter than on the physical, though it could not be done away with entirely. Only in the higher Inner Worlds was time— and space— left behind.

"Welcome to the Astral, Mrs. Frumpwooler," Commander Blevins said. There was some trumpeting off in the distance, and the little purple flowers began beating themselves with small appendages. "I think we are in for a sound storm."

"Sounds more like a parade to me, Commander Blevins. And I must say you look dashing." He did, in fact, look quite handsome. Gone was his old robe and slouching posture. In place stood a trim, erect figure glimmering with a solid coat of sparkles. Mrs. Frump-wooler found herself similarly transformed.

Ignoring the personal comment, Commander Blevins said, "Well, things are different here, Mrs.

Frumpwooler. "They aren't always what they seem." The trumpeting grew louder, and the flowers divided into two choruses: one beat fast staccato rhythms of three runs of three beats each, with the accented beat rotating. The second chorus provided a slow, steady background beat that gradually rose in intensity. It would peak periodically with the last accented beat of a set of three threes by the first chorus. This went on for a while, then dimmed somewhat, then got louder again, but coming from a different angle.

Suddenly all was quiet. A point of light hovered on the horizon. It grew to show a brilliant orange center surrounded by luminescent green circles. Then it came nearer quickly and filled out to become a solid-looking sphere. Mrs. Frumpwooler shrieked when she first saw it, hovering in the near distance.

Commander Blevins said quietly, "It's all right, Mrs. Frumpwooler."

"But it is coming straight at us, Commander Blevins!"

"Yes, it surely is."

"But it looks like it is going to eat us," Mrs. Frumpwooler said, standing up and looking around frantically.

Before she could do anything provocative—such as running amok though through the little purples flowers —Commander Blevins gently gripped her arm and said, "Please do get a hold of yourself, Mrs. Frumpwooler. It is not going to eat us, though I do hope we will be able to use it to our benefit." His hand glowed brightly, where he touched her. She did not notice. She noticed the gently tickling sensation that came from her arm and, torn between investigation and the crisis at hand, Mrs. Frumpwooler's knees became wobbly.

Gripping her around the waist with his other arm, Commander Blevins continued, "As we go higher in the Inner Worlds, our thoughts will manifest more quickly. This is one of the secrets to living on the physical: what we think manifests in our lives. It does not happen quickly enough for most people to make the connection. Our manifestations also involve what we are doing in the Inner Worlds, so not all the forces in the physical are readily apparent while locked into our human consciousness." He paused for a moment. The brilliant orange sphere was hovering in front of them; a small pebble toss away. "Are you with me so far?" he asked.

"Uhhh, yes, I think so." Mrs. Frumpwooler forced back a giggle.

"Good. Now keep this in mind. Controlling the mind is a matter of attention, not effort. I will help you for the next little while." Commander Blevins pressed his right index finger against the ridge that ran behind Mrs. Frumpwooler's right ear, and he hummed a simple little sound. Sparks shot from the point of contact.

"Oh, that is better," she said at once. Her urge to giggle, or do anything but smile, dissipated.

"Good. Now relax into the feeling of serenity while we step into the next world. Transitions are the most tricky, but I will be here with you every step of the way." As he was speaking, a large orange tongue unfurled from the center of the sphere. It spread out before them, stopping about shoulder height. Three green lines ran straight up the middle of the tongue and disappeared into the brilliant orange sphere. They looked like racing stripes.

A moment later, there was a faint crackling from the end of the tongue. Two little doors opened outward, and a set of steps unfolded from the inside of the tip of the tongue. The steps stretched out into mid-air and down, completed their extension, stopping just before crushing several purple flowers. The steps had a purplish cast to then at the bottom, which turned to crimson, then red-orange as the steps neared the tip of the tongue from whence they came.

"Hold my hand, and here we go," Commander Blevins said.

Mrs. Frumpwooler, wide-eyed, did as requested. They stepped in unison onto the first rung on the stairs. The sky hue changed immediately, and the orange sphere shot out away from them toward an increasingly chartreuse sky. The tongue, trailing the sphere, further unfurled at a now furious pace. Still standing on the first rung of the stairs, they watched as the tongue laid out a long straight road before them. The road led up and into a suddenly pinkish-red sky.

"Wow," said Mrs. Frumpwooler.

"See, this is jolly fun, isn't it?" Commander said. As they mounted the steps, he held fast to Mrs. Frumpwooler's hand, but the finger on his other hand slipped from the ridge behind her ear monetarily. A thousand two-inch Pterodactyls instantly swarmed around them, diving and biting Mrs. Frumpwooler.

"Oops, sorry about that," he said, regaining his balance and repositioning his finger behind her ear, unaware of what had just materialized.

Mrs. Frumpwooler watched as the little Pterodactyls disappeared one by one in grey puffs, like victims of unseen and unheard anti-aircraft fire. With a bit of prodding from Commander

Blevins, she finished climbing the stairs: eyes wide, mouth open, a guttural scream frozen on her lips.

They stepped onto the tongue, something began whirring, and they began to move ahead. Mrs. Frump-wooler decided to keep her attention only on what was directly in front of her. Commander Blevins could deal with the rear. Their movement increased in speed. The orange tongue rolled up fast behind them, becoming larger and larger and pushing them along. To someone uninitiated in the Inner Worlds ways, it looked like it was about to squash them flat.

Commander Blevins hummed merrily and chatted about whatever crossed his mind while keeping his finger on the ridge behind Mrs. Frumpwooler's ear. Her panic dissolved. At one point, his comments about the nature of a person's past lives and how choices made manifest in both Inner and Outer Worlds caught Mrs. Frumpwooler's attention. The event on the little steps took on new meaning. She also listened to Commander

Blevins' contention that e-v-e-r-y-t-h-i-n-g—he had spelled it out for emphasis—which comes into our world is there because we create it on one level or another.

"And if we create it," he said, "we are also responsible for it."

SIX

THE DOWNSIDE OF FOCALSHIFTING

Suddenly they were flying through the air in an elongated arc. Puffy, light blue bushes reached up and caught Mrs. Frumpwooler as she entered the final approach to her landing. She was all akimbo as she came down: her arms and legs flailing, her mouth open, and she was unable to suppress one of her guttural screams completely. As she landed, she got a glimpse of the brilliant orange spheres's center opening, which puckered, then closed. The sphere's tongue tip poked through the opening and then retracted just before the sphere closed up. Then the sphere was gone. In its place, spread a lovely lavender sky. Mrs. Frumpwooler had the distinct impression they had been spit out of the orange sphere and into this world. Something pushed at her gently.

Commander Blevins landed neatly on his feet a few meters away and inhaled deeply. Off in the distance, a large pole split the horizon. He glanced in Mrs. Frump-wooler's direction and saw the blue bushes gently righting her. He focused his attention on the pole. Immediately he was standing in front of it.

It was as he had hoped, a signpost. Large arrows were attached at different intervals and pointing in many directions. He walked around it slowly, reading each sign. Some seemed almost familiar. Several were printed in German and a few in English. "Mench-gruten." "Slippery Pete." "Bal." "The Dump of Dumps." "Fantasy Number 9." Some of the characters printed on the signs were unknown to him.

"Eureka!" Commander Blevins shouted. He glanced toward Mrs. Frumpwooler. She was standing up, looking around and swatting at something behind her. She held one hand against her forehead over her eyes. He thought he could see her mouth moving. He directed his attention upon the area next to her and was there.

"Oh! Gracious Commander Blevins, you've done me out of years of good health!" Mrs. Frumpwooler cried out. "I was worried sick you'd been eaten or something and left me here at heaven-knows-what's mercy. Some-thing keeps poking me in the back. Then you pop up next to me without even a modicum of warning. Gracious!" Her breast heaved. "Where are we anyway? And where are we going?" She looked him up and down. "And why are you all stripy!"

Commander Blevins WAS stripy. Mrs. Frump-wooler was stripy, too. Gone were their transparent, shimmering bodies of a thousand sparkles. Instead, they both wore oblong orbs of striped light. Little stumpy legs and feet protruded from the bottoms of their orbs. Their faces shone with light, extending beyond the tops of their heads. Or where the tops of their heads would usually be.

"And you don't have any arms! And I don't either. What's going on here? My nose itches...oh, there's my arm. And you have one too!"

Commander Blevins had raised his arm to show her that he still had one. He also had not heard a word of what Mrs. Frumpwooler had said. He nodded, reading her lips as she moved her mouth. Neither had she heard what she said, in the normal way. She was not talking so loudly that her speech's internal resonation blocked out any awareness that her vocal cords no longer function-tion. Commander Blevins was relieved to see that she appeared to be basically in control of herself. He elected not to place his finger behind her ear, lowering his arm instead. It blended into his orb again.

"Mrs. Frumpwooler," he said. His voice came through very clearly to her, slightly deeper and with more warmth than before. The sound seemed to resonate from within her rather than from him. His lips did not move, nor did his mouth open.

She moved her lips, though, jumped and stammered, "What, what was...how did you do that!" Of course, he did not hear her, and she did not hear herself, but he knew what she was saying.

Commander Blevins continued soothingly, "Listen

to me for a moment, please, Mrs. Frumpwooler. We cannot communicate with our mouths here. As we travel closer to our destination, our mouths will blend into the rest of our faces as we become more light and less matter. Sound does still play an important role but will be different and resemble the Inner Sound you have heard many times before.

Mrs. Frumpwooler cocked her head like a puppy trying to understand. Commander Blevins continued. "For example, remember when you were walking around the Palace of Fine Arts? You know, the reason you came to see me...?" Mrs. Frumpwooler nodded her head so vigorously the light orb around it left tracers to each side of her head. "...and the sound you heard just before you rejoined your body. Do you remember that?"

Mrs. Frumpwooler nodded yes, slowly, her lips pressed firmly together.

"Good. That sound is the Inner Sound I'm talking about, which takes many forms. In the Inner Worlds, and we are now in the second of the lower Inner Worlds, the Sound is more readily available to us. By vibrating with it, we can talk without needing vocal cords and all that. In fact, we don't even have them."

Mrs. Frumpwooler's eyes shot open, and she clutched at her throat.

Blevins ignored her dismay. "Now, I want you to remember our little experiment in my apartment when you first left your physical body. Remember when I asked you to focus your attention on the far wall. The next moment you were there, right?"

Mrs. Frumpwooler nodded again, still holding her throat.

"Well, we have left our Astral bodies back in the Astral Worlds, just like we left our Physical bodies back in the Physical World. You'll notice you have no silver cord anymore."

Her mouth opened, she released her throat, looked down, and felt around on her stomach. Her hands sunk into her body a little.

"The silver cord is used to connect the Astral and Physical Bodies. We now have only our Causal bodies and our Mental bodies between our present consciousness and our true selves, sometimes called our higher selves or Soul. These bodies are like overcoats. They protect us from the harsher vibrations of the respective lower worlds. When we pass into the next higher world, we cannot take our coarser body with us. It is like pushing ourselves through a finer and finer screen, shedding the larger dross each time." He paused. "Are you with me so far?".

Mrs. Frumpwooler's eyes were a little glazed, but she bravely nodded yes and stopped looking for her silver cord.

"Grand! I knew you were a trooper. Since we are one step closer to the Mental Worlds, we have one less layer between our minds and our consciousness of the moment. What we think, therefore, will manifest even more quickly. To talk, you only need to think of what you want to say and to whom you want to say it. To move, you only need to think about where you want to move."

Mrs. Frumpwooler's eyes widened: she was momentarily overwhelmed.

"Now, please don't get alarmed." He gently took hold of her arm. His hands sunk partway into her body glowed slightly, and the stripes on her arm diverted around where he held her. "Here in the Casual Worlds, we are limited. For example, we can only communicate with someone we can see. This has something to do with discrete materialization, I think. At any rate, in the worlds of pure spirit, above the Mental Worlds, all limitations are removed. Here, though, we also must be able to see our next destination, and we cannot manifest something which will harm us. There is still illusion here, though, so keep that in mind."

Mrs. Frumpwooler relaxed a bit, began to move her lips, but then stopped. Slowly, but clearly, her voice filled Commander Blevins. "Wha, why did--can you hear me, this feels so silly," she said.

"Yes, yes. I can hear you fine. Please continue."

"Well. I wondered why we hadn't used the thinking way of moving since our apartment that one time. It seems that we have walked so very much, needlessly."

Commander Blevins was quiet for a moment, then said without speaking, "That was a great job of using the Inner Sound. I can see that you are right on top of things, and that is terrific. Keep in mind, though, that we need to learn many things that may not seem relevant at the time. We haven't done any focalshift traveling until now because I wanted you to get used to being out of your physical body without having to deal with too many things at once. I often lose my perspective with a new traveler. But are you ready to try it again now?"

Mrs. Frumpwooler looked around for a moment. No orange sphere loomed anywhere in sight. The lavender sky was calming, and no other life forms were in view "Why yes, I believe so," she said without saying.

"Transborneo!" Commander Blevins exclaimed. "Let's get on with it then. Do you see that tall pole off in the distance there?" He pointed toward the signpost.

"Yes, I do."

"Well then, follow these instructions. Place your attention gently on that pole and drop all else from your mind for a brief moment. At that moment, simply visualize yourself standing next to the pole or wherever you want to go. Got that?"

"I think so."

"Ok, now you can go first, or I can, which would you like?" Commander Blevins didn't say.

"Well, why don't you...oh no, then I'd be left...but I don't want to go by myself." Mrs. Frumpwooler looked at him with despair.

"I'll tell you what," he said. "We shall both go first. On the count of three, we will both momentarily clear our minds and picture ourselves by the pole. All right?"

"All right."

"Ok. One. Two. Three." Just as Commander Blevins

said "three," a large red rabbit whizzed by on the right side of Mrs. Frumpwooler, heading in the general direction of the signpost. It stopped about two-thirds of the way there. Commander Blevins materialized five meters to the left of the signpost. He had wanted to give Mrs. Frumpwooler plenty of latitude. Mrs. Frumpwooler appeared a hare's breath away from the rabbit, which then shot skyward in reaction to the sudden company.

The rabbit came straight down, bounced first on top of Mrs. Frumpwooler's head, and then landed on the ground. It immediately ran back the way it had come. Mrs. Frumpwooler screamed and fainted. Her stripy body became hazy as it sunk to the bottom, but held its shape. Little stumpy legs and feet stuck straight out of one end, held off the ground by the firm orb of light. Commander Blevins sighed, and focalshifted over to her. He waited the few minutes needed for Mrs. Frumpwooler to regain her wits. Her stripes were still cloudy when he heard her not speak to him.

"What...oh my...something hit me. A red blur! Are there Communists here too?"

Commander Blevins placed his right hand under Mrs. Frumpwooler's neck and let his index finger rest on the ridge behind her ear. He pressed slightly. The stripes cleared, and he thought to himself that despite her distraction with the red rabbit, she did very well to speak to him without using her mouth, while she was still half-conscious.

"Oh...hello Commander Blevins. Why am I here on the ground?"

Silently, he expressed undying gratitude for the Point of Infinite Peacefulness, then didn't say, "You are fine. Just rest a moment. A one in a million occurrence caught you just as you were about to focalshift to the signpost."

"What signpost?" she asked.

"The post over there, which was our destination, is a signpost." He released his pressure on the ridge behind her ear, helped her up, and pointed to the post. "I think we had better walk to it while you regain your equilibrium."

"Thank you," she said. They began walking. "What was it that hit me, anyway? And why didn't I go to the signpost? Did you?"

"Yes, yes. I made it fine but came back to check on you. Just as you were about to shift over to the pole, a shooting hare zipped by you. I kept my attention on the signpost. You did not, so you went where you were looking and focusing: to the rabbit. Your sudden appearance startled the bunny. It jumped straight up and then came down on your head. I imagine its little heart was racing as fast as yours at that point. I can't imagine how the rabbit knocked you out. They are soft as feather pillows and weigh about as much."

They were nearing the signpost when Mrs. Frump-wooler asked, "What happens if someone looks somewhere but puts their focus somewhere else?"

Blevins chuckled. "You are a marvel, Mrs. Frumpwooler. Hopefully, you will never have the experience. Usually, nothing happens. The person shifting simply goes to the point that they locked onto the strongest. Once in a great while, however, the locks will be evenly balanced. Then we have the Ping-pong effect. The focalshifter goes from one spot to the other, back and forth."

"How does this 'Ping-pong effect' end?"

"Usually, an outsider steps in and neutralizes one lock, so the Ping-ponger stops at the other point."

"What's an 'outsider'?" Mrs. Frumpwooler asked.

"In this case, it's a person outside the Ping-pong effect. I have heard that in truly extraordinary cases, the lock was so balanced that the person split in two and went to both places, then switched back and so on."

"But how could that happen? Does the person die or get back together or what?"

"I don't know. I've never seen it. Here we are now." They were standing at the base of the signpost. Commander Blevins walked around to the far side of the signpost. Mrs. Frumpwooler followed, reading the signs that were intelligible to her. "Here it is," Blevins did not say.

"Here what is?" Mrs. Frumpwooler asked as she joined him.

"Our next port of call," Commander Blevins explained as

Mrs. Frumpwooler looked up. This sign read "AKASH" and pointed in the direction of a low-rising mountain.

"Is that mountain called 'AKASH?'" she asked.

"No, I'm afraid not. I think that must be the Nodule Range. Akash is across several more valleys and a great desert between the Shining Shores Sea and us.

Akash is a port town on the Bay of Bubbling Lights. Are you up to some more focalshifting? I think you will be fine this time."

"Ok, I'll try again. Those certainly are silly-sounding names."

"Silly is as silly does, Mrs. Frumpwooler." Commander Blevins grinned at his silly comment. "Now let's shift to that first peak up ahead of us. You focus on its right side, and I'll take the left. Ready?" She nodded. "Ok. On the count of three: one; two; three."

They both stood in a pale raspberry meadow lining a small dip on the mountain top, dotted with little dark grey toadstools. "Congratulations, Mrs. Frumpwooler!" Commander Blevins said. Mrs. Frumpwooler smiled and glowed proudly. "Let's try it again now. You pick a spot over there, go first, and then I'll join you." He pointed slightly off to their left toward a gap between two peaks where a valley dotted with swaying trees and large, stationary boulders stretched out before them. A moment later, Mrs. Frumpwooler was a small waving figure in that valley between the two mountain tops. Another second later, Commander Blevins joined her.

"Wheee, this is fun," she chortled.

"Glad you are enjoying yourself." Blevins smiled.

"Shall we go for that next peak?"

They hopped from mountain top to mountain top,

their stripy bodies disappearing from each peak almost as quickly as they arrived. Mrs. Frumpwooler followed Commander Blevins to a very lofty summit and braced herself against a strong wind blowing at them. "When are we going to get there?" she asked without saying, then looked at the strangely-colored valley floor below them. "Oh, mercy! That is so beautiful. What sort of land is it?"

SEVEN

PTERODACTYLS, HEROS, AND RUMPS

" **A** desert."

"But it has so many colors, and they are all moving!"

"Yes, it's called The Collage. Though it IS a desert, some also think of it as a Sand Lake. Sand is continually brought up to the surface from its depths, moves about from one place to another, then slips below the surface again. The flowing colors make this valley floor unique."

"Oh, look," Mrs. Frumpwooler said, pointing to a geyser of forest-green sand.

"That is often the way sand comes back to the surface," Commander Blevins said. "If you watch that geyser until it stops, you will be able to see that the sand does not blow and scatter, even in this wind. It acts much like a highly viscous liquid, like molasses."

"Oh, I see what you mean," she said as the geyser

stopped erupting, sank into the desert floor, forming a pool that first collected on top of the sand, then blended into it.

"The desert is remarkable not only because there are different colors of sand, but because there are also different breeds. Each species of sand has its own color and cycles, so the different patterns are limitless."

They both stood and watched as long fuchsia tendrils of sand sprung from the green pool left by the geyser. The sand tendrils moved out like the spokes of a wheel. Marbled patches shifted in trapezoids of multiple hues. A whole section of ultramarine moved in a quilt-like pattern, a blueprint of dark and light tones. Other areas sported colors and designs that neither Mrs. Frumpwooler nor Commander Blevins had words to describe.

"Can we walk on it?" Mrs. Frumpwooler asked.

"No."

"Well, then how are we going to..."

"The Sand Lake Express runs straight across the desert and into the suburbs of Akash."

"Suburbs?" Mrs. Frumpwooler asked.

"Yes, suburbs. You know, outlying areas away from the central hub of activity. You haven't forgotten those sorts of things, have you Mrs. Frumpwooler?"

"Well, no. I'm just surprised to find something so..."

"So normal? So Earthly? Here in the Causal Worlds?"

"Yes, I guess that's it," she said.

Commander Blevins puffed up slightly, his stripy, luminescent body noticeably bloated. "Well, don't fret a moment. It's a prevalent assumption that the Inner Spiritual Worlds have to be totally different than life in the Physical World. But, the situation is nearly the opposite. The Inner Worlds, the lower ones at least, are quite like each other. There are differences, of course. Did you know that Heaven, such as it is, is ever-changing? The Heaven many religious people in the physical talk about—the one with people walking around with long white robes, and all that— is at least two thousand years out of date, and it's hardly higher up the spiritual ladder than the Mental Worlds. There are many Heavens, you see, and where one goes after leaving the physical realm is to an Inner World for, very probably, another lifetime. Then back to the physical for more doom and gloom." Commander Blevins leaned close to Mrs. Frumpwooler and whispered, "I call the Physical World 'Spiritual Boot Camp." Chuckling, he winked, deflated to his previous state, and began walking down a path running along the mountain top. The wind blew in hard from the desert. Absorbed in her thoughts, Mrs. Frumpwooler had to run to catch up with him.

"Commander Blevins, I disagree with you that the physical, that Earth, is all negative. Not everything is 'doom and gloom.'" She moved her mouth as though she was shouting over the noise of the wind. No words came out, of course, but her thoughts resonated within Commander Blevins more forcefully than usual. Sparks bounced off her cheeks. Surprised at the sparks, she looked down, noticing she had a hold of Blevins' arm.

She let go immediately. Her fingers tingled strangely and glowed where they had touched him.

He had stopped and turned around. Looking at Mrs. Frumpwooler, he said softly, "You are so right again, Mrs. Frumpwooler! There is plenty of beauty and love in the Physical World. There also is an equal amount of negative energy. There has to be. That's the nature of the physical. By design, it is the negative repository in the many worlds of positive and pure positive energy. God, by whatever name you choose, has set it up so that we—each of us as Soul, our higher selves— will learn, grow and mature while living in the Physical Worlds. That act of maturing does not, alas, take place in the worlds of pure spirit for unmatured Souls. In the worlds of only positive energy and Divine Love, the young and inexperienced beings tend to languish. Therefore, you and I must wind and bump our way along the road of our choosing, having our rough edges ground smooth by being continually pulled back and forth between the positive and the negative. The negative force is as much a part of God as anything and everything, doing the job it was meant to do. And a wonderful job it is Mrs. Frumpwooler. For without this training, you and I, and myriad other beings, would suffer from narrow vision and over-involvement with the little self—the human conscious. We could never grow to find our way home to the pure spiritual worlds, where each of us has work to do."

Commander Blevins paused for a minute. They both looked around and then at each other. A little

spark of recognition ran between them. Mrs. Frumpwooler smiled shyly. Commander Blevins said, "I
usually don't talk this much, but I seem to know so
much more when I am here in the Inner Worlds." He
then blushed, quickly turned back to the path, and said
so quietly that it barely resonated in Mrs. Frumpwooler, "We must be on our way."

Distracted by her thoughts once more, Mrs. Frumpwooler was surprised to suddenly find herself a long
way behind Commander Blevins and wondered why he
was walking and not focalshifting from place to place.
Feeling confident, she decided to shift to a point about
a hundred meters ahead of him. As she flew through
her unseen arc, a raucous "caw" shattered the serenity.
Commander Blevins stopped, turned in his tracks, and
acted quickly. He had to.

The moment ended with Mrs. Frumpwooler
standing next to Commander Blevins, in the spot
where he had stood the moment before she launched
herself. He had an arm around her waist and was
visibly holding her up. Little sparks were shooting out
from underneath his arm in a steady stream. She had a
crease where her behind would be if her body were not
a shapeless light orb. It was wide and deep but was not
bleeding, and she did not appear to be severely injured.
A large winged creature was crumpled on the desert
floor, far below them, slowly being bled dry of its color
by the sand around it.

"Good grief. What happened?" Mrs. Frumpwooler
asked.

"It is my fault, dear Mrs. Frumpwooler." Commander Blevins did not say. "I walked on without taking proper note of your joining me."

"I seem to remember being grabbed by something. Oh, my tushy is so sore." She ran her hand over her backside, "And dented! What did happen, Commander Blevins?"

"Well, what I neglected to tell you was that we do not focalshift near the desert, under any circumstances. Some extremely large Pterodactyls live just on the other side of the veil here. They can cross over in an instant to catch anything that moves through the air. That's why there are no birds or other winged creatures near the desert." He paused for a moment, then added, "Though I can't remember anyone grabbed so quickly as you. Usually, the Pteras stalk a while before striking."

"You mean to tell me that a PTER...O...DAC...TYL grabbed me and dented my tushy? But I wasn't flying. You said yourself that focalshifting was being one place one moment and another the next."

"True, that is what I said. Again, you are too clever to hide any truth from Mrs. Frumpwooler. When we focalshift, as long as we have a body of any kind, we travel through space. The movement happens so quickly that the normal laws of displacement do not apply. These crossover Pterodactyls, however, are amazingly swift. That one caught you in mid-flight and was about to be off with you."

"Which one? And be off to where with me? Good Grief."

She sat down on a nearby boulder, her stripy body shuddering all over. Her stripes wobbled like unset jello on a paint mixing machine.

Commander Blevins pointed toward the desert. Mrs. Frumpwooler looked around slowly. "Oh, Mercy!" she exclaimed. What is happening to that creature? And it looks so small. How could it possibly carry me and dent my tushy like this? Oh, it's still so sore, and...."

Commander Blevins saw that Mrs. Frumpwooler was heading straight into a crisal vortex. He placed his free hand on her neck and pressed his index finger onto the Point of Infinite Peacefulness, the ridge below her right ear. She quieted instantly, meowing softly. He felt it was vital for her to retain her general awareness of what had just happened—to grasp the danger of focal-shifting near the desert—and, therefore, released his hold on her neck almost as quickly as he had applied it.

"Oh," Mrs. Frumpwooler said and burped. Her body, and stripes, no longer shook.

"The creature you see down there on the desert floor was the one who grabbed you in mid-flight. It does look small from here, but remember we are many thousands of meters above it."

"Why is it half maroon and half that bleached eggshell color?" she asked.

"That is one reason why we cannot walk in the desert. It absorbs the color of anything that touches it."

"Oh," Mrs. Frumpwooler said again and then was quiet for a while.

Just as Commander Blevins was about to suggest

they begin walking again, Mrs. Frumpwooler asked, "If that thing had me in its mouth," she shuddered for a moment. "Why is it down there, while I'm up here with you? I was aiming for a point farther up the path, I think."

"Well, once the Pterodactyl caught you and your focalshifting arc was interrupted, your destination no longer mattered." Blevins was then silent.

Impatient, Mrs. Frumpwooler asked again, "Well then how DID I get back here."

Commander Blevins blushed and kicked some pebbles at his feet. "Uh, I er...I brought you back here."

"YOU brought me back here. From where? And how?"

Reluctantly he explained, "When I heard the screech of the Pterodactyl, I knew what had happened. I turned and focalshifted to a point just in front of where I saw it flying. You, I, and the creature arrived at nearly the same point in time and space simultaneously. I grabbed your arm, was swept along with you as the Pterodactyl's huge wings beat for a brief time. I then managed to convince the Pterodactyl to release you. As soon as it did, I focalshifted us back here, to keep from plummeting straight down to the ground. We were extraordinarily lucky there were no other Pteras in the area."

"My, Commander Blevins, you are a living Hero!"

Commander Blevins' stripy body blushed the length of its orb. His stumpy little legs were unaffected by Mrs. Frumpwooler's sudden adulation, except that they quivered slightly. "I'm only doing my job, Mrs. Frumpwooler," he said. "And it was necessary only because I didn't do my job right in the first place. I should have warned you."

"Oh, I think you are doing just fine, Commander Blevins." Mrs. Frumpwooler's orb pulsed with deep vibrations. Holding her beating heart, lest it rip from her luminescent breast, she shifted gears quickly and asked, "Just how did you 'convince' that thing to let go of me?"

Commander Blevins was silent for a moment. Then he said, "Oh, let's just say that I intruded upon a rather sensitive and personal area of its body in a way that completely diverted its attention. The Ptera opening its jaw to protest was a lucky break. Exactly why the bird landed in the desert is a complete mystery to me."

They both stood quietly for a moment. Blevins then asked, "Are you ready to push on Mrs. Frumpwooler?"

She wanted to ask more questions, to find out exactly where and how Commander Blevins had intruded upon the horrid bird's body but felt it was impolite to press further. She said, "Yes, I believe so."

Push on, they did. Blevins led the way. Mrs. Frump-wooler, preoccupied and rubbing her behind, was nonetheless careful to follow Commander Blevins closely.

They wound their way along the top of the ridge. The wind died down. Suddenly Commander Blevins got shorter and shorter, then disappeared altogether. Mrs. Frumpwooler was keeping only one eye upon him, still trying to fit together all the pieces of her mental puzzle. When she finally noticed he was shrinking and was then gone altogether, her distress was intense. She came to the point of his departure and peered down a graceful stairway cut into the mountainside. Commander Blevins was a couple dozen steps ahead of her. She hurried along to catch with him, very relieved.

"Hey, wait a minute, Commander Blevins," she said, panting as she caught up with him. "Where are we going now?"

"Down the stairs, Mrs. Frumpwooler," he said. His eyes were slightly glazed.

"Well, yes, I can see that. I am not a total ninny."

Commander Blevins was jolted slightly by Mrs. Frumpwooler's sarcasm. He stopped and turned back toward her and said, "I am so sorry, Mrs. Frumpwooler. It seems I'm getting a little too absorbed in the journey. Yes, of course, you can see that we are going down the stairs, and no, I do not think you are a ninny, or anything remotely close. We are heading down the stairs to the desert floor. It is time for us to cross The Collage and head for Akash."

"But you said we could not cross the desert," Mrs. Frumpwooler said with a whine in her voice. She was still a little annoyed.

"I think you are mistaken this time, Mrs. Frump-wooler. I said we could not walk on the desert floor. But we can cross it on the Sand Lake Express."

They locked eyes. Mrs. Frumpwooler seemed unwilling to relinquish her irritation, so Blevins waited.

Finally, she sighed and said, "Oh, I am a pill. Of course, you mentioned the Sand Lake Express. You haven't mentioned what it is, though. Do we find it at the bottom of these steps?"

"More or less. Follow me; it will be a surprise," Commander Blevins said, and started down the steps again.

"I'm not sure I'm up for another surprise just yet, thank you." Still feeling cross, Mrs. Frumpwooler set off after Commander Blevins, keeping him in close sight. Rubbing her still tender rump, she followed him along the stairway, which led around an outcropping. A splendid view of the desert unfolded in front of them from their vantage point a couple of hundred meters above the valley floor.

Mrs. Frumpwooler gasped at the vivid colors of The Collage. The sight restimulated her overactive mind, and she asked without saying, "Commander Blevins, where was that thing taking me?"

Caught in his reverie, he said, "What thing, where?"

"That horrid Ptera-ptooey thing that dented my tushy!"

"Oh, sorry," he said. "The Ptera was taking you back to its lair."

"To its lair. Where in the world is that?"

"I don't know. Probably in some of the less accessible regions of the Moondog World."

"Oh, that sounds awful. Why 'inaccessible'? Can't we go anywhere if we choose to?"

"No, not by a long shot. There are power curtains

and monkey windows and all sorts of traps to capture the unguided inner traveler."

"That gives me the willys," Mrs. Frumpwooler said, shivering.

They padded down the stairs. Mrs. Frump- wooler, still preoccupied, brought up the rear. The steps led into a narrow tunnel. Commander Blevins stopped and waited for Mrs. Frumpwooler. When she caught up with him, he said, "This is the last stretch before the Sand Lake Express. We must move through here quickly and quietly." Before Mrs. Frumpwooler could object, Blevins took firm hold of her squishy striped hand and set off at a fast trot. She started to protest, then remembered Commander Blevins' orders and swallowed her complaint.

Wispy things passed by her, whispering little sounds she could not quite hear. Something tried to pinch her, she thought, but they trotted by so quickly the moment passed before she could swat at whatever had grabbed for her.

The pathway turned to the right, and a soft blue light filled the end of the tunnel ahead. Then they were out of the tunnel and standing in a large blue under- ground cavern. A small lake lapped at the shoreline, not far from their feet. They both gasped, their stripy bodies heaving from the exertion.

After he caught his breath, Commander Blevins said, "That was the smoothest trip I've ever had through the tunnel."

"Oh, why?" Mrs. Frumpwooler asked, breathing only a little heavier than usual.

"The spiders are such nuisances. They can cause all kinds of problems."

"Spiders! What spiders!" Mrs. Frumpwooler's eyes grew large, and her breathing accelerated.

"Bigmouth," Commander Blevins muttered to himself as he put his hand on Mrs. Frumpwooler's neck. Touching behind her ear, Blevins was relieved to watch her regain her composure. "The Whispering Spiders in the tunnel," he said, testing her.

"Oh, that's nice. Where do we go next?" Mrs. Frumpwooler was calm, with a detached look and a semi-smile on her face.

Commander Blevins released her neck and watched her closely for a moment. "We go to the other side of the lake. Are you ready?"

"Sure, let's go." Mrs. Frumpwooler focused her eyes as they walked around the lake. The sand near the water shone a deep azure blue, sprinkled with shimmering silver slivers.

"Hey, what's that," Mrs. Frumpwooler pointed toward a short dock protruding into the lake.

"That is The Sand Lake Express," Commander Blevins said with a smile.

"The Sand Lake Express! It looks like the roller coaster from the old Land's End Funn Palace, without the track. How can that get us across the desert?"

"Mrs. Frumpwooler, never underestimate anything in the Inner Worlds. First thing: it IS the old roller coaster from the Land's End Funn Palace. Second thing..."

"Wait a minute, how could this possibly be that same old roller coaster, and furthermore, how do YOU know that it is?" Mrs. Frumpwooler's moodiness had resurfaced.

"It IS the same old roller coaster. You may check it out for yourself. I know because I brought it here myself."

"I find this incomprehensible, Commander Blevins. How on earth could you do such a thing?"

"On earth, I could not, my dear Mrs. Frumpwooler. Shall we go have a look?"

"Not on your life, boopsy. I never trusted roller coasters anyway, especially one that's in the water." Mrs. Frumpwooler's stripes were rising from the rest of her orb, pulsing rapidly.

Blevins sighed and squeezed Mrs. Frumpwooler behind the ear again. The stripes quieted down, and the vacant look returned to her eyes. Leading her by the hand, Commander Blevins walked along the remaining beach. He stepped on the boardwalk near the dock, turned to help Mrs. Frumpwooler negotiate the three steps, and cooed, "Upsy daisy now."

"Why thank you, Commander Blevins, you are such the gentleman." Mrs. Frumpwooler was as close to calm as she was likely to get at this point in the Journey. Their little stubby feet clumped along the boardwalk, echoing in the cavern. A white, hand-lettered sign was tied to poles, standing about head height. It announced

"Sand Lake Express." Smaller letters underneath it said, "Donated by Commander Blevins."

"Commander Blevins, you donated this? Why you are full of surprises! Wherever did you get it? And how did you get it here? You know it looks just like the old roller coaster at the Land's End Funn Palace. Do you remember the Funn Palace, Commander Blevins?"

Blevins let all of Mrs. Frumpwooler's chatter sail past, grateful she was in a pleasant mood. "If you will step over here, we can get on our way."

"Oh sure, Commander Blevins. I wouldn't want little old me to hold us up." He rolled his eyes. Leading her by the hand, he walked over to the middle of three bobbing cars. "SLE" was painted in blue letters on the side of each one. He stepped in first, helping her settle onto the soft cushions, then sat down himself. A round metal bar lowered onto their laps, and three blue lights lit up on the console in the middle of the little car's instrument panel.

"This is exciting, Commander Blevins. I always loved the rides."

"Well, I'm happy to hear that, Mrs. Frumpwooler. Just sit back now and relax. Blevins punched a few buttons. A backlit monitor came to life. Questions began appearing on it: "Pilot?" "Stability Required?" "Speed?" "Originating Locale?" "Number of Passengers?"

Commander Blevins punched in: "Creator, Yes, Level 3, Spider Tunnel Lake, 2".

The monitor responded: "Kosher & OK'd. Where to Commander Blevins?"

Commander Blevins punched in: "Records, Quadrant 17.863."

"Roger Dodger, CB. Akashic Gardens or Bust!" the monitor typed out.

Mrs. Frumpwooler watched in silent fascination.

Just as quietly, the whole side of the mountain rolled back in front of them. Brilliant light poured in through the opening, blinding both Mrs. Frumpwooler and Commander Blevins. The Sand Lake Express rocked slightly, the mountain disappearing from around them, and the desert beginning to move by, underneath the old Funn Palace Roller Coaster Cars.

EIGHT

AKASHIC GARDENS OR BUST

"Commander Blevins, what on earth is happening?" Mrs. Frumpwooler said without saying.

Smiling, Commander Blevins explained patiently, "Mrs. Frumpwooler, we are not on earth. That is why this can happen."

Three blue and white roller coaster cars rocked serenely in the gentle waters of Spider Tunnel Lake, looking as though they had been manufactured soon after World War I and refurbished recently. Mrs. Frumpwooler was able to stretch her already strained comprehension powers far enough to encompass the roller coaster cars. The lake itself nestled the three cars and two passengers comfortably in its waters, rolling along at a brisk clip ON TOP of many colors' desert. This development proved difficult for Mrs. Frump-wooler to accept.

"'This. What is this?" She was nearly frantic again. Commander Blevins had only to bend his wrist slightly. His right arm was lying across the back of the seat, putting his hand in easy reach of Mrs. Frumpwooler's neck. He pressed her Point of Infinite Peacefulness. She cooed a descending scale and settled into contentment.

"We are skimming over the desert in a lake of modest proportions. Any problem with that, Mrs. Frumpwooler."

"No, why none, Commander Blevins. It is a lovely day for a ride." Mrs. Frumpwooler said.

"Good, I'm glad you can enjoy the trip. It is a unique way to travel." He kept his finger firmly on her neck. "I'm sure I'm somewhat less that one hundred percent objective, but I do think it is the finest mode of travel available in the lower worlds, which rely on exterior devices, of course."

Mrs. Frumpwooler agreed.

They whizzed along for many kilometers. Commander Blevins had released his grip on Mrs. Frumpwooler sometime earlier. Soon after that, she said, "My, Commander, this is pleasant." He was amused at her familiarity. She was unaware of her boldness.

The lavender sky backlit several geyser eruptions: three cherry ones had gone up nearby, and Mrs. Frumpwooler had oohed and aahed. A multi-colored geyser sprang up just ahead of them as they passed over a series of gullies. Mrs. Frumpwooler clutched the lap bar, saying, "Oops see doop see," and then asked

Commander Blevins why the geyser had not affected their travel.

"The water of the lake deflects anything that hits it," he said. "The energy is absorbed and directed out to the side. That geyser is no wider than normal puddle behind us."

Mrs. Frumpwooler looked around behind them, but they had already traveled too far for her to see the flattened geyser. She settled back down. A short time later, she said, "Commander Blevins, remember the time that horrible creature grabbed me and dented my tushy?"

"Wouldn't forget that for the world, Mrs. Frumpwooler."

"Well, I was wondering what would have happened to me if that thing had...if you had not so gallantly rescued me?" She shuddered slightly.

Blevins took a deep breath. "It's a little difficult to say, Mrs. Frumpwooler. I haven't been party to a similar situation."

"Well, what would have happened to my physical body that we left sitting in your apartment? It is still there, isn't it."

"Yes, without question, though I imagine you are still standing. You were doing so when we left. If there were any intrusions there on the physical, we both would be pulled back from here immediately. But whether someone could be pulled back from the other side of a veil, much less from the digestive tract of a Pterodactyl, I really couldn't say."

"Ugh." A violent tremor went through Mrs. Frumpwooler.

"Well, what would happen to my body, the one still standing in your apartment, if I couldn't come back?"

"Oh, it would remain there."

"For how long?"

"Indefinitely, I suspect."

"Are you sure?"

"No."

"Would you come back to get me?"

"Of course, Mrs. Frumpwooler. It would be my professional duty to exhaust all possible avenues to return you to what is rightfully yours."

"But if you just couldn't find me, what then? What would you do with my physical body?"

"Oh, I'd probably put you in a closet for a while," Commander Blevins said. He had a sly smile on his stripy lips.

"Oh, you're awful," Mrs. Frumpwooler said in a huff.

"What would you like me to do, anyway? You brought up this subject in the first place."

"Well, you don't have to put me in the closet, for heaven's sake!"

"I repeat, 'what would you like me to do?' Leave you standing in the middle of the room and dust you once a month, whether you need it or not?"

"Well, that would be better than standing in an old dark closet, Commander Blevins. Really!" Mrs. Frump-wooler was quiet for a while, then said, "Maybe you could find a rest home for me. One that wasn't too particular, but would keep me warm and dry, feed me, and bathe me. You know, they take care of a lot of people who are lying down and can't fend for themselves, why not one that is standing straight up and can't fend for..."

Commander Blevins pressed Mrs. Frumpwooler's Point of Infinite Peacefulness again. She whistled a plaintive tune for a couple of kilometers, then fell silent. The remainder of the trip over the desert was uneventful.

NINE
OLD TRADERS AND ROGUES

Signposts zipped by occasionally on the outside of the Lake as it rolled across the desert. Mrs. Frumpwooler was oblivious to their passing. One sign went by in a moment of lucidity, though, and she commented to Commander Blevins, "What on earth does that mean?"

"On earth, Mrs. Frumpwooler, that would seem surreal. Here, it is simply a directional indicator for beings who wish to find the causes behind those particular facets of their lives."

"Oh, right. I see," Mrs. Frumpwooler said and silently vowed never to say, "What on earth does that mean?" again. The sign had said, "Nightmares & Follys," and had pointed away from the direction they traveled.

The Sand Lake Express, with Mrs. Frumpwooler and Commander Blevins firmly in tow, approached what appeared to be an oasis in the middle of the desert. It grew larger and larger as they drew nearer. Beyond the oasis, but hidden from view, lay the Shining Shores Seas. Pure white buildings dotted the area. Many had spires, domed roofs, and parapets. Lush greenery, in a full range of tones, filled wide spaces between clusters of the white buildings. The air around the whole sector crackled with blue, yellow, and burnt orange streaks, which shot through the atmosphere from points high and low, in a random pattern.

They rolled straight toward an outer forest of dense growth. "Are we going to..." Mrs. Frumpwooler then squealed. Spider Tunnel Lake looked as if it would crash into the trees and bushes now clearly visible. Before Commander Blevins could clamp down on Mrs. Frumpwooler's Point of Infinite Peacefulness, the greenery parted majestically, revealing a broad water-way, awaiting their arrival.

"Oh! How delightful, Commander Blevins," Mrs. Frumpwooler said, shifting from high anxiety to glee with amazing dexterity. A sign off to their right announced, "Akash Metro Canal" in vivid orange lettering on a grey background. The Lake rode from the desert into the Canal and blended without a ripple. Commander Blevins and Mrs. Frumpwooler found themselves cruising along the waterway through a lush forest, trailing a small wake behind them. The blue, yellow, and burnt orange streaks continued to bisect the lavender sky.

"Is this where we are?" Mrs. Frumpwooler chewed

on the knuckle of one hand and pounded on the lap bar with the other.

"Yes, I certainly cannot argue with that, Mrs. Frumpwooler," Blevins said.

A little confused, Mrs. Frumpwooler said, "Well, I mean, where are we, Commander Blevins?"

"I see. We are in Akash. The suburbs, to be exact. The name of this specific suburb is Akashic Gardens."

"Oh, I remember you mentioning that name earlier. Who made these wonderful little rivers. They are so nice and straight. Did you make these too, Commander Blevins? Don't be bashful now. You can tell little old me."

Commander Blevins looked closely at Mrs. Frump-wooler. He decided she was being playful, not getting out of hand.

"These are canals, Mrs. Frumpwooler. They were built by the Old Traders of Akash, long ago. I certainly did not make them. Getting these little cars up here and refurbished is quite all I'm up to, thank you."

"I think you underestimate yourself, Commander," Mrs. Frumpwooler said. Commander Blevins noted the familiarity again and smiled. Mrs. Frumpwooler continued, "What did the Traders trade?"

"They traded past life experiences."

"Oh." Mrs. Frumpwooler thought for a moment. "How did they do that, Commander?"

"Well, not very prudently, I'm afraid. The traders were known as the Naacal Raiders in their day, for they had developed the ability to snatch previous life experiences from unsuspecting travelers. This, of course, caused untold repercussions in those affected by the events of any given snatched lifetime, not the least, of course, the snatchee, so to speak."

"That sounds dreadful, Commander Blevins. Are we likely to encounter these Nasal Raiders of yours?" Mrs. Frumpwooler was genuinely concerned.

"Nacaal, Mrs. Frumpwooler. N-A-A-C-A-L: Naacal. And no, not here. They were banished long ago. I only learned about them by accident when I was adjusting the vibrational harmonics of these lovely old Funn Palace cars. They had to be tuned to the inherent interplays of both the Spider Tunnel Lake and what we are riding on now the Akash Metro Canal."

"Oh, that reminds me, Commander, where did that lovely lake go. It was so nice and blue. This little river is a pleasant looking green, but I like blue better. And where did those nasty Raider boys go to anyway."

"Mrs. Frumpwooler, you continue to amaze me. Nothing gets by your keen powers of observation. The Canals are green but don't fret. When we get to the Records, there will be enough blue to last you a lifetime —even a lifetime here, which can go on for many thousands of Physical World years. The Akash Traders, or Naacal Raiders, whichever you like, were sent to various subworlds. There are a few in the Moondog World, but the Moondog keeps them easily under control and out of the way."

Mrs. Frumpwooler had a vision of that great white dog, herding a pack of tattered pirates across a barren landscape, away from the scarlet trees and white rippling paths of motion that she had seen there.

Uninterrupted by Mrs. Frumpwooler's speculations, Commander Blevins continued talking without speaking, "I've also heard that many of them were sent back to the physical to start their spiritual training all over again. Apparently, their rogue tendencies have not been completely worked off, for in transition between lifetimes, they, or so I've heard, often slip out of the transitory pathways and spend their time tapping into the physical bodies of unsuspecting beings who leave themselves open in various ways."

"Gee, how does someone know if they have been tapped into? It gives me the willys, just thinking about it."

"Yes, it is quite a sticky wicket. The best way to avoid contact is to lead a life of moderation and provide service whenever possible. Purportedly, these renegades cannot attach to someone while that person is giving. Only when the intended victim is taking or trying to take will their aura open sufficiently to let in impurities, including contact with these Takers. A really accomplished Taker may attach itself to someone and derive vicarious experiences through the unwitting host person with a sufficient invitation. Or so I've heard. The Takers' desires filter into the host, who is motivated to indulge in certain activities, usually, to excess, I might add, which may well prove injurious to the unwitting person. The result is often destructive. Of course, the Rogue is happy as a rat in a sewer as it sucks up energy and thrills through its attachment to the attachee. Supposedly."

Mrs. Frumpwooler looked nearly as green as the bushes on the shoreline of the Canal, passing by steadily. Commander Blevins noticed her condition, put his arm around her, which produced little tickly arcs of electricity and a shower of sparks. He said, "Sorry if I've overloaded you. I always seem to get verbose when I'm in the Akash. Anyway, Mrs. Frump-wooler, this isn't as bad as it sounds. We do each create our own worlds, remember. I've overstated the role of the host as a victim. This only happens to people who richly deserve it through their blindness and greed. Don't fret. You are much too kind too ever to attract this kind of problem."

Mrs. Frumpwooler whimpered, then began giggling as the sparks from Commander Blevins' arm tickled her shoulders.

TEN

THE PASSION PIT REHABILITATION

"Are we there yet, Commander. And why haven't we seen anyone here?" Mrs. Frumpwooler complained. They had just come to a fork in the Akash Metro Canal and had taken the lane marked both "Stairway to Heaven" and "Records." The other arm of the Canal led to "Baby Dreams," "Whithered Transgressions," and "Central Hub." Colored streaks still filled the sky, and they had not seen anyone at all since entering Akash. "We haven't seen anyone or anything since that dreadful creature almost broke my rump. Oh." She rubbed her bottom. "Say, it doesn't hurt anymore," Mrs. Frumpwooler said, pleased. " I can't remember when it did hurt last. And that awful dent is gone, too."

"Injuries to bodies behave in a much different manner here than in the Physical Worlds, Mrs. Frumpwooler," Blevins explained. "I'm happy you are well now."

"Thank you, Commander Blevins. You are so chival-rous." Mrs. Frumpwooler was unable to keep her grip on cheerfulness and abruptly assailed Blevins, "Except when you wanted to put me in the closet, you dreadful man! And you never did tell me where the Lake went!" She slapped him hard across his face. Her hand, though, didn't strike a solid surface, but bounced off, gently, giving Mrs. Frumpwooler the impression that she had just hit a rubber band. Sparks flew everywhere from the contact, tickling both of them.

"Steady now, Mrs. Frumpwooler." Commander Blevins had placed his hand on the back of her neck when he felt her attitude shift. "Things get trickier the closer we come to the Records. Mood swings are to be expected." He held her Point of Infinite Peacefulness firmly and chuckled while she let out great peals of laughter. The little sparks soothed her and tickled them both. "And the Lake went back home where it always has been," he added.

"Of course, I should have guessed that. But how will we get home?"

"There are many ways to accomplish that. Don't worry about it for now."

"You are such a dear, Commander," Mrs. Frump-wooler cooed. "It would be nice to see some other people, though."

Instantly the Canal was populated.

People were gliding in both directions along the waterway. Some traveled on small chairs, skimming over the water, leaving barely a ripple behind them. A group of people was on the shore just up ahead, laughing and dancing. Two youngsters raced by on skates, kicking up small jets of water with each stroke of their legs, joking and yelling at each other. Everyone had bodies similar to Commander Blevins and Mrs. Frumpwooler, with one striking exception: their stripes rotated.

"Where did they all suddenly come from, Commander Blevins? And look, everyone's stripes are spinning around. Why don't our stripes spin?" Mrs. Frumpwooler wanted to know. She thought the spiraling stripes made the people look like shiny barber's poles. "Yoo-hoo. Hello there," Mrs. Frump-wooler waved to the group on the shore.

"These people were always here," Commander Blevins said. "I usually find it simpler to filter out other life forms while passing through populated areas. Approaching the records is taxing enough, in itself, without undue stimulation. And they can't see or hear us anyway, Mrs. Frumpwooler."

"Oh, gracious. Does that mean we are invisible? Are we ghosts, Commander Blevins?" Mrs. Frumpwooler's eyes became very wide at the thought.

"No, no. Don't get ahead of yourself, Mrs. Frump-wooler. We are guests here. They call us 'Readers.' The Council, who reside in the Central Core, decided a long time ago to shield residents from the unpredictable energy of the many Readers who move through here. The people you see around you exist at a different vibrational rate. We are only a passing haze to them.

They can tell we are here only enough to avoid direct contact with us."

"Is that why their stripes are turning?"

"No. But that's a good guess, Mrs. Frumpwooler. Their stripes are rotating because they are happy."

"Does that mean we aren't happy?"

"No, not at all."

"What happens when they are mad? Do the stripes get dark or stop turning?"

"No. Well, really, no one is sure. People don't get mad here."

"Oh, you mean this is one of those good worlds with no bad that you mentioned?"

"Well, not quite, though I am impressed you remember my mention of the positive and pure positive worlds, Mrs. Frumpwooler. The people here can get angry and do have conflicts with each other sometimes. The catch is that whenever their negative emotions or actions surface, they simply go poof; they are no longer where they were."

"Well, where are they then, Commander Blevins?" Mrs. Frumpwooler was intrigued.

"They are in the Passion Pit," explained Blevins.

"The what?" Incredulous, Mrs. Frumpwooler was unable to prevent her mouth from hanging open.

"The Passion Pit. Whenever someone chooses to let the passions of their mind take over, they are whisked away from the general populace to an area called the Passion Pit."

"Oh, a Rehabilitation Pit. It sounds dreadful."

"No, not at all," Commander Blevins said. Rehab is an enjoyable place where people can vent their steam in a way that burdens them less karmically. Then they have a chance to reflect on their actions, learning how better to detach from their passions."

Mrs. Frumpwooler considered this. "That does sound like a pleasant way to handle things when they get bothersome. We should have a place like that back home."

Commander Blevins chuckled, "Ever the thinker, Mrs. Frumpwooler."

Off to their right, several large people were detaining three smaller persons. Mrs. Frumpwooler stared, then asked, "What's going on over there, Commander Blevins?"

"The local authorities are rounding up some aliens, it looks like."

"Aliens!"

"Yes, people from different areas of the Causal Worlds often come here to Akash. There is lots of work here, and the environment is more peaceful than where the smaller people come from."

"What are they going to do with them?"

"The authorities will try to send them back home."

"Where's home?"

"I don't know. And neither do the authorities. The little people slip in through harmonic portals that close up and vanish moments after the openings appear."

"So, what do they do with them?" Mrs. Frump-wooler asked.

"They just hold them for a while, then let them go. That's all they can do."

"Why on Ear...why do they do that? It sounds so pointless."

"No more so than some of our practices back in the Physical Worlds. The people in control here are just exercising it, their control, or the illusion of it."

They were near a group of people now. Mrs. Frumpwooler exclaimed, "Look, they have bumps all over them."

"That's how people here can tell they are aliens. That and the fact that they are shorter than the residents."

The three bobbing cars passed through the area where the large people still held the smaller people. Mrs. Frumpwooler contemplated. Then she said, "How do the aliens get here, Commander Blevins? How do they find those harmonic potholes?"

Before he could answer, the control panel on their car beeped twice and a message scrolled across the monitor. "Approaching Gardens. Specify Quad-Sector CB." Commander Blevins punched in "FRUM.../currently active."

"What does that mean, Commander Blevins."

"Pretty basic stuff, Mrs. Frumpwooler. 'FRUM' is your sector. Things are organized in many ways here, but for you, coming from the Physical World's hard-shell side, an alphabetical listing is the most direct. 'Currently active' means you are running a physical body. If you had already shed that body, I would have entered 'limbo,' 'en route,' or 'assigned,' depending on your status.

"What's 'hard shell' mean. And 'limbo,' 'rerouted,' or..."

"Can't answer that just now, Mrs. Frumpwooler. Please hang on tight. There will be turbulence as we approach the Records."

Mrs. Frumpwooler grabbed ahold of the lap bar just as the three little cars began pitching to and fro. The water in the Canal churned, turning a pale, whitish-green. Off to the left ahead of them, a glistening white spire shot hundreds of meters into the sky, twirling. From it's top exploded a shower of azure blue streaks. The yellow, blue, and burnt orange streaks, which had been a constant fixture against the lavender skyline, faded and were gone in moments. The light purplish-blue streaks erupted in all directions, growing larger as they moved out from the spire.

The spire expanded as it twirled. It became a tall, thin pyramid, then shifted to a round-domed temple. Next, it fattened, looking like a Physical World 21st century skyscraper, only much larger. The azure blue streaks had reached the horizons by this time, impacting them like rockets with warheads of concentrated blue dye, and were spreading their color over much of the lavender sky.

Mrs. Frumpwooler was in awe. She twisted her head in one direction, then the other as she followed the coloring of the skies and the spire's transformation, which now stood as a towering mountain of shining white. Its sides were multifaceted, shining with pale blue light. The Canal twisted around it, churning violently, and angled up as the waterway climbed the white face of the towering mountain.

"Wowser, Commander, this is quite a doozy," Mrs. Frumpwooler shouted. Commander Blevins smiled as he punched additional information into the console.

A stream of blue water jetted out from the side of the mountain, meeting the climbing canal in mid-air. The canal calmed noticeably. High above the city, Mrs. Frumpwooler watched as a round doorway opened in the side of the mountain. The canal—carrying the three roller coaster cars and their passengers, and now merged with the jet stream—ran smoothly through the doorway and spilled into an awaiting pool, splashing up the back wall just slightly, before finally settling down.

Mrs. Frumpwooler looked around gleefully and said, "Hey Commander, the water is blue again. How nice."

Commander Blevins flipped three toggle switches. The monitor flashed: "Welcome to 'FROM/active.' Have a pleasant Reading. Catch you on the way back, CB." A small blip appeared in the middle of the screen, ran around eating up all the letters, then burped and sucked in all the light on the screen as the system shut down.

"Well, welcome to the Records of Akash, Mrs. Frumpwooler," Commander Blevins said. The old Land's End Funn Palace Roller Coaster cars came to rest at a dock on the pool's far side. Pale blue light bathed the area. An arched doorway led away from the

Docking Site and the Dock. Beyond it, Mrs. Frump-wooler could see a blue and white checked hall winding around until it disappeared.

"Oh, Commander, I can't tell you how exciting this is," Mrs. Frumpwooler smiled happily. Her stripes pulsed.

"Well, the real adventure has yet to begin," Commander Blevins said, hopping onto the dock. The car rocked as he pushed off from it. Mrs. Frumpwooler stood up to follow him and nearly fell backward into the pool. Overcompensating in her effort to maintain composure, she lurched, falling forward, then landing flat on her face at Commander Blevins' feet. "Oh, Mrs. Frumpwooler, are you all right?" Commander Blevins scooped her up and held her steady as she regained her balance.

Sparks flew everywhere, covering the Dock and spilling over into the Dock Site Pool. Mrs. Frump-wooler was only partially dazed from her fall, leaving most of her powers of observation intact. Giggling, she pointed back toward the pool and said, "Commander, look at what happens when these little sparky things land in the water."

Sparks continued to pour from their bodies' contact points. The sparks that fell into the water sat still for only a moment, then began swimming in circles like small fish and soon were chasing each other madly. The Pool was turning into sparkly chaos, and Mrs. Frump-wooler and Commander Blevins convulsed in laughter. Fortunately, their belly laugh convolutions caused them to part. The sparks stopped spewing forth, Commander Blevins and Mrs. Frumpwooler sobered up, and the Pool absorbed the frolicking sparkles.

Catching his breath, Commander Blevins said without saying, "My that was a curious sensation, don't you think Mrs. Frumpwooler."

She was still breathing heavily and said nothing. Had Commander Blevins been a more worldly man, he would have noticed the Causal equivalent of arousal in Mrs. Frumpwooler's look. He was not, though, and he continued, "I wonder what caused it?"

After looking around a bit, he shrugged his shoulders, smiled, and said, "Oh, well. We should get on with it, don't you agree, Mrs. Frumpwooler?"

Still overcome with her unexpected sensations, she could only manage, "Mmmmmm."

He started to take her arm, thought better of it, then said, "I shall lead the way." He walked through the arched doorway and into the checked hall. Each square he stepped onto lighted up, in either blue or white, and sent corresponding bands of light around the hallway's curved outer wall. Mrs. Frumpwooler followed, and a similar effect greeted her. Still somewhat dazzled, and now partially mesmerized, she walked on, prepared to trail Commander Blevins into the bowels of hell itself.

ELEVEN
THESE ARE YOUR LIVES

Commander Blevins walked through a second arched doorway, and Mrs. Frumpwooler followed. The hallway curved around to their left then went straight for a long way. Long rectangular windows cut into both sides of the walls, spaced about a meter apart. The panes of the windows were frosted over. Every seventh window on Mrs. Frumpwooler's right side was a doorway with a small sign mounted at eye level, which read, "Viewing Room."

"Not too much further now, Mrs. Frumpwooler," Commander Blevins said.

"How do you know that?" Mrs. Frumpwooler asked.

"As you pass each repository, look directly at the bottom of the recessed window panel. You will see a name or part thereof."

"Oh, you're right, Commander!" Mrs. Frumpwooler had just passed "FRUMMILDEW." As she passed more frosted windows, she read, "FRUMMILTON, FRUM-MOLTEN, FRUMMULLEN, FRUMMY, FRUMNOT, FRUMNUT, FRUMNUTTON, FRUMOPO, FRUMOPOT. "Commander Blevins, I don't think we are getting close very quickly. And why are all my lives listed under Frumpwooler? Why not under one of my other names?"

"They are. You are completely cross-indexed here. Now, be patient, Mrs. Frumpwooler, and you shall be rewarded."

Mrs. Frumpwooler sighed and walked on. Gradually they passed "FRUMQUERT... FRUMRUMM... FRUM-STONE...FRUMTRONE... FRUMUS... FRUMVITE...FRUMWASTE ...FRUMWA-TERS...FRUMWET... "Oh, Commander, we are getting close now."

Near the end of the hallway, and just past a Viewing Room, Mrs. Frumpwooler let out a whoop, "FRUMP-WOOLER! Commander, you've gone past it!"

"Just seeing if you are on your toes, Mrs. Frump-wooler," Blevins grinned.

"Oh, you sly dog, you," she said, winking at him. "What do we do now?"

"Well, we have a choice. Only two kinds of people can access the records here; first, the person in question, reviewing their own records. Second, a Verified Viewer. Since we have both types of people here, at least in how it affects the viewing of one Gladys Frumpwooler's Akashic records, we can choose."

"What's the difference, Commander?"

"Well, you can view your records, and I can view your records. That's the similarity. I can also view other people's records in this file, and you cannot. That's the difference."

"You mean you could pull out Malvandian's records."

"Of course. Would you like that, Mrs. Frumpwooler?"

"Uhh, no, I think not. I'd rather leave his memories alone for now, thank you." Thoughts of Malvandian rippled through Mrs. Frumpwooler, interrupting her infatuation with Commander Blevins.

"Ok, by me, Mrs. Frumpwooler. So now our question is which one of us will do the selecting?"

"Why don't you, Commander," she offered with a little wave of her hand.

"Why don't we both," suggested Blevins, spreading his arms.

"Oh, grand," she said. Malvandian faded.

"First, put your palm squarely on the middle of the repository window."

Mrs. Frumpwooler did so. The window felt cool to her touch, and the change was immediate and startling. The frosted panes of the repository cleared. Inside was a tall rotating blue fixture that contained many small dark blue trays. Each tray was labeled. As Mrs. Frumpwooler watched in fascination, she noticed that the labels were all the same. "Look, Commander, they are all called FRUMPWOOLER. How can we tell which is mine?"

"Yours will have your full name on it. Watch this."

Commander Blevins put his palm on the window beside Mrs. Frumpwooler. The tray labeled "FRUMP-WOOLER" immediately changed to "ERONK SILAS FRUMPWOOLER" directly in front of his hand. The next one said, "ETHYL PIL FRUMPWOOLER."

Mrs. Frumpwooler cried out softly, her hand quivering on the glass. Commander Blevins turned toward her to see what was the matter. In doing so, he removed his hand from the glass. The labels changed back to "FRUMPWOOLER" only.

"Oh, thank you, Commander. I really don't want to run into Malvandian just now." She shuddered a bit, then quieted down. Suddenly the carousel stopped turning. The tray immediately in front of Mrs. Frumpwooler said only "FRUMPWOOLER." Why has it stopped? This one's no different than any other."

"Your observations are quite keen as usual, Mrs. Frumpwooler," said Blevins. "If you look further, however, you will see the reason for its stopping."

Mrs. Frumpwooler looked up, then down. "Oh, goody," she said. At just above her knee level, a tray was labeled, "GLADYS PERIWINKLE FRUMPWOOLER."

"Are you ready for the next step, Mrs. Frumpwooler?" Commander Blevins asked.

"Most certainly," she said.

"Then touch the window immediately in front of your tray with your other hand."

Mrs. Frumpwooler bent down and did so. For a moment, nothing happened. Then the tray began moving out toward the window. The window section in front of the tray slid back into the wall. A small pulsating charge went through both of Mrs. Frumpwooler's arms. She shrieked and pulled back her hands. The tray reversed its direction, reseating itself in its original position, and the missing section of the window reappeared from inside the wall. A moment later, the label on the tray changed back to "FRUMPWOOLER."

"Oh, gracious, what have I done?"

"Nothing that can't be undone. Let me help you." Commander Blevins placed his hand on the window in front of Mrs. Frumpwooler's tray. It had just begun to refrost itself but rapidly cleared up again. Mrs. Frumpwooler's full name appeared for the second time, and the tray started to slip out toward the window again.

"How did the tray know it was the one you wanted, Commander?"

"Oh, that's part of the Verified Viewers Training. I'm sorry, but I must keep the technique confidential."

"Oh. I see," Mrs. Frumpwooler said, feeling a little slighted.

The window section disappeared into the wall once more, and Commander Blevins let the chosen tray slide neatly onto the palm of his hand. He turned slowly away from the window, raising the tray up to eye level. Mrs. Frumpwooler followed his every move. The tray was about as long as Commander Blevins' forearm, medium width, and not too high. It appeared to be made of shiny blue metal, which pulsed gently. Mrs. Frumpwooler thought it looked wet and alive, like a dog's nose. As Commander Blevins lifted the tray, Mrs. Frumpwooler saw a bead of moisture drop toward the floor. She watched it fall. It disappeared in mid-air with a little bright twinkle. Looking back up to the tray, she wondered about the vanishing drop only until she saw the tray's contents. Lined up neatly from front to back, like extra wide file cards, were wafer-thin, pearl white rectangles.

"Here we go," Commander Blevins said, holding out the tray for Mrs. Frumpwooler's inspection. "These are your lives."

"Gracious, that's all. I mean, how can those little squares be my lives. Was I trash compacted or something? Can I touch them?" Mrs. Frumpwooler was losing her composure as she became excited.

"Yes, in fact, you will need to touch them. They are nothing like what you are thinking, so please hold your imagination at bay for the moment." Commander Blevins gently took Mrs. Frumpwooler's arm with his free hand. Ignoring the sparks, he said, "Let's go into the Viewing Room here." The door next to the now refrosted window opened as he placed a foot in front of it. With a giggling Mrs. Frumpwooler firmly in tow, and leading with the tray marked 'GLADYS PERI-WINKLE FRUMPWOOLER,' he entered the room and led her over to a long couch against the left-hand wall.

Blevins indicated she should sit. She plopped down in the middle of the couch next to a dividing console, saying, "Oh, this is so soft. You should get one of these for your apartment, Commander."

Commander Blevins gently sat the tray of files into a sunken area of the console and clipped it into place. "Good idea Mrs. Frumpwooler. I'll work on that when we get back home."

Misreading Commander Blevins' use of the word "we," Mrs. Frumpwooler tittered. He looked at her closely, then sat down on the opposite side of the console. "It is important to frame the proper attitude before going further, Mrs. Frumpwooler. Are you with me?" he said.

"Forever Commander," she solemnly pledged, sighing.

He sighed too and was quiet for a moment. "Please let your mind relax. Let all those interesting and bushy thoughts of yours simply take a vacation. They can do anything they like, be involved in whatever they like, only you choose to be occupied with what we have at hand, letting the thoughts have their own world." He was silent for several more moments.

Finally, he opened a small door behind the tray and extracted a cupped armrest. One end of the armrest remained anchored to the console's inside; the other end swung freely in mid-air. A small shelf extended from the arm rest's tip. He put his hand around a lever inside the swinging arm's cavity and pushed it forward, which advanced the tray. As the lever stopped, two additional, lower armrests rose on either side of the console.

Commander Blevins glanced at Mrs. Frumpwooler and was relieved to see her sitting quietly, gazing at the wall across from her. The wall was blank and light blue. He touched her gently on the shoulder, then let his left arm lay on his armrest and said, "Place your right arm in your armrest here, as I am doing." She smiled and did as he asked.

"Ok, now we are ready to begin. Our first step is to look at your Past Lives Index Record Card, which should be here at the front of the row." Commander Blevins lifted the thin wafer and placed it carefully on the small folding shelf atop the upper armrest. The Card sat upright on a narrow grooved strip, supported by two metal fingers in back.

"Now, I can do this, but it is important for you to at least look through the Index. Many of the lives you have previously led do not have any particular impact on this current lifetime. The trick is to figure out which ones do and to scan them for telling features."

"But I want to see them all!"

"Impossible. That would take far too long, and the strain on your present consciousness would be over-whelming." Mrs. Frumpwooler started to protest, and Commander Blevins cut her off. "That goes for every-body, Mrs. Frumpwooler."

"Oh, well," Mrs. Frumpwooler sighed. "How do we discover which cards to check. And how do these little cards tell me about a life I have lived before, anyway," she asked.

"I did promise to tell you that, Blevins said. "I think, though, that it would be better to *show* you first. Depending on who last worked your files, we may find the significant lifetimes already marked. At worst, the implant codes will make sorting easy."

"How do we start?"

"It is quite simple. First, you rest your right arm in this upper armrest." Commander Blevins helped Mrs. Frumpwooler position her arm on the swinging armrest and then said, "Yes, that's it." She laid her hand just below the small shelf. A couple sparks flew. "Next, you place the middle finger of your right hand on the small white dot in the middle of the Record Card."

"But the whole card is white. I don't see a dot."

"Oh, of course. I'm sorry. Just turn your wrist slightly, so the heel of your hand touches here." He guided

Mrs. Frumpwooler moved her hand into position, so it rested in a contoured area of the armrest just below the Record Card holding shelf. Deep midnight blue bathed the room. The Card glowed noticeably, pearl white, and shimmered. At its bottom, directly in the center, a small white dot was visible. It glistened as though damp.

"I see it. Oh, goody." Mrs. Frumpwooler said, rejoicing. She moved her finger toward the white dot, then hesitated. "Shall I do it?" She looked a little awkward.

"Go for it, Mrs. Frumpwooler," he smiled and urged her onward.

Mrs. Frumpwooler uncoiled her middle finger and firmly touched it to the white spot. "Oh, it feels cool and wet. Just like a doggie's nose," she cooed.

Chuckling, Commander Blevins watched as the

Card filled with waves of light pulsing across its surface, which was now a screen. "It should clear momentarily." The screen did clear. A pale blue sky filled most of it. A short rock ledge appeared at the bottom of the picture. "My this is unusual," he said, "I've never seen an Index Card begin with a landscape. Perhaps this is a new..." Commander Blevins never finished his sentence. Two raucous shrieks filled the room. Across the screen flew a very large Pterodactyl, growing larger until only the belly and feet of the enormous bird could be seen, as it came to rest on the rock ledge. The creature had emitted the first cry. Mrs. Frumpwooler had joined in with the second screech. She was squatting on the couch, with her left arm bent and sticking out from her body in wing-like fashion. Her right arm was still in place on the swinging armrest, middle finger firmly planted on the white dot of the Record Card. Her mouth was opened and moving, but released no further sound.

"Holy Zoider!" Commander Blevins was stunned. He was sure he had heard the noise—both noises—with his ears, coming from outside himself. This was so far from norma. He had no idea what to do next. He could barely see Mrs. Frumpwooler in the dark blue room. She sat stone-still. On the card, the Pterodactyl scratched at the stone ledge and sat down. Its large leathery tail filled the small screen.

Jerking awake, Commander Blevins came out of his shock. He grabbed the Card from its shelf. The Pterodactyl faded. He squinted at the Card for an Index

Code, which wasn't there, and then put it away in the tray. Mrs. Frumpwooler's right arm and finger remained motionless, and Commander Blevins gently moved her hand away from the Record Card holding shelf and the contoured hand rest. Dark blue turned to light blue, and Commander Blevins gasped as he fully realized Mrs. Frumpwooler's condition, perched as she was on the viewing sofa. He jumped up from his side of the console and hurried over to her.

Muttering to himself, "Well, that explains the Ptera popping up so quickly in the desert. Poor Mrs. Frumpwooler." He sat down beside her and placed his hand on her neck, found the Point of Infinite Peacefulness, and pressed. She made several small birdlike sounds and slid back down to a normal sitting position, with both hands folded in her lap.

Commander Blevins sat quietly with Mrs. Frumpwooler until he was sure she had recovered from her identity shift. He then returned to his side of the couch, sat down, and looked through the many cards in the tray. None of the codes were there. Puzzled, he decided to run through a few Cards in an attempt to solve the mystery.

Picking a Record Card several Cards in front of the Ptera "Index," he pulled it up and set it on the shelf. He laid his left arm and hand on the swinging armrest and touched the white dot along the Card's bottom. The room was dark blue before the Card flickered. The Card became a screen. After a moment's ripple, the screen cleared to reveal a small baby playing with a stick in the dirt outside a bamboo hut. The child was naked and had something bright red in its hair. Behind the baby, he could see a leg and foot, perhaps belonging to its mother. The sun was shining, and Commander Blevins could hear singing in the background. The voices came from outside of him. His mind started to boggle, then he remembered: In a viewing room, sound from the Cards did appear to come from the outside, instead of resonating from within like everywhere else in the Causal Worlds.

"Silly of me to forget," he admonished himself. "But that still doesn't explain how Mrs. Frumpwooler's Ptera cry came from outside."

The mother moved her leg behind the baby in rhythm to the distant voices. Suddenly there was a loud cry. The leg disappeared. There seemed to be a commotion nearby. The baby played on with its stick, unconcerned. A loud crash shook the ground, a shadow fell across the baby, and it screamed in terror.

The next moment the baby on the screen was replaced by a huge dull grey stump. "No, its a leg," Commander Blevins said to himself. "Probably a rampaging elephant's leg." With horror, he then watched as the elephant's leg left the screen. The realization of what he had just seen was confirmed by the sight of a squashed, pulpy, mound where the little baby, then the elephant's leg, had just been.

Pulling his finger off the Card's white spot, he looked at Mrs. Frumpwooler, who appeared to be unaffected. Grateful, and feeling queasy, Blevins sighed and replaced the Card back in the file. Light blue light returned. "Her first life a Pterodactyl. Then squashed as a baby by a rogue elephant," he muttered to himself, shaking his head with compassion. Not wanting to leave Mrs. Frumpwooler with only those two experiences, though one of which she probably was not aware, Commander Blevins felt he must press on: surely there would be positive experiences ahead.

Another Card, more deep blue, and then slaughter on an ancient battlefield. Jerking that Card from the holder, Blevins picked up a handful of Cards and impatiently threw them on the shelf one after the other in rapid succession: a sinking ship, a volcano erupting, a landslide, a cholera epidemic, another animal stampede. The array of carnage was deafening. Though everyone moved from lifetime to lifetime by one device or another, and physical death could be bloody, Commander Blevins had never seen a series of Cards open with only death and gore as he was now witnessing.

He pressed on. A murder then suicide, caught in the reins of a runaway horse, pulled under a calm lake by something unseen, poisoned, ripped apart during torture, strangled over a card game, an abusive jailer hanged by inmates...on and on. Blevins' mind reeled at the carnage.

Supposedly the Cards would open with whatever was pertinent to a viewer's current lifetime. If there was little connection between the lifetime represented on the Record Card and the viewer's present life, then happy scenes of carefree times would flicker by, or at least that was what Commander Blevins had learned at Verified Viewers Training. And that had been his experience, for the most part, to date.

Commander Blevins pulled the hair in his right ear. "Something is amiss here," he muttered aloud.

"What was that, Commander. When are we going to start this, anyway?" Mrs. Frumpwooler was back, demanding an explanation as usual.

"Oh, pardon me, Mrs. Frumpwooler. I was just talking to myself. Yes, well, we can...er...start right now, of course. Sorry to keep you waiting." He was stalling for time, unsure whether or not to continue the Viewing.

"I feel stiff all over, Commander Blevins. This little blue room must not agree with me." Mrs. Frumpwooler stretched her arms, especially the left one. "But I do want to see what this is all about. Why is your arm on that contraption? And what are those little shiny things in your hand?"

Commander Blevins raised his left arm from the swinging armrest and held it up to Mrs. Frumpwooler. "One question at a time, Mrs. Frumpwooler," he cautioned her, still holding the last Record Card. It contained the records of Mrs. Frumpwooler when she had been burned at the stake as an evil sorcerer.

"Oh, is that one of my file cards? Let me see it." She plucked it from Commander Blevins before he could protest.

"Perhaps it would be better if we skipped this part of

the tour and..."

"Not on your life, Commander. I may be a little stiff and sore from our Journey here, but I am most certainly prepared to find out just what I may have been about in other times." She looked the Record Card over and said, "This looks like a dull one. Pick another, and let's get the show on the road."

Commander Blevins accepted the Card with relief and inserted it, along with the stack in his hand, back into the Tray. Picking a new card from near the front of the row, he took a deep breath and placed it in the holder. He laid his left arm on the swinging rest, carefully put his middle finger in front of where he knew the white dot to be, and then looked over at Mrs. Frumpwooler.

"Well, I'm waiting," she said, pouting.

A vision of devising a permanent pressure pad for her Point of Infinite Peacefulness, and then strapping it onto Mrs. Frumpwooler's neck, flickered through Commander Blevins' imagination. Brushing temptation aside, he reminded himself that the Client's mood swings were part of the job and pressed his finger squarely on the dot. The room turned deep blue.

"Oh, this is exciting, Commander." She was cooing once again.

The screen sprang to life. A narrow uphill street disappeared at the top of the screen. A curious slot divided the road into left and right lanes. On the right, debris tumbled into the street from somewhere off the screen. A man's legs ran by and a scream pierced the

Viewing Room. Commander Blevins quickly glanced at Mrs. Frumpwooler, expecting the worse. However, she was sitting calmly with her chin resting on her closed hand, watching the screen intently.

"So far so good," Commander Blevins thought to himself. He looked back to the screen. The scene had shifted. At a distance, buildings could be seen half standing. People were running around, yelling, and crying. "Great Zoids!" Commander Blevins said aloud.

"What was that, Commander?"

"Uh, this is the San Francisco Earthquake...or just after it."

"Of course, it is," Mrs. Frumpwooler said with sudden authority.

Commander Blevins looked at Mrs. Frumpwooler and thought, "It must be a pertinent event in her past life for her to know so readily, but they usually don't pick-up that quickly...."

Mrs. Frumpwooler shook her head as if emerging from a trance, then looked at Commander Blevins with a puzzled expression. "How did I know that, Commander? I was born twenty-nine years after the San Francisco Earthquake. Now how did I know that? And in Des Moines, not in..." She trailed off and looked back toward the screen, her face a mask of unanswered questions. Commander Blevins also turned back to the screen.

They both watched as a young man hid behind an arched trellis of roses and spied upon a woman prying bricks loose from a wall across the garden. Both Mrs.

Frumpwooler and Commander Blevins gasped in unison, neither looking at the other. The city rumbled in the distance. It was night time on the screen, but the scene was light enough to make out what was happening.

The woman worked quickly with a chisel and hammer. Vines grew up the wall where she worked. Sweat lines streaked her face. She managed to get two bricks out and then bent down and hacked at them with her chisel. The young man moved over behind a birdbath in a small pool and crouched down low.

A woman upstairs in the house cried out,"Iiiito. Where are you?" Ito looked around but did not move. He watched intently as the woman stuffed a linen pouch into the hole where the bricks had been and held up one brick, slopping some mortar on it with her other hand. He could see that a corner of the brick was missing. The woman stuffed the first brick back into place, then the second. The other woman's voice called out, "Iiiito" again, this time from nearby. The young man stood up to look for a safer hiding place when the woman at the brick

wall turned around and saw him and let out an involuntary squeak. Their eyes met. The voice of the woman calling Ito grew nearer.

An involuntary squeak had also escaped from Mrs. Frumpwooler. She felt movement in the room and looked over at Commander Blevins. He was no longer on the couch, but standing up in front of it, and he, too, turned to look at her.

TWELVE

DIAMONDS IN THE WALL

The woman at the brick wall continued looking at
the young man. Mrs. Frumpwooler continued
looking at Commander Blevins: a moment later, she
became the woman at the wall. The Viewing Room of
deep blue dropped away to reveal pre-dawn darkness.

Commander Blevins went through a similar transformation and became the young man, Ito, whose
spying was discovered. Old Frau Swope was bearing
down fast on the backyard. He dropped all shyness and
blurted out, "Gwenny! What are you doing? Was that
one of Von Blume's pouches?"

"Hush Ito and come here," Gwendolyn answered,
and ran around the corner of the brick wall. Ito
followed her. They both hid behind the coal shed and
waited for Frau Swope to pass by. The large German
woman pounded down the back steps of the kitchen,

yelling, "Ito! I know here you are out. This is not the time for games! To do we—"

Her shouting was cut short. The ground shook again. Bricks and glass crashed into the street in front of the house. Frau Swope shrieked and ran around the other side of the house, away from Gwendolyn and Ito hiding behind the carriage house. Gwendolyn came out from behind the coal shed in a flash.

"That was only a little one," Ito said. "Think there'll be another?"

"Hush." Gwendolyn picked-up the small bucket of mortar and slapped some into the empty grooves between the bricks. Ito watched silently as she worked the mortar into the cracks. Rearranging the vines to cover her handiwork, she paused, picked up some dirt, and rubbed it all over the just-set bricks.

"Gwenny, someone's coming," Ito said.

She brushed away the large clumps of dirt and moved the vines back over the bricks. "Thanks, Runt." They both disappeared behind the carriage house again and hid silently as excited voices passed near them in the neighbor's yard.

"Boy, that was close, Runt," Gwendolyn said. "Thanks for the warning. And yeah, that last shake was smaller than the first."

"Don't call me Runt," Ito said.

"I'll call you whatever I want to, Ito-san, Jap-boy. Why were you spying on me anyway?"

Ito glared at her and said nothing.

"Tell me what you saw, Ito." They stared at each other. "Oh, all right, I'm sorry I called you Runt."

"And you said 'Jap-boy', too."

"Yes, yes. I'm sorry I called you Jap-boy." Gwendolyn was beginning to feel uncomfortable. "Tell me what you saw."

"I saw you hide a sack of diamonds that belongs to Mr. Von Blume," Ito said.

Gwendolyn gasped. "How did you know that? Come on, tell!"

"I watched you take one of the sacks from the strongbox. How'd you get the key? And why didn't you take all of them, while you were at it?"

Gwendolyn looked at him hard for a moment, then said, "Because I don't want him to think someone took them, that's why! Who else knows? Did you tell anyone?"

"How are you going to keep him from finding out? "

"Who else knows!" Gwendolyn was almost shouting.

"Tell me how Von Blume won't know. Then I'll tell you who knows." Ito was beginning to feel that he had the upper hand.

"You'd better. It's simple: he had seven bags. Last night I took a little out of each and made an eighth bag. Tonight I snuck down after he went to sleep and got the extra bag."

"I know all that, Gwenny. How will *he* not know? That's what I want to know," Ito said.

"How do you know about the extra bag? Tell me."

"You aren't the only one up in the middle of the night."

"Oh." She glared at him, then relaxed. "He's too dumb to know anything. And now he's probably too scared. Tell me who else knows."

"I think he'll find out. Anyway, no one else knows."

"The only way he'll find out is if someone tells him. He hasn't *weighed* the diamonds yet. I heard him tell Master Peter. You're not thinking of being that someone, are you Ito?" Gwendolyn let the words linger, menacingly.

Ito raised his eyebrows and said, "Noooo, but..."

"But what!"

"What are you going to give me," Ito said.

"I'm not going to give you anything, you little..."

Ito stood up and said, "Then, I'll go tell him now."

Gwendolyn grabbed his wrist. "No, you won't." She looked him in the eye and said, "I'll give you a third of the diamonds."

"More." Ito pulled his wrist away from her grasp.

"Half."

"Closer," Ito felt power for the first time in his life.

"No more than half, period. I'm the one who did all the work, anyway," Gwendolyn said, standing up and looking down at Ito.

Looking her up and down slowly, Ito said, "Throw in some spiff, and I'll consider it."

Gwendolyn raised her arm to slap him and said, "Why you..." then paused and looked at Ito, who smiled back at her. "You're too young to..."

"Oh, yeah? Been doing it with the Whittier's down-stairs maid for six months now." Ito puffed out his chest and stood straight and as tall as his five-foot frame permitted. "Let's see your caboose, sister. You want my silence; you got to haul the ashes."

"Where did you learn such language!" Gwendolyn stared at him in disbelief. A fortune in diamonds danced in front of her eyes. She had been discretely servicing the master's guests for three years, in exchange for a handsome reward. She thought the situation over. Diddling with this little man...boy!...would not be as bad as that fat old Von Blume, or the others before him, at least, she thought and laughed. "All right, Ito-san. You tell me what you like."

Ito lost his bluster. Turning bright red, he could not utter a sound. His heart pounded.

"Well?" Gwendolyn challenged. Gathering his courage—he had lied about the downstairs maid—he motioned for Gwendolyn to raise her skirt. Moving a step away from him, she curtsied slightly and slowly lifted her skirt and petticoat. As she revealed her ankles and calves, Ito's eyes grew huge. Now enjoying the seduction, Gwendolyn raised her skirts higher and turned around slowly.

Her bloomers ended in frills just above her knees. Ito saw the dark patch where the legs of her pantaloons joined. He went into orbit. Gwendolyn kept raising her skirt until her entire dress was over her head, and then she dropped it on the storage shed. "Want to touch, Ito-san?" She leaned over toward him and shook her breasts. They were heavy and pressed into the thin cotton of her bodice. "Come on, lover. Show me what you can do."

Ito raised his right hand and, trembling, touched Gwendolyn's right breast. He gasped. She feigned a moan and squeezed harder. In a moment, he had untied her bodice and had filled his small hands with her full, white breasts. He squeezed one then the other.

"You do know a woman, Ito-san," Gwendolyn said, mocking him. "Please forgive me for ever doubting you." Ito was oblivious to her sarcasm. He was now sucking on the distended nipple of one breast and continuing to squeeze the other." Despite his clumsiness, Gwendolyn leaned back against the carriage house's cold brick wall, beginning to enjoy his attention. She felt a small hand crawl up her thighs and dig into her soft down. The sudden roughness caused her to cry out.

"Ah-Ha. So are you there! And Got-in-Himmel's name doing are you what?" Old Frau Swope stomped into the narrow passage behind the garage.

Ito was in a heaven heretofore only imagined. Gwendolyn was in a flurry of panic. Ito firmly clutched her breasts and pawed at her House of Jade, as he had once heard it called. The sight of Frau Swope thundering down upon them promised Gwendolyn relief from Ito's frantic attention, but she knew Frau Swope would punish her severely.

Frau Swope immediately sized up the situation: Gwendolyn barely dressed and leaning back against the carriage house, groaning, and Ito pawing at her like a small satyr incarnate. The old woman acted quickly, seizing Ito by the scruff of his sweaty collar and him pulling back.

Ito hung onto Gwendolyn for dear life. She shrieked. Frau Swope pulled harder and was rewarded by a resounding "pop." Ito clawed the air trying to return to heaven. Gwendolyn slid down the carriage house wall, clutching her body at the places from which Ito had just been torn.

"Hussy! Bastard! You both I'll have to the street beaten and thrown." Dragging Ito by his collar, and shaking with anger, Frau Swope turned and spat at Gwendolyn, "Yourself dress and house march, Hussy!"

The shock of their parting reversed the identity shift: Commander Blevins found himself standing, observing the scene; Mrs. Frumpwooler sat in silence, watching the Viewing Room screen as Gwendolyn was literally thrown out of the house and banned forever, such was the force of Frau Swope's outrage.

They both watched as Gwendolyn stumbled passed debris in the street on her way down to the next corner. She stopped and looked back. The screen showed what Gwendolyn saw, and Commander Blevins and Mrs. Frumpwooler got a glimpse of the house Gwendolyn now fled. The mansion sat above the sidewalk on its own bed of walled and packed earth, reaching tall into the sky with a stacked set of gables and turrets. A large corner turret on the top of the house was most impressive and distinctive, its windows reaching higher than imaginable.

Gwendolyn turned and continued walking away from the house. She passed a second street crossing, then two more, finally coming to an intersection at a broad cross street where tracks ran down the street's center. A small bench sat on the road's side, near a sign that was only partially visible on the screen in the Viewing Room. The sign read "nia Street Cable Car S." It was a cable car stop, but no cars were running. Part of the city was in flames in the background.

The screen flashed black letters across the bottom: "RECAP."

"That's weird," Commander Blevins mumbled to himself as the Recap began. "Usually, this is an option."

The text on the screen scrolled up slowly. It said, "Soon after that Gwendolyn O'Reilly was forced into prostitution at the sprawling and filthy tent city set up south of Market. "Ito Takahashi was sold to one of the many builders who helped rebuild San Francisco. Life in disease-ridden tenements was hard. Neither Gwendolyn nor Ito survived the year, nor were either able to return for the hidden diamonds."

The screen turned white, and the Viewing Room traded dark blue for light blue. Commander Blevins sat down, too stunned to notice that the Record Card had played out its story without anyone's middle finger pressing against the white spot on the bottom, which could not be seen now. He had never experienced an identity shift. He also had never run across a past life of his blending with a Client's past life.

Mrs. Frumpwooler, fresh from her Pterodactyl ID shift and unaware of any Viewing Room norms, snapped back without introspection. Diamonds dominated her thoughts. She wondered how she could get out of there and back to the Physical World. Glancing at Commander Blevins, she headed for the door. He was roused by the racket Mrs. Frumpwooler made trying to open the door. "Where's the cursed doorknob," she yelled. There was a quality to her voice he had not felt before, and her stripes pulsated violently.

Commander Blevins stood up to help Mrs. Frumpwooler with the door, still puzzled. "Patience, patience," he said. She elbowed him in the ribs. He absorbed part of the blow but was thrown back by the force of it. Mrs. Frumpwooler's arm was flung forward toward the door, hitting it hard. She screamed. It was an involuntary scream, for she did not hurt herself. The door opened.

THIRTEEN
THE WEBS WE WEAVE

Mrs. Frumpwooler flashed through the door. Blevins stuck his head out of the room and watched her focalshift down the hall: on the ceiling, then back on the floor, then halfway through a wall, then back to the ceiling, finally disappearing around the corner that led to the Dock.

Blevins was torn between two responsibilities. He needed to watch over the safety of the guest he had brought to the Causal Worlds, but would lose his Verified Viewers rating if he left the Viewing Room in its current disarray. Commander Blevins decided to attempt both. He quickly folded up the console's three armrests, smoothed out the depressions on the couch's cushions, assembled the stack of Record Cards, and returned them neatly to Mrs. Frumpwooler's Tray. That accomplished, he focalshifted to the end of the hall, then around the corner and to the Dock.

At the arched doorway to the docking area, he watched as Mrs. Frumpwooler punched away madly at the Sand Lake Express's console to no avail: the SLE sat motionless, unresponsive. He decided she was harmlessly trapped at the Dock until he activated the SLE.

Blevins quickly returned to the Viewing Room and resisted the temptation to inspect the Records Cards and the Viewer. He wanted to know how the Record Cards could have gone so awry. With great discipline, he neatly replaced the Cards in the Tray, closed up the Viewing Room, and walked the few steps to the frosted recessed window marked "FRUMPWOOLER." He placed his hand on the windowpane at knee-level, where he remembered the empty chamber to be. The glass cleared, then disappeared into the wall. He slid the Tray neatly into its slot and removed his hand. Once the window resealed and refrosted itself, Blevins focal-shifted to the end of the hallway, around the corner, and was dockside again. Mrs. Frumpwooler was gone.

Commander Blevins' chin dropped: it was indeed a remarkable day. The Sand Lake Express was there. The Dock and Dockside Pool were there. Mrs. Frump-wooler was not. Scratching his head, he turned by chance to his left, away from the Dock and the arched doorway leading back to the Records.

"Great Jumping Zoidifers!" He saw an open door across the Dock Site Pool. Above the door, a small lime green sign flashed the word "Exit."

Commander Blevins shifted to the doorway and stepped through. A long circular stairwell wound down and down. Peering over the stair railing's edge, he caught a glimpse of erratic movement. Mrs. Frumpwooler was bouncing off the walls again, focal-shifting from point to point in the stairwell. He could think of only one way down. After a brief review of his options with a deep sigh, he put one hand on the railing and vaulted over and into on open-ended focalshift.

Commander Blevins knew open-ended focalshifting was tricky. He thanked himself for neglecting to teach it to Mrs. Frumpwooler. "No telling where she would be by now," he said to himself as time stretched out in front and behind him.

As his mind went on stand-by, he watched the world around him with 360 degree Inner Vision, unfettered by normal mental demands. The stair spiraled downward, Commander Blevins fell like a stone. A passing blip showed where Mrs. Frumpwooler zigged and zagged. Another irregularity caught his attention. He strained to hold his focus on that point as he continued falling. Stretching in two dimensions—Time and Space—was difficult even in the Causal Worlds, and Commander Blevins was not able to keep his anchor point for long. He did, though, manage to perceive a closed door with a small sign near one edge that read "High Balcony - No Unauthorized Entry, Please."

Sensing a mass of compact energy not too far ahead of him, Commander Blevins pulled up a few levels above the bottom of the stairwell. He paused and listened carefully. A door clicked closed above him, then silence.

Guessing who had closed the door and where it led, he shifted back to the High Balcony area. His concentration was split, and he missed the doorway to the balcony by two levels. Blevins shifted again, climbed over the stair railing, and stepped across the stairs to the door, which he opened onto the Balcony.

A too familiar, "Caw!" greeted him. He saw large wings flapping near the balcony and above a grove of trees near the canal. The beast shrieked and plummeted to the ground. Another immediately appeared, cawing, and then it, too, met a similar fate. When he heard a third, "Caw," but no anguished screech, Blevins focalshifted to a point just in front of the creature. He stood still in mid-air at the moment, watching in amazement as the large Pterodactyl flew by with Mrs. Frumpwooler standing triumphantly on its back. Her stripy body was erect, her arms were folded, and she stared straight ahead.

He shifted beside her. "Oh there you are, Ito-san," she said without saying. "I was sure you would show up soon." She was very calm.

"Mrs. Frumpwooler, I beg of you. Please do not mix incarnations. The resulting karma can be devastating."

"Hah," she mocked, but thought to herself that he did still have his uses: whether as Commander Blevins or Ito-san.

"You continue to amaze me, Mrs. Frumpwooler, though I do wish you would consult with me before moving about on your own," Blevins suddenly felt unsure with Mrs. Frumpwooler.

"Right. So you can get them first. No way Ito...Commander. Those are mine. You saw me take them *twice*, and I won't let you muck things up a second time." Mrs. Frumpwooler had taken another turn in her Records-induced instability and was now self-assured, even militant.

Commander Blevins was befuddled. "I'm not sure I follow, Mrs. Frumpwooler." Another Pterodactyl flew in front of them and cawed to the big bird they were riding. "And I don't think we should stay here for much longer."

"Of course you do. You follow all too well." Three more Pteras sailed by. "Though you may be right about getting off this thing. I'd rather not go at it hand to...whatever...with another one of these creatures."

The Ptera suddenly settled the matter for them, doing a violent barrel roll that spun Commander Blevins and Mrs. Frumpwooler off its back. Blevins grabbed her hand as they fell and shifted to a spot below and near the canal. They landed amid the beat of wings as a squadron of the huge Pteras just missed swooping them up for a midday snack.

"Well, now what do we do?" Mrs. Frumpwooler asked, becoming abruptly passive, fully expecting Commander Blevins to get them out of their predicament, even though moments before she had been abusing him.

Blevins flowed with her change and reasserted his

guidance. He felt exceptionally alive today in the Causal Worlds, more fully in touch with Knowingness than he had experienced before. He knew that the higher one travels in the Inner Worlds, the more their motivations purify, and that purification, even in the smallest of doses, causes upheaval. He saw a small clearing nearby, with a picnic table in its center. Commander Blevins motioned for Mrs. Frumpwooler to follow as he walked toward it. He sat down on the far side.

"Oh, great. Now you want to rest," huffed Mrs, Frumpwooler. She put both hands on the table and leaned her face down close to his and said, with building fury, "When I asked what we should do, I did *not* have in mind sitting here in this little par.k. I want to go back home *now* to my normal body. And then I am going to leave your presence forever. Do I make myself clear, Commander Blevins!"

"Quite clear, Mrs. Frumpwooler," Blevins said evenly.

Though he had seen many erratic mood shifts in Clients as he brought them nearer and nearer to Akash, he had never seen the violent extremes he was now witnessing in Mrs. Frumpwooler. "I think we had better abandon the normal return route," he said.

"Will that be faster?" she hissed.

"Yes, it will take no more than a moment."

"Do it then," she said.

"You must sit down first."

"Well, why didn't you say so," she said and sat down.

Sighing, Commander Blevins said, "Please sit over

here by me. We will need to be touching to make sure we return to the same point in time and space."

Mrs. Frumpwooler got up and walked around the table. Sitting down, she warned him, "None of your tricks, now."

Ignoring her, Commander Blevins said, "Just sit quietly and breathe deeply."

"You said this would only take a moment."

"It will, Mrs. Frumpwooler. It will. But only if you cooperate."

"All right." She straightened her back and began to breathe deeply. Commander Blevins watched her until he trusted she would continue.

"Put your right hand on the table," he said. S he did so. "Now, let your mind go, just let it think whatever it wants to. We will let this happen quietly for a moment." They both sat in silence, breathing deeply. "Now, picture a blue light swirling in front of your eyes and slightly above them." After more silence, he said, "Do you see the blue light?"

"Yes, I do," she answered, mellowing slightly.

"Good." Blevins knew Mrs. Frumpwooler would have a hard return unless she released her anger. "Now let it grow larger and larger until the blue light over-shadows everything." More quietly, he then said, "Let yourself be submerged in the swirling blue light." A long moment passed, then he asked her, "Are you submerged in the blue light?"

"Yes, I am," Mrs. Frumpwooler said. She sounded far away and nearly peaceful.

"Good. Now out of the middle of the swirling blue light, watch as your physical body walks toward you."

Mrs. Frumpwooler watched as she walked toward herself. Commander Blevins also watched as his rumpled body lumbered straight for himself. He broke the silence quietly. "In a minute, reach out and touch yourself...not yet... we must do this together." He spoke without speaking, but for the first time on this Journey in the Causal Worlds, his words did not resonate within Mrs. Frumpwooler. "I am going to touch...."

Commander Blevins did not finish his sentence. He felt he was alone and opened his eyes. He was. He quickly closed them again, re-established the swirling blue and

it.

FOURTEEN
RUCKUS IN THE BATHROOM

B levins was aware, but not fully conscious. Points of light and images of other forms passed by him. He traveled down and down the bright blue tunnel. In his awareness, he knew he had come this way before. He felt himself sliding, yet without any sensation of motion. A brilliant, almost blinding orange ring shot by him, followed by an equally bright pink one and then a silver streak, all flashing by.

Then a growing heaviness began to seep into him. He felt the weight as a tangible sensation, spreading from the center of his being outward: weight upon weight. Something soft pushed up against him. He heard a noticeable 'pop' as the bright blue tunnel dimmed and was gone.

He opened his eyes. Commander Blevins was home. The first thing he noticed was the loveseat. It was turned over on its back. There was a cup of tea on the floor nearby, spilled. Full consciousness returned to him as he thought, "Mrs. Frumpwooler! Where is she!"

Commander Blevins stood up and groaned. Physical reality had returned quickly. His legs felt numb. He remembered to check his clocks. One said 1:37, the other 3:24, changing to 3:25 as he stared at it. He tried to remember which one had been the Journey clock this time. Most trips lasted about a half-hour. He had never been gone more than two hours before, let alone three and a half, so it had to be the clock that read 1:37.

"Remarkable," he said to himself, "a near-record. But where on earth is Mrs. Frumpwooler!"

"Mrs. Fruuumpwoooooler," he called out loud.

As if in response to his call, he heard a racket from the bathroom, which was located past the front door at the end of a short hallway. He walked stiffly across the main room--stopping to turn up one heater--and into the foyer, with the two light cords following. The small square of hardwood flooring served as the hub of the apartment. This axis separated the kitchen from a large walk-in closet, from the small, front door coat closet, from the living-sleeping room, from the short hallway that led to the bathroom. Peering around the corner of the short hallway, he flinched as he heard, "Get away from me, you horrid thing." Something crashed. He had found Mrs. Frumpwooler.

More cursing and banging echoed from the closed bathroom door. Commander Blevins found himself stymied: he could not just go barging into the bathroom with a lady inside; she *had* shut the door. On the other hand, she was definitely not tending to normal business.

"Try that again, and I'll clobber you good," Mrs. Frumpwooler yelled from inside the closed door.

"Well that settles it," Commander Blevins said to himself. He marched the few steps down the hallway, raised his fist to pound on the door, and opened his mouth to announce his intentions. Before he could do either, the bathroom door opened, and Mrs. Frump-wooler stormed out.

"So there you are!" she said, pushing by him. "*You* can deal with that *thing* now." The light cords whipped around as Mrs. Frumpwooler elbowed him. Commander Blevins looked back into the bathroom. The window over the tub was open about two inches. The white tile floor needed cleaning and repairing in a few places. The toilet seat was lifted to a forty-five-degree angle, something he had not seen before. He stepped in and looked up at the ceiling. The cracked paint festooned over the tub, hanging down in several places. Cautiously he peered around the door, moving it back from the wall a few inches. A magazine lay on the floor, crumpled, and the toilet brush had fallen out of its caddy. Nothing unusual. The toilet seat was at a curious angle, but that did not seem significant to him, and certainly not grounds for Mrs. Frumpwooler's outburst.

He turned and headed back to the main room. As he entered the room, he saw Mrs. Frumpwooler sitting on the up-turned edge of the love seat, rubbing her calves and feet. "My God, but I'm sore and achy," she said. "My arm feels like I've been loading bags of cement." Without looking up, she added, "Where did you hide my hat, Blevins. I must get out of this oven before I die of perspire—" The next word out of her mouth was a scream, followed by, "Get away from me with that thing, you monster."

Commander Blevins was at a loss. He stood in the middle of the living room with his two light cords swishing behind him. He, of course, wasn't aware of this. Nor did he realize that Mrs. Frumpwooler had made such a hasty and unguided return to the Physical World that she had ripped her aura. A new friend had found her condition too inviting to pass up and was in hot pursuit of her, trying to make contact.

In the confusion of Mrs. Frumpwooler leaving the bathroom just as Commander Blevins showed up outside it, her new friend--in pursuit of her--stopped to sniff at the light cords of Commander Blevins' two unknown MEs.

Mrs. Frumpwooler's impatient reentry had also left her Inner Vision wide open, a condition guaranteed to affect the most stout individual's balance. Running about the Physical World with the spiritual eye wide open was the equivalent of sniffing everyone's dirty underwear. Hidden thoughts, Misplaced Entities, warped auras, and distorted energy fields were just a few of the unseen aspects of Physical World life on full view to someone whose third eye has been unexpectedly opened.

As Commander Blevins stood in front of Mrs. Frumpwooler, the newcomer, her unwanted paramour, was drifting lazily around the two light cords coming out of Commander Blevins' back. Having satisfied Itself of the nature of Its unseen cousins, It again spied Mrs. Frumpwooler and, leading with Its unconnected light cord, headed straight for her.

All this happened in a flash. The newcomer, which was about twice the size of a hand-held vacuum, green and very ugly, came around the side of Commander Blevins. To Mrs. Frumpwooler, it looked as though Commander Blevins held Its light cord and was bringing It over to her, as though It were a balloon on a string. For the first time, she also saw the two other light cords and immediately presumed he was in league with the awful thing that had accosted her in the bathroom.

She bolted for the door and for freedom. Diamonds danced in the back of her mind, blind fear hovered in front of her, and the purple hat, so dear to her a moment before, was gone from her thoughts entirely. Commander Blevins stepped aside to avoid being run down. She jinked around where he had been and ran smack into him, knocking him back, almost bowling him over. The green ME used this moment of impact to plant its cord deep into Mrs. Frumpwooler's back.

She and her light cord were out the door a moment later. Confused and stunned, Commander Blevins regained his balance and called to her, "Won't you stay for some more tea?"

The terror drained away as she charged down the stairway. When the new ME attached to her, it drew a great deal of energy. Since she had her physical and emotional energies fully occupied, the only place from which the ME could draw additional power was from her spiritual eye, which immediately locked down in reaction to the pressure. So, as Mrs. Frumpwooler burst through the front door of 600 Page Street, her spiritual eye closed and she was not, therefore, overwhelmed with all the unseen things that bounce around, unseen, in the Physical World.

FIFTEEN
AND GREENY MAKES THREE

"Something is sniffing at me," said Ember.

"That won't last long, I'm sure," Pins said.

"Jealous."

"Am not."

"Are too."

"Puddle and poop. At least the Old Lush is back," Pins said.

"Reformed Lush, you mean."

"Well, not for long if I have anything to say about it,"

Their bickering went on, rarely stopping. The two light cords—one well-defined and dull-red, the other fuzzy, dark grey and dirty—which connected these two ill-tempered cousins with Commander Blevins, swayed in an unseen, gentle breeze. At the same moment, the other wind, which caused people to bundle up, was coming off the ocean wet, cold, and brisk.

Ember was plumb, red-orange, and sat easily on the

wire, waving Its stumpy little arms. There was a vague head-like shape to the upper portion of Its body. When needed, It could squeeze-out a face, legs, and a more defined torso. At the moment, however, It was resting and happy to be Its blobish self, waving Its little stumps, which caused the wire to vibrate at an irregular rate, incessantly annoying Pins.

"Hey Maggot Breath, there ain't no parade today," Pins said. It was not very fit and hung tenaciously to the wire, afraid of falling off. In past times It had been fat and sassy in Its black and grey pin-striped body, relishing vicarious thrills from Commander Blevins' near-constant drinking and frequent visits to the world of titillation. The appearance of Ember, however, slowed their host considerably, leaving little remaining energy to satisfy Pins. It was withering and not a pretty sight.

"Hey, looky-loo," Ember said.

"Where, where?"

"Above the place, Eagle Eye."

"Oh, yeah. Wonder what he is."

"Well, if he's got anything to do with our friend, he can't be good news," Ember said. "Feeling any loss in juice?"

"I've felt nothing but a loss of juice for quite some time now," Pins said.

"I mean any sudden change just now, Jerkoff."

"No." Pins searched Its list of deities to plead for help in getting rid of Ember. "Hey, look, he disappeared."

"Maybe he hasn't hooked on yet. Shake it, Commander!" Ember had now materialized short legs and jumped up and down on the wire, Its light cord whipping around frantically.

"Wa-Wa-Watch it, Dummmmm...." Pins lost Its grip on the wire and went sailing downward. Its light cord got tangled with Ember's, sending It back up then down again on a whiplash ride.

The door to 600 Page Street opened, and Mrs. Frumpwooler walked out. She pulled her collar tightly around her neck and marched across Page Street without looking in either direction. Trailing behind her was a bright green line of light, coming from the back of her knee-length mauve coat and disappearing into the doorway she had just left.

"Hey wowser, look at this, High Wire," Ember said, and stopped jumping up and down. It studied Mrs. Frumpwooler and her light cord intently. The diversion allowed Its light cord to slowly stop whipping around.

Pins grabbed hold of Its companion's swaying light cord as soon as it slowed down enough to do so, and began climbing up with Its stumpy little arms.

"Hey, ow...oohh. Cut it out...that tickles...hahaha," Ember said, Its attention split between the sensations coming up Its light cord and watching Mrs. Frumpwooler.

The green light cord which came out of her back had strung out behind her as she crossed Page. In a quick motion, it cut up through the apartment building like steel cable slicing a cloud. When she had reached the corner of Page and Filmore, a small green ugly balloon popped out of a second-floor window, looking bedraggled. The Third One was slowly learning the ropes of maneuvering while attached to a physical body.

Mrs. Frumpwooler crossed Page Street and walked down Filmore directly across the street from the two squabbling Misplaced Entities. Her new-found friend floated along behind her, looking like a wilted St. Patrick's Day balloon with stumpy little arms.

Ember, now tickled unbearably, forgot about Mrs. Frumpwooler and began dancing wildly. It heard a small voice down below It say, "Quit jumpin'." A thousand daggers speared Its light cord. Distorting in pain, It looked down to see Pins grinning hideously behind a colossal mouthful of bared teeth. Reddish light spilled out around Pins' mouth, where many pointy teeth gripped Ember's light cord.

They looked at each other, their four beady eyes meeting and locking. Whimpering, Ember watched as Pins reached up above Its mouth with Its hand and grasped the wounded light cord. Pins opened Its mouth and pulled Itself up a stumpy arm's length.

Ember moaned.

Slowly Pins opened Its now huge mouth again and positioned Its teeth around the cord.

"Nooooo, please, please, please don't bite again," Ember said. Pins hung motionless for a long moment, then pulled back Its mouth, closed it, and hauled Itself up Ember's light cord hand over little hand, keeping eye contact the whole time.

Hopping up on the wire, Pins felt reinvigorated from absorbing the spilled light from Ember's wounded light cord. Its dull black color had some shine, there was a hint of grey pinstriping, and Its beady little eyes sparkled in a way they had not for a long time. It looked over at Ember and said, "Now what's the news, Frozen Ovary."

Trembling from both fright and a leaking light cord, Ember could only hold Its stumpy little arm out and point across the street to a hurrying figure wearing a mauve coat and sporting a bright green light cord coming straight out of her back.

"Holy Light Sucker!" Pins said, "A new kid on the block. So that's what old What's Its Face brought back with him. Wonders and wonders. Do you think the old crustacean will ever learn?"

"I ho-o-ope no-o-t." Ember's teeth were chattering from cold, and Its body had turned pale pink.

Mrs. Frumpwooler was jostled by two people carrying groceries. Diamonds had been on her mind since watching herself, as Gwendolyn, hide them. Now she had Diamond-fever. She did not watch her. The neighborhood where she had worked so long ago unfolded before her mind's eye: large extraordinary homes; chilly walks through Lafayette Park; catching the cable car down on California Street; people going to parties; kitchen help, like herself, working hard to serve all those people who stood around and smiled down their noses at her; the men who regularly made advances: some subtle, some not so subtle. And the Diamonds: those amazing little stones of pure light.

She had watched from the kitchen as Mr. Von Blume had carefully emptied the bags out in front of old Peter Haas late one night. She had overheard Von Blume tell tales of his mine in South Africa, but she heard very few words. The sight of the diamonds had choked her mind. Had she known of them the night before when old Peter showed Von Blume to her room and told her, with a wink, to "entertain our distinguished guest"—it was disgusting for her to think about, the man was so fat and reeked from drink—but if she had known about the diamonds then...

Tires screeched, and a horn honked. "Hey, watch out, lady. You crazy?" someone yelled. Mrs. Frumpwooler shook off the memories flooding her and found herself standing in the middle of Haight Street. The light had turned red against her, but she had walked into the street anyway. Now there was a white van blocking her retreat and cars zipped by in front of her.

"Looky. Looky. Green-Greeny ain't gonna have juice for long. That broad's gonna get herself killed. Wheeeee, what fun," Pins said.

"Yeth, your rith," Ember said softly. It was sitting a couple meters farther away from Its companion and was sucking on the wounded part of Its light cord. "Ann noh looky-loo," It said, pointing back toward 600 Page Street.

Commander Blevins pushed through the door with

two worn cardboard boxes, one inside the other. Both had handle cutouts had been ripped-out and taped over repeatedly. One of the outside box's handles needed repair again. He held the bigger box by the good handle and the bottom corner on the other end.

Dressed as he was in a long waterproof cape over wool coat over a short leather jacket, two sock caps pulled down low on his forehead, and a six-foot crimson and grey striped scarf coiled around his neck, dragging on the ground behind him, he looked amazingly strange and awkward, a sight even to street people. Commander Blevins struggled with the empty boxes in his ongoing attempt to pull his coats tightly around him.

Of course, the two light cords followed him and easily shortened as he, and they neared the perch of the MEs. "What a crazy woman," he muttered. "She didn't even pay me."

"Its a party," yelled Pins.

By this time, Mrs. Frumpwooler had cleared Haight Street and was marching further down Filmore, intent on catching the N Judah trolley out to the Sunset. She wanted to get to the solitude of Ocean Beach to consider her options, then intended to head back to the Marina, and home to formalize plans to recover her long-lost diamonds. She stopped in her tracks, however, and shouted, "My hat! That greedy old man kept my hat!" She turned around and set off back up Filmore to confront the thieving Commander Blevins and rescue her purple hat. Her green friend navigated the "U" turn with only minor difficulty and was soon merrily in tow, smiling a satisfied, ugly smile.

"Now, Greeny's coming back," said Pins, continuing the narrative for Its wounded fellow wire-sitter.

Mrs. Frumpwooler and Greeny hit Haight Street in full stride. Looking up, she was amazed to see Commander Blevins coming down the hill towards her. "Thief! Thief!" she yelled and sprinted across the street after him; he would not escape if she could help it.

Commander Blevins heard a commotion and some yelling. He ignored it; there was always yelling and bedlam on the streets these days.

"Hey, Bro, wanna score?" a tall man in dreadlocks whispered as he brushed by. Commander Blevins pushed passed him and turned the corner.

"Come back here, you—" Mrs. Frumpwooler's oath was cut short. She felt her shoulder meet with resistance. A small question formed in her mind before bright blue and very familiar light flooded over her.

"Holy Holy, did you see that, Frozen Ovary?" Pins asked. Ember opened Its mouth, and Its light cord dropped out. Pink was darkening to red in most of Its body as Its healing efforts took effect. Its mouth remained open, but no sound came forth.

Commander Blevins heard more commotion behind him but ducked into the laundromat, anxious to see if his clothes were still there.

SIXTEEN
NO. 7 HAIGHT MAULS

Muni Victim No. 7

In the lower right-hand corner of the next afternoon's Examiner, a two-column headline would read: "No. 7 Haight Mauls Muni Victim No. 7". The story would be noteworthy enough to garner front-page space because the local municipal transit system had just run down its seventh San Franciscan of the year. Of course, her name and address would be printed, but little else of import was to be disclosed about Mrs. Gladys Periwinkle Frumpwooler, of 3513 Broderick Street, San Francisco. Diamonds would definitely not be mentioned. Neither would a Misplaced Entity, forced to leave home.

Commander Blevins did not read obituaries, the

financial section, or the newspaper's front page. He also studiously ignored conflict and commotion. This, along with his current fixation on his laundry, narrowed his opportunity to learn of his most recent Client's unexpected detour. Entirely absorbed in the moment, he rushed to the narrow hallway of dryers in the back of the laundromat. Machines numbered seven, and nine were spinning. "Great," he said to himself as he opened the door to number seven, "But I don't think I put that much money in it."

"Hey, you, crazy person, what you think you doin'?" The woman who spoke to him was well over six feet tall, dark-skinned, dressed in full leathers, and standing right behind him.

"III...yeek!" Commander Blevins shrieked as he turned around and found himself eye to eye with jutting, leather-covered, rhinestone-studded breasts. He looked up, opened his mouth but could say nothing. The dryer door softly closed behind him, and the clothes began to spin again.

"Well...little man, you trying to steal my clothes?"

"Noooo!" he protested and jumped back against the dryer.

"Tyrone. Get the manager. This little miserable honky is stealing my clothes." She looked down, straight into his eyes, grinning a mean. "I'm going to eat you" grin and added, "Aren't you."

"No, I wasn't. No ma'am. I made a mistake. I thought these were my clothes," Blevins protested.

The woman pushed him aside, opened the door, and

reached into the dryer. The clothes stopped spinning. She pulled out a white lace bra with holes cut in the tips. "I suppose your gonna tell me this is yours. You a faggoty maggot too?"

Commander Blevins stared at the bra.

"Here's the manager, Simone." A little shrimpy black guy was standing behind the manager, jumping up and down like a pogo stick. "Here he is. Here he is."

"What's the matter," the manager began to say.

"Shut up, Tyrone. I can see that," Simone said.

The manager looked back and forth between Commander Blevins, Simone, and Tyrone, who had now squirmed in beside the woman. He rubbed up and down against her side, smiling in all directions. The manager wished he was still in Denver, but said, "Now what is the problem here?"

Commander Blevins opened his mouth and said, "I..."

"This little weirdo is stealing my clothes." Simone had put her hands into the lace bra. Her two index fingers stuck through the holes, and she twirled her fingers around in circles as she stared back at the manager.

Sighing, he turned to Commander Blevins and said, "Did you take this woman's clothes."

"No, I did not. They are right there." He pointed to the dryer. Inside, he was shaking.

"Are these your clothes, ma'am?" the manger ask Simone.

"Of course they are," she said.

"Well, I don't see—"

"He opened the door to *my* dryer and had his thieving hands on *my* clothes. He is stealing my clothes. Arrest him!" Simone said.

"Yeah, arrest him. Arrest the..." Tyrone began, still rubbing against Simone.

"Shut up, Tyrone," she said and elbowed him in the chin.

"Ow, that hurt, Cookie-Nookie. You shouldn't hurt your..."

"Please." The manager glared at Tyrone. Turning to Commander Blevins, he asked, "Do you have an explanation for this?"

Blevins said, "I thought they were mine."

"Yours!" Simone said. I been here for two hours doing laundry. Where you been? I didn't see you come in here and put any clothes anywhere. You just come in here—"

"Hold it," the manager yelled. "I saw this man in here earlier." He turned to Blevins again and asked, "Why did you leave for so long? You know store policy is to stay with your laundry until it's done and then leave. We do not allow any loitering here."

Commander Blevins racked his brain. "I was on an errand with a...friend. And we couldn't...get back in time." Sweat ran down his back and sides. His arms were shaking now.

"Next time, tell me if you are going to leave for more than a minute. Now, look over in that corner. I think you'll find your clothes in the big basket with the hanging bar. I unloaded this dryer when it stopped because someone else needed it. And you," he said, turning to Simone, "Please try to be a little nicer. We can all get along if we just try."

The manager turned and went back to the front counter.

Commander Blevins scurried back to the basket of clothes pointed out by the manager. Relieved, he saw that they were his. His boxes, though, sat on the floor near Simone. He looked at them and then at her.

She turned and glared at him. "Weirdo Honky, how come you wear so many clothes anyway? You a *real* crazy person. Come on, Tyrone, baby, let's take some air." She threw the bra back in the dryer and slammed the door. It began spinning again.

Commander Blevins eased his way over to the cardboard boxes as Simone and Tyrone walked away. Quickly he pulled the boxes apart and stuffed his clothes in them. Piling one atop the other, and grabbing the bigger bottom box by its bottom corners, he pigeon-walked through the front of the laundromat, avoiding the eyes of the manager, and out onto the sidewalk along Haight Street. A large crowd had gathered down by the corner in front of the natural food store. Sirens wailed in the distance.

Shrinking behind his boxes, Commander Blevins walked as quickly as he could. He bumped into someone every few steps but ignored their protests. Turning the corner, he headed up Filmore. His arms ached from the weight of the clothes; his body still reverberated with tension, and his legs cramped as he struggled to take each step.

"Never seen such a deal," said Ember, quietly. He was not back to full strength yet, but he was rapidly on the mend. The two MEs had been engrossed in the spectacle down on Haight Street. They had edged along the wire toward the intersection and now sat on a ringside perch over the corner. Neither had said a word for the past several minutes.

"Lookeyloo at old Greeny, he's juicing for all he's worth," Pins said. Greeny was doing just that. It hovered over the people huddling over Mrs. Frumpwooler, with Its light cord reeled in short. Its little sides around Its Yahooney were going in and out like bellows. Try as It did, though, It was getting little nourishment. At the moment, Mrs. Frumpwooler was barely cooperating in the physical, and Greeny was turning a sickly yellow-green.

"Here comes old Step 'N Fetchit again," said Pins. Commander Blevins was barely visible behind the mound of clothes as he bumped from one person to the next. Since everyone else was gawking at the human theater on the street, he was tolerated and drew only an occasional, "Watch it, fellow."

The two MEs were not alone in noticing Commander Blevins. Greeny perked up like a lost dog when It spied Blevins, Its only other acquaintance in the Physical World. Taking a last look at Its current patron as she was lifted onto a stretcher, Greeny decided to cut loose. It reeled in Its light cord and set off for a new conquest. Only two other beings heard the distinctive suck-pop that happens when a light cord is pulled out of a host. The sound got their attention.

"Whoa, Lookeyloo here," Ember said. "Old Greeny's unplugged from What's Her Face. Wonder what he'll do next. Sure are a lot of prime ones down there." The two MEs watched in silence as Greeny floated over the crowd and paused near a seedy-looking fellow standing on the Haight Street side of the corner that Commander Blevins had just rounded.

"That one will do, Greeny...go for it," Pins cheered. Greeny inched Its way along until It came to the very edge of the building, playing out Its light cord, which sniffed around like a long, thin, green elephant's trunk. It checked out the seedy fellow and two women standing by street lamp pole. Then slowly, it worked its way up the hill to another woman dropping some mail in the mailbox on her way down the street to check out all the commotion.

Greeny then came around the corner and watched Commander Blevins trudging up the hill directly in the path of two large black men, who saw a puny little white guy all bundled up and carrying a pile of clothes. An afternoon's entertainment was walking right up to them while everyone else watched something down on Haight Street.

"Something's gonna happen," said Pins. "And it ain't gonna be good."

"Yeah, I can hardly wait," said Ember.

"Idiot. Lunch, dinner, and all the snacks in between

is right in the thick of it. You want to wind up like old Greeny."

"Oh. No way. See the point." Ember sobered up quickly, then said, "What's to do."

"As much as I hate it," said Pins, "let's do a Wrap on those two big ugly ones."

"Oh yech," Ember grimaced. Its light cord was sore, and It was still a little weak from the loss of energy, but It pushed the discomfort aside.

"Come on."

"Ok." The two light cords began winding around themselves, coiling and knotting as they did so, like muscles trying to contract and extend simultaneously.

Commander Blevins dragged himself up the hill, light cords in tow. The two big men walked straight down at him, smiling. One had a knife in his hand. Greeny was slowly narrowing the distance between It and Commander Blevins. It saw the large gap in his aura where two light cords already attached. A third would make no difference.

Greeny was a naive, though crafty, ME. Mrs. Frumpwooler had been Its first host. Its motivating passion was a carry-over from a just-completed lifetime spent hoarding money and living off others. The attachment to Its fortune had been so great that It was unable to transit normally, which arrested Its development—the result: another ME.

There was a slight film over the gap in Commander Blevins' aura, and Greeny waited for it to clear.

The men were almost upon him when Commander

Blevins realized they existed and meant him harm. One stepped around behind him, grabbed Blevins' scarf, and wound it around his eyes. The other put a hand on the pile of clothes and was about to sweep them to the ground.

As this happened, Commander Blevins almost swallowed his tongue. He felt the men's intentions; fear froze his mind. The light film over the tear in his aura disappeared, then the gap widened. Greeny was buoyant. It shot Its light cord deftly into the opening and sunk it home.

"Uhhh. Oh," said Commander Blevins.

"Hey, what the crap is happening," said Ember.

"Quiet and concentrate," Pins said.

"Yeah, but..."

"Yeah, but nothing. It's now or never."

Ember gave in, and a massive surge of energy flowed down the two light cords. Another energy wave followed. As the big men set upon their feeble white-guy-for-lunch, a jolt stopped them both cold. Commander Blevins' momentum carried him forward and beyond their reach. He continued walking, stone-blind from the scarf around his eyes, scrunching his jaw, nose, and forehead furiously to shake off the scarf.

The two big men were not so fortunate. The first Wrap from the coiled light cords had momentarily shorted a particular set of synapses in their brains. They became briefly, but violently incontinent, deaf, dumb, and sightless.

When the second energy surge hit them, they went

flying back against the wall of one of the many apartment buildings fronting Fillmore. The building was built right up to the sidewalk, and that is where they landed in a pile, unconscious, and smelling poorly.

Greeny waltzed through this war zone without hesitation. Everyone was Its friend at the moment as it juiced deeply.

Commander Blevins unwound his scarf in time to prevent another vehicle-pedestrian encounter and reached his front door, puffing heavily. He propped the boxes against the wooden window trim next to the lobby door and fished in his pocket for his keys. Just as he closed his fingers around the keyring, he heard the front door open.

A man's voice said, "I will hold the door for you."

"Oh, thanks. I can't tell you how much I appreciate it," Blevins said over the pile of clothes as he walked through the open doorway. A shaft of light shimmered on his left as he stepped over the threshold. Halfway across the foyer, Blevins stopped and whirled around: he had not seen anyone hold the door open. The man's words echoed in his mind, and he realized the sound of the voice was familiar to him.

Blevins watched as the hydraulic door opener, wheezing, slowly closed the door. Floor to ceiling windows flanked the front door on both sides, spanning the entryway's entire width. No one was there. He could see through the windows and across the street to the buildings beyond. They were bathed in sunlight. He looked to the right side of the door where the shimmering light had been when he came in and saw a dark corner: no ray of light to be seen. With sunlight falling on the other side of the street, the sun could not have been shining into the foyer.

Commander Blevins shook his head, confused about the shimmering light he had seen, and turned to the stairs. Greeny flowed through the door behind him.

"Way to go, General Custer," Ember said. Pins said nothing. They glared at each other.

The ambulance left Haight Street, its siren wailing. The crowd dispersed, Muni Bus No. 7 Haight rolled on, and the two would-be muggers lolled slack-jawed like winos on the way down. Ember and Pins moved back to their usual perch halfway between Page and Haight Streets on Filmore's downtown side.

Soon Greeny popped up over the far back corner of 600 Page, floating leisurely in an unseen, gentle breeze. It smiled at the two other MEs across the building, the intersection, and the half-block that separated them. They did not smile back.

SEVENTEEN

WINDSURFING IN A FIRESTORM

Commander Blevins settled into his overstuffed chair. The heaters in the apartment all hummed away. His Goofy slippers peeked out from under his long robe; he had a steaming cup of Mugi-Cha in one hand; and three light cords ran out of his back, through the chair and up into the ceiling. Perplexed, Commander Blevins reviewed the day's events.

The trip to the Records had been a little out of the ordinary. Mrs. Frumpwooler was a unique Client, to be sure. The confusion began with her Record Cards: they were out of order and uncoded. He could not remember the Cards being jumbled before.

In Verified Viewers Training, someone had mentioned karmic bonds between Viewers and their Clients. There was a strict code of conduct governing Viewers. One complete section of the manual covered the relationship between Viewers and Clients, and he made a mental note to reread those chapters.

His tea finished, Commander Blevins leaned back, closed his eyes, and fell asleep. He awoke a few minutes later and said, "She didn't pay me." This bothered him. Mrs. Frumpwooler owed him some money, quite a lot of money: his services did not come cheaply. He could not let the matter go, so he got up from the chair and walked toward the kitchen. His clothes still sat in the foyer, unfolded and spilling out of the boxes. Making a face, he decided to deal with them tomorrow.

The kitchen table was still covered with adding machine parts, just as it had been when Mrs. Frump-wooler knocked on his door a scant few hours ago. "Time. It sure is a fooler," he said.

He peered into the box of parts sitting on the chair between the built-in china cabinet and the table and rummaged through them. Nothing sparked his interest, so he sat down on the other chair facing the china cabinets. A draft from the leaky window frame cooled his legs and ankles. He got up, turned the oven on low, and opened its door.

The adding machine parts were spread out neatly on an old towel. Near the window was a jumble of springs, long metal arms, short knurled connectors, and several hundred other shapes and sizes, many smeared with grease. The pile of pieces had been a large machine. Along the opposite end of the table lay three or four dozen paired metal shapes. They had been picked from the jumble, matched, and then cleaned in the half-gallon plastic yogurt container that now sat across from Commander Blevins. It was filled with Fantastic Household Cleaner, and its lid was on tight. When he had found the collection of storage containers during a visit to a Napa County hot springs, he had rejoiced. Containers of any kind were a find. Yogurt tubs were especially useful but so icky to cleanout. He took seven of these, which had been empty and clean. Commander Blevins ate no milk products of any kind. Dairy made him blow his nose.

"Music." He always forgot something. Sighing, he stood back up and shuffled over to the little green table in the hall. The three light cords followed along in unison. He bent over the tape deck and rewound-Mozart's 40th and 41st Symphonies, back to back on one cassette. He had last listened to the 41st. "I must get a deck with auto-rewind," he mumbled to himself, not for the first time.

Back at the table, he set to work. When he had begun using adding machines as raw material, he'd worked them methodically: disassembly, cleaning, sorting the parts into matching pieces, then putting ear wires on them. Now he liked to vary the process. This machine had been only half taken apart first. Bits of it were tossed into a big box as he stripped the machine. He then had scooped piles of the greasy parts at random from the tub and plopped them down on the end of the table nearest the window. Picking out interesting singles and pairs, or sets that worked together, he cleaned the pieces and laid them out to dry.

This method held his interest longer. Putting ear wires on the eclectic metal shapes made them instant earrings, which kids in the City loved. Commander Blevins gave the earrings away like candy. Giving naturally made him smile, though now he felt curiously unenthusiastic about it.

Humming along with the violins, Commander Blevins worked steadily. He wondered if maybe he should charge for these earrings. This machine had some exceedingly wicked shapes in it. "I bet they'd pay three, even five bucks a crack for these," he said to himself as he held up two pieces in front of him. One metal part had a toothed arm curving up and a long spiky shaft, like a miniature Viking ax. The other metal piece was like a double-pointed pike with a star-shaped burst of points in its middle.

The phone rang.

He shuffled out to the main room and picked up the phone. "Blevins, at your service," he said.

"Commander Blevins, this is Earl Roy Tickle, Vice-Counsel of the Society for Verified Viewers Accountability."

"Why yes, Vice-Counsel Tickle, to what do I owe this honor?" Commander Blevins asked, puffing up.

"Well, er, it seems we have had a protest lodged..."

"Protest? Why, whom, how? Commander Blevins deflated, quickly humbled.

"A complaint actually," Vice-Counsel Tickle said. A complaint was more serious than a protest. Commander Blevins sat down. Vice-Counsel Tickle continued, "It seems that you passed through the Astral and re-entered the Physical in such a manner that you interfered with another Viewer."

"Well, I did just return. But, I don't think my..."

Commander Blevins was interrupted before he could go any further.

"We're all sure there is a proper explanation for this, Commander Blevins. It is just that another member was jolted by the sudden intrusion into passageways deemed navigatable, and this resulted in a certain degree of discomfiture. There was also a matter of their Client and a loss of professional regard if you catch my drift."

"Yes, I get the picture."

"The Society would like to address the matter at the earliest convenience. Would tomorrow at three o'clock be suitable.?"

"Yes, yes, of course, I will be there."

"We appreciate your cooperation, Commander Blevins. And we look forward to a satisfactory resolution for all concerned. Have a good evening."

The phone clicked in his ear. Forty-five seconds later, it began a shrill tone, designed to alert people when their phones were off the hook. The noise brought Commander Blevins out of his reverie. He replaced the receiver and sat down on the love seat. He rarely sat there; his posture was as uncomfortable as his thoughts. He could not imagine what Mrs. Frumpwooler had gotten into on her direct leap home. Yes, taking Clients to the Records did violate the letter of the Society's Articles, but he had been doing so for more than three years now, and no one had mentioned it. He had to admit that this was the first time a Client had bolted and returned on their own, though rapid retreats by Viewers did occasionally happen. What had she done?...and WHO had she tripped up? And she had not even paid him! His irritation grew as he mulled over the situation.

He sat and stared at the clothes in the hallway for a long time. Finally, realizing he was uncomfortable, he stood up, stretched, walked into the kitchen, and made another cup of tea. Carrying the tea back into the main room, he flipped the cassette again and fell back into his overstuffed chair.

Commander Blevins turned up the heater closest to him. He was quickly mesmerized by the swaying branches of the tall pine tree in the yard next door, which filled his third-floor window and gave him the feeling of living in a treehouse high in a forest of pines. The fog hung over Twin Peaks beyond the tree. He slowly became lost in his thoughts and the evening floated by.

Very tired and soaked with sweat from the heat, tea, and a parade of fears, Blevins decided to turn in at 9:30. He slid the loveseat back in front of the window. Trudging over to the walk-in closet, he dragged his futon back along the hardwood floor, which left a clean streak on the floor behind it.

When he had made the bed for the night and set the electric blanket at seven, he turned down the three heaters in the main room, turned off the oven, closed its door, shut off the lights in the kitchen, and shuffled by the clothes in the foyer and down the hall to the bathroom. Remembering Mrs. Frumpwooler's battle in the bathroom, he reinspected the scene. He found no evidence of intruders. He closed the window tightly over the tub, bent down, turned on the hot water handle full blast, then squatted down to turn on the heater under the porcelain sink. He poured in a long stream of Bath Therapy and watched as the green powder swirled in the wake of the water flowing from the tub spout.

Slowly he stripped off his robe and outer layers of shirts. He flipped off his Goofy slippers, peeled off two pairs of long-johns, and kicked the whole pile behind the bathroom door.

The tub was about half full when he shut off the hot and turned on the cold. He put one foot into the tub after it had filled some more. The water was too hot, but not scalding. He swished the cold water to the back of the tub with his foot until he could stand the temperature.

Sighing deeply, he lowered his skinny body into the hot water, stretched out, and put his feet up on the tile behind the faucet. The three light cords ran up the wall behind the tub. Two of the cords pulsed more than the other, and the red one now began throbbing even harder. Steam rose and filled the room. The paint on the ceiling peeled a fraction more—brown spots collected on the walls and ceilings. Commander Blevins relaxed, too warm to hold any tension.

Twenty minutes later, he pulled his pink sleepy skinny self out of the tub, dried off hurriedly, raced thorough the cold apartment, and crawled into a comfortably warm bed. Sleep came to him quickly. Dreaming followed sometime after that. Commander Blevins usually sweated when he slept. This night was no exception.

Out on the wire above Filmore, three MEs sat glumly. MEs always were glum when their hosts slept: nothing happened. The MEs' attachment was only to the physical body. When people slept, their physical bodies were at rest, providing no stimulation for attached MEs.

Ember was bright red and glowing. It had sucked up enough heat from Commander Blevins' bath to keep It fueled for many hours to come. It was not glum from lack of satisfaction, but from boredom. The other two were even glummer. In fact, Pins was extraordinarily glum because It had taken the arrival of Greeny hard. Pickings were slim since Ember had arrived, and additional company was not welcome. Ember was more philosophical about the arrangement. It could afford to be.

With its new host, Greeny could feel the mixing of energies and reshifting patterns already taking place and was glumly happy. By morning when Commander Blevins would begin a new day, Greeny would undoubtedly shed Its gloomy night mood the most quickly of the three.

Commander Blevins found himself wide awake and sitting straight up. He walked across the room to the window and watched the moon through the edge of the fog, partially hidden and fuzzy-edged. Then he turned back toward his bed. Two things struck him at once: he was not cold, even though he was naked, and someone was sleeping in his bed. He walked around to the foot of the futon, and the person in his bed rolled over and snorted. It was himself. "How silly of me not to realize that," he thought.

Blevins checked his Inner Awareness. It was a blank screen. The world was as it should be, and there was a reassuring calm inside him, a blank reassuring calm, which he surrendered to without any other consideration, like being on automatic pilot.

A surfboard came through the wall and stopped at his feet. It was yellow with orange fins. He stepped onto the surfboard, and the room fell away. Fog lapped at the sides of the board, and he began moving steadily through grey waves. The waves became bigger, and he cut through them faster.

He wished he had something to hang onto. A sail sprung from the center of the board, and he grasped the bowed sail-bar. He leaned back against the pull of the sail. It shone a fiery red. Splashed with water, the red sail glistened, stark against the grey sea. There was no sun or moon. The sky and sea met somewhere ahead, the horizon an indistinct blending of different shades of grey.

Soon he was being pulled along faster. The muscles in his legs and arms ached from exertion. He wondered how much longer he could hang on. Fear began to creep in as letting go of the sail seemed more and more dangerous. His speed increased again.

Now he was going faster than the wind. Instead of feeling the wind from behind, pushing him along, it blew directly against his face as he cut through both the sea and the wind. He blinked as he thought he saw a dark line stretch out in front of the board through the swell ahead of him. Water drenched him as the waves became larger.

Suddenly a large black shape surfaced ahead of him. The dark line ran back from the black form, back to the front of the board. The black shape plunged into another wave. He was pulled ahead as the pace quickened to an impossible speed. He thought his grip would surely fail him at any moment. Fear spread, and panic nibbled at his feet.

The sea erupted in flames, yellow-orange jets of fire shooting straight up all around him, the grey surface of the sea becoming pockmarked with pools of fire. A huge swell rose in front of him, and he topped it, finding himself completely engulfed in fire. Then the sea fell away, and the sail-bar turned white-hot in his hands. The sail burst into flames. Sweat poured out of him, and he was pulled along faster than thought possible.

Blevins awoke. The bedding was tangled, and most of it was thrown off him. The sheet under him was soaked. His body glistened with sweat, yet he was freezing. An image of his dream journal floated by in his mind. He was unsure who or where he was, though, and was in no shape to find the book, let alone record the dream. He sat still, teeth chattering.

EIGHTEEN
CAYENNE, WATER, THE CHRONICLE

"Hey, Lookeyloo," Ember said. It pointed down to the front door of Commander Blevins' apartment house. Blevins was checking his mailbox. There was no mail yet, so he turned and looked across the street.

Commander Blevins wore his grey and red-striped scarf, a knee-length grey leather coat, mid-calf burgundy boots, and dark green corduroy pants tucked into the boot tops and spilling over in baggy folds. He looked like a well-dressed and well-muscled man ready for a morning stroll through a snow-covered park. Hidden beneath his carefully chosen outer layer were many unseen clothing layers and the skinny body they covered.

He was acutely embarrassed about the amount of clothing he had to wear. The last-minute comment by the women in the laundromat the day before had cut into him deeply. Though the ocean's wind was often cold, he knew there was a limit to just how cold seventeen degrees Celsius should feel.

Commander Blevins topped off his winter wardrobe with an oversize blood-red stocking cap. Behind this hat, a sliver of blue plastic poked out from underneath. This liner, fashioned from a cut-up windbreaker, provided a windbreak for his head and separated the oversized outer cap from the wool stocking cap underneath.

"The old turkey is all dressed up for plucking," said Pins.

"Must be his Sunday-best," said Ember.

"Yep, must be," said Greeny. Ember and Pins looked hard at Greeny. It had joined them on the wire in the middle of the night. The reception that morning had been less than cordial. Antagonism was nothing new with MEs. Most of their feelings toward fellow usurpers were malevolent. The least Greeny was expected to do was to shut-up when It obviously did not know what It was talking about, like now.

Commander Blevins walked across Page Street and down Filmore. The three light cords slowly shortened.

"Wonder where the Bundle is headed today," Pins said. "Maybe the grocery."

"Nope. Too dressed up," Ember said.

"Could be having company later today," Pins said.

"Nope."

"Could be."

"No way, Fuddlebutt. That Old man has never looked this presentable," Ember said.

Commander Blevins walked across Haight Street and continued down Filmore, passing the Haight Street Natural Foods Store on the corner. He looked over the tomatoes and avocados on the outside racks nearest the corner and then continued down the block. The Filmore end of the grocery was solid stained wood, as though a wrap-around storefront had been carefully boarded up. On the sidewalk, built as part of the wooden wall, was a coffin-sized storage cabinet. Its lid was on top, and the cabinet looked disconnected from the rest of the business. Commander Blevins pulled at the lid, out of habit, as he walked by. He had long wondered what the box was used for. The cover did not budge.

"See," Ember said.

"Yeah, see," Greeny piped in. Two stares stopped It from further babble.

Commander Blevins walked down the hill past Sticks and Stones, a newly opened business that provided stuffed scorpions and human bones—among other items of similar taste—to a unique clientele. He shivered, as much from the events of the past day as from the store. Usually, he crossed the street to avoid the little black store.

"I think he's going on Safari," Ember said.

"Which means we are going on Safari," Pins said.

"Come on, Greeny, if light cords get too strung out, they may pop," Ember said.

"Big Mouth," said Pins.

"Give it a rest." The three MEs sailed up on unseen thermals and soon were dancing along over Commander Blevins.

To someone who could see the unseen, he looked like a man walking his balloons: three strange, misshapen balloons with uncommonly thick strings which were translucent, glowing, or both.

Unaware of the MEs, yet feeling their effect, Commander Blevins walked on, troubled. He had never been admonished by the Society. Occasionally he had heard of someone who had been irresponsible in their conduct in the Inner Worlds, but that was rare. And he had never heard of any punitive action taken by the Society.

Blevins thought about his Dream. He had sat immobile in the middle of the bed, soaking wet and naked, for so long that he had gotten deeply chilled. A second long soak in the tub had warmed him, but not before his viral syndrome kicked-up again. He had chewed a large clove of garlic each hour for the rest of the night and morning, which had quelled most of the symptoms. His head, though, was fuzzy, and he felt more susceptible to the cold. He knew the dream was important, but he had yet to figure it out.

And Mrs. Frumpwooler had not paid him!

Lurking in the shadows of his mind, as always, was his nagging fear of sliding backward: of getting one chill after the other and one viral attack after another, which had happened a few years earlier, and he had almost been institutionalized. Luckily he had pulled out of that downward spiral with a prolonged fast, an action too extreme for him to repeat, and had stabilized. He knew he needed to leave San Francisco. The weather was just too cold for him, yet he found his old haunts hard to leave.

A friend had told him about a community living at a hot spring just north of Napa County that sounded interesting. Perhaps he would investigate that area sometime.

He stepped across the tracks where the N Judah trolley pulled up to its last stop on Duboce Street, and he continued on the sidewalk, rounding the corner of Church Street. The J Church trolley was just slowing for its turn into the Muni Underground. At Market Street, Commander Blevins waited for the light to change. The wind picked up, and he hunched his shoulders against it. He knew he ought to stay at home and keep warm, not go out gallivanting. He had nearly four hours before his appointment with the Society; leaving the house this early had been dumb. He debated whether to go to Rainbow, another health food store in the Mission, now or after his meeting. Many bulk things were much better buys at Rainbow, and he especially needed some miso, kombu, and hijiki.

"Later," he decided. The light changed, and Commander Blevins and his three attachments crossed Market Street. The flowers were lovely at The Church Street Peddle Pusher, spilling out onto the sidewalk.

Two storefronts ahead, he opened a steamed-up door, stepped in, and sighed with relief at the warmth.

An "L" shaped food line greeted him. Behind the counter stood a woman in her early twenties. One side of her scalp was shaved to the skin, except for three angled stripes of hair, each about a quarter-inch wide and a quarter-inch high. They began over her ear, disappeared behind her head, and were green, red, and black. The rest of her hair was a flat grey—the color a seventy-year-old anemic woman would change at any cost—-and all one length, chopped off square with the bottom of her other ear. She wore a white apron over a ripped T-shirt and had a jagged metal earing hanging from her exposed ear. She smiled.

"Whacha want?" she asked quietly.

"Oh. I'll have the number one and soup, thank you," Commander Blevins said.

"Which kind of soup: Split Pea or Adzuki-Barley?"

"Adzuki, please. And that is a wonderful earring you have on."

"Thank you. Some man gave it to a friend of mine," she said and gave him the soup. "Lemon butter sauce on your veggies?"

"No thanks."

She handed Commander Blevins a plate piled high with brown rice, garbanzo-tomato stew, steamed carrots, broccoli, green beans, onions, and some other vegetable kingdom bits. Most of his friends found Amazing Grace either too dull or too garish. Blevins, though, was always satisfied by the food and rarely spent more than five bucks. He continued through the line, smiled at the cashier, wondered how much she would pay for one of his new earrings, and then found a back booth away from the door.

He set the tray down and slid in, then got right up again and went back to the front room for a glass of water. Someone had left a Chronicle on top of the trash container. He was in luck since he hadn't remembered to buy a paper. That fact startled him: he always bought a newspaper at the little corner shop catty-corner from the apartment building. He made a mental note to pull himself together.

Back at the booth with water and paper, Commander Blevins doused his plate with cayenne and tamari and opened the paper. The lime green walls and orange booths did not please him visually, but he could overlook this minor shortcoming of the restaurant. Three light cords ran out of the back of the booth up and out through the building and found their way to their three creators, now sitting patiently on an overhead wire on Church Street watching the J Church Car unload at Market.

NINETEEN
UNEXPECTEDLY VISITING CLUB PARADISE

Nestled in an out of the way recess, down the hill and around the corner from City Lights Bookstore, a faded blue door stood, locked. Its square window was silvered and reflected the image of whoever happened to peer into it. "S. V. V." was printed in Gothic script underneath the silver window.

Commander Blevins stood outside the door, in the heart of North Beach. It was 12:35 pm, and there was no beach in sight. Many people, including Commander Blevins, would be dismayed to find a beach anywhere close to North Beach. The North Beach neighborhood was named for the beach that, at one time, skirted the bay just a block and a half from where he now stood. Fill, earthquake rubble, bricked-over muddy streets, paved-over brick streets, bones of dogs lost or eaten: all of that and much more caused the North Beach of today to be landlocked. The TransAmerica Pyramid stood, smack in the midst of the lapping Bay surf, for an illusionary moment of a century.

Blevins had eaten lunch, endured an uneventful ride downtown on the Muni Underground to Montgomery Station, had walked up to the Post/Montgomery side of Market Street, and a block back up Market to Kearny. He had found the 15 Third Street bus almost ready to leave. Five long minutes later, the bus had stopped just short of Broadway. Commander Blevins had gotten off and walked the longer, back way around to get to where he was now.

He was far too early to consider entering and waiting. He tried the door handle anyway, which did not turn. He walked down Columbus Avenue, passed by a bar at the corner of Pacific. The bar was welcoming business, and the doors and windows were wide open. Commander Blevins marveled at how people could be comfortable wearing only a T-shirt when the temperature was in the fifties. He knew he was extreme, but the only place where fifty degrees was T-shirt weather was in San Francisco. Next to the two guys drinking at the bar--in T-shirts--was a man who wore a leather jacket, buttoned, and a scarf. Commander Blevins did not notice him.

The light turned. He took the path of least resistance, crossed Columbus, and walked up the other side of the street. He was stopped by traffic at Broadway. Feeling insignificant and vulnerable among the number of cars and people, he spied Coit Tower peeking over the buildings across the street. He considered going there and taking a look at the city from the tower. Climbing the many steps would probably make him sweat, though, and then he would get chilled. Already cold, he vetoed the idea and crossed Columbus Avenue in front of some girlie joints.

He wandered on, not paying much attention to the people sweeping the sidewalk or passing by or talking on the curb. A taxi pulled up next to him and honked. A woman came out of the doorway, almost knocking him down as she yanked open the back door of the taxi and jumped in the back seat. After a moment's hesitation, the cab and the girl sped off. The image of the woman, as she slipped into the car, burned into Commander Blevins' mind: she was wearing a red leather halter, a red leather mini skirt, black heels, dark glasses, and no panties. The fact that he had known – not guessed – about her underwear, or lack thereof, stopped Commander Blevins in his tracks.

High overhead Pins perked up. It felt a surge of energy that had been missing for a long time. Encouraged, It focused Its full attention on Its host and began drawing in long deep pumps. The light cord had only passed up a trickle of energy in the past three years. The cord responded to the new sensation by turning a shiny charcoal grey but then collapsing in places.

"Drat," Pins thought. "This is going to take some coaxing."

Commander Blevins watched the street by the curb where the taxi, and the red mini-skirted woman, had been. An old urgent feeling flooded his solar plexus.

"Well, why don't you come in and watch the show." Someone was talking to him.

He turned around, hunching over slightly, wondering if he had been caught. Another woman stood in the same doorway, and she did have on panties, along with tall black boots and a very green thigh-length coat, unbuttoned and held back by her elbows. She had vivid green eyes, and underneath the coat, she wore a sheer white push-up bra and white bikini panties. Commander Blevins was very sure just how sheer they were, for her jet black hair falling on her shoulders echoed quite noticeably behind her panties.

Commander Blevins felt a wildness course through him, and his trousers become tight.

Pins got a blast of energy that over-juiced It. The light cord had repaired its collapsed areas, and the sudden increase in energy flow caused the ME to flash glossy black and swoon. All three MEs were hovering a couple hundred feet above their mutual host. Pins slowly floated down, Its light cord coiling neatly beside Commander Blevins. Finally, It landed on the coil.

"What's gotten into him?" Greeny said.

Ember was silent, too involved in monitoring the energy flowing Its own way to respond. Either Pins had suffered a psychic short, or their host was up to old tricks. The latter would not bode well for Ember's future.

Blevins still stared at the second woman.

"My name's Estel," she said. She quickly scanned the

area and then said, "Would you like to come inside," she ran her hand slowly over her stomach, "and sit with me?" As she said "me," her fingers slid inside her panties and moved in little circles.

"Yes!" Commander Blevins blurted, staring harder. He walked into the club behind the woman. A heavy black drape caught him in the face as it swung back into position after she passed through. Fumbling his way around the curtain, he found himself in a room so dark he could not see where he stood. Across the room was a stage with a high stool sitting in the center. A woman was on the stool. Unseen and clustered around the ceiling like sentry gargoyles were fat black Misplaced Entities. Their light cords were black, then red, changing as they undulated and crossed the room in a shiny spider web pattern. They all were juicing heavily from four men up front near the stage.

The woman on the stool sat poised with both legs wrapped around her neck. One man up front—Commander Blevins could only see his dark outline against the stage lights—was yelling in a mushy voice, "Take it off. Take it off."

His companion laughed, "She already has, Harry. You're too snookered to see, you old coot." His words were slurred, too. The two other men snickered.

Outside, a man walked across the place Commander Blevins had been standing, passing through the area where Pins lay on Its coil of light cord. The man hesitated two steps later, looked down at one leg, shook it as though something clung to it, and then shivered all over.

Pins was brought back to Its senses by the energy field passing through It. It had to make a conscious effort to keep from attaching itself to the new potential host. For a ME, connecting to two physical bodies at once was a sure way to gluttony and spontaneous division, if the two hosts got too far apart. This usually led to a ME losing control and often becoming the slave of another, stronger ME.

Commander Blevins felt a firm grip on his arm. "This way, Sugar," a woman purred into his ear. The music was loud, but her voice pierced it easily. He let himself be guided, but his eyes did not leave the stage and the woman of many postures on the stool who continued to find positions that defied gravity, modesty, and Commander Blevins' imagination. Three light cords followed. One pulsed heavily.

"Here, this will do, won't it, Honey." Blevins felt himself being pushed into a booth. She sat down next to him, very close to him. Perfume assaulted his senses. "What would you like to drink, Handsome?"

"Uh, orange juice."

"Would this sexy man buy Estel a drink?" She put her hand on his thigh.

Outside, Ember's fears were confirmed. Pins rose high into the air, a vibrant gloss black, with smart grey pinstriping. Its light cord had now turned coal-black too, looking and twitching like a stalking panther's tail still damp from a rainstorm.

"Yeah, sure, okay." The Society, Mrs. Frumpwooler, earrings, his dream: all--everything that made Commander Blevins' world function and approach balance--had been left outside.

"I'll be right back, and then we can talk," Estel said.

As she started to leave, she let her hand glide farther up his leg and across his crotch. "Ohhhhh," she said as her hand brushed his pants, "A big, handsome boy."

Commander Blevins jolted when Estel touched him. After she left, he tried to look around him but could see little.

The woman on stage was now standing in front of the stool and looking over her shoulder. She turned back around on the stool. Bending down slowly, she reached around into a shopping bag that sat on the floor. Straightening up, she looked over her shoulder again and, with a teasing look on her face, revealed a large cucumber that she held in one hand. Slowly she began licking the tip of the cucumber.

Two huge MEs began drifting over toward Commander Blevins and the three light cords. They both had bright red circles under their eyes and lumps all over their bodies. One of them, the largest, trailed strings of shiny grey drool.

"Here we are now."

He heard the voice but did not associate it with anyone in particular until a hot body was pressing against him.

"Here are the drinks, Hon. That'll be fifty bucks. Ten for yours and forty for mine."

The woman on the stage was now sliding the massive cucumber into her mouth as far as possible, which was not very far. Blevins reached into his front left pants pocket and pulled out the little wallet he carried. He had been paid two days earlier by the Client before Mrs. Frumpwooler and had not deposited any cash. He pulled out three twenties and handed them to Estel, expecting change.

"Oh, thank you, Sugar." She quickly added the bills to a small wad, twisted a rubber band around it, and shoved it into a Collins glass on her tray, which was on a chair next to the booth. "Now, where were we?" she murmured as she snuggled against Commander Blevins and began once again running her hand over him.

Blevins' inner voice, small and faint, protested at the idea of paying so much and receiving no change. Commander Blevins ignored it. He was entirely focused on two sensations: one, which his eyes brought to him, and the other, which Estel's hands provided. He took a long drink of his orange juice. It rolled down his throat, hit his stomach, and burned everywhere. He had not had any orange juice in three years. It made him feel colder in a world that was already too cold for him. The voice grew louder inside, but he pushed it away.

"My, but we have a lot of clothes on, Honey. Is it that cold out today?" Estel was becoming very familiar with Commander Blevins. She had his two pairs of pants unzipped and was now fishing through his longjohns. "I know you are in here somewhere. I can feel that big boy of yours, Handsome."

Commander Blevins squirmed and took another long drink of his orange juice and felt more fire. The woman on stage was bent entirely over now, head almost touching her knees, which were nowhere close to touching each other. She had the cucumber positioned in such a way that there was no doubt where it was going next. He took a third big drink from the glass.

"Ahah!" Estel said. "Here you are." Flesh met flesh.

On stage, the cucumber disappeared, mostly, to shouts from the men upfront and an extended stage groan from the woman.

Commander Blevins yelled, "Booze!" and stood straight up, knocking the table over in the booth.

"Careful, Honey. Sit back down." Estel looked around, worried, but still retained her grip.

"You put booze in my orange juice!" he shouted. His pants fell partway down his legs. The three light cords whipped behind him as he gyrated, trying to shake loose from Estel's lock. The big black MEs, just starting to sniff the light cords, were caught by surprise. They were not able to avoid being brushed by them.

Outside, Pins sailed higher, dancing in unseen jet streams, oblivious to what was going on inside.

Ember felt the sniffing and the proximity of other MEs, guessed what was happening, yelled to Greeny, and poked Itself through the front wall of Club Paradise. It screamed. As quickly as It went in, It withdrew. Greeny was nearby, looking like a dog called by

Its master. Its eyes were huge, and Its greedy little heart was thrilled at being called upon.

"Of course, the bartender put booze in your Orange Juice." The situation was rapidly deteriorating for Estel.

"I can't drink!"

"Could've fooled me, Honey," Estel said.

The gang of MEs in the club all perked up when Ember suddenly appeared and screamed. They began moving toward the door, and Commander Blevins.

The woman on stage stopped in mid-stroke and peered between her legs at the commotion in the back.

"Hey now, no slacking on the job," one of the ring-side drunks yelled.

"I can't drink!" Commander Blevins yelled again.

Estel finally released both her eyes from the other bills in his wallet and his appendage of the moment.

"And you owe me money. I gave you sixty bucks and did not get any change," Blevins added.

Estel quickly pulled up his pants, buttoned them, zipped the fly, slid out of the booth, and yelled, "Georgio!"

"We've got do a Wrap, Greeny," Ember said.

"What's a Wrap, and what about..." Greeny pointed up to where Pins sailed, lost in euphoria.

"Forget it. Too far gone right now. Listen carefully and do exactly what I say."

In a heartbeat, Georgio was at Estel's side and said, "What's the matter, Hun?"

"This creep's outa hand. He won't keep his hands offa me."

Georgio looked at her carefully. He did not want to rile a customer unnecessarily. His girls were not supposed to do half the stuff they did, but stiffing a john was bad business.

"She owes me money," Commander Blevins said. He was weaving a little bit. His pants were lumpy and uncomfortable around his crotch and upper thighs. The alcohol had started to get to him. He had developed a sensitivity to alcohol even before his training in Inner World travel. Now it was a violent shock to his system.

The gang of MEs clustered around him, poking and prodding with their light cords.

Georgio wondered if this guy was a big man or just had on many layers of clothes. Deliberation was not one of Georgio's talents. When his mind got as far as it could go, he simply decided. Usually, his decision was based on his own mood at the moment. "Outa here, chump."

Expecting justice, Commander Blevins said, "What?"

Two black light cords scratched at the center of his back, where the hole in his aura was wide open. Their tips glowed red.

"I said leave, dude. Outa here." Estel was now behind Georgio but under a small light. She had dirty blonde hair, was far from young, and wore jeans and a long-sleeve black blouse.

Commander Blevins saw her. "What the..." he began to say, but found himself pushed along by strong hands. A black wall parted before him, and outside, the light was blinding as he stumbled toward the sidewalk. The

MEs inside the bar were also blinded. Ember and Greeny had combined for a mighty Wrap, negating any possibility of Commander Blevins becoming a new host.

"Steady, now." Another voice said and touched him enough to help him stabilize. "Some visits to Club Paradise last longer than others."

He looked up as he got his balance and found vivid green eyes staring back at him. The woman put one arm around his shoulder like he was her kid brother, and began walking him away from the Club. Behind them trailed an unseen fourth of July: Greeny had found a new thrill.

"Sometimes we get what we want, and sometimes what we want gets us," Estel said as they walked along. "I'm sure you will have a fine day ahead of you. Please come back again when you have more time to spend. Maybe I will sit with you then."

Stunned and silent, Commander Blevins stood on the corner and watched as she returned to the Club. Her long legs ran into her high boots and stepped out gracefully from beneath the hem of her green jacket as she walked back down Broadway.

"Slow down, Wyatt. That's enough," Ember said. Greeny grinned and did several barrel rolls.

TWENTY
READJUSTING THE

Strategic Appendage

Commander Blevins stared after her until she disappeared into the strip joint. Over the doorway was suspended a big green Palm Tree painted on a vertical sign. Lettering ran up by the trunk and said, "CLUB PARADISE," in purple letters. Underneath the painted sand was the promise: "Where Dreams Come True."

Shaking his head the way a dog does when ear mites bite, Commander Blevins tried to break free of the spell. He gazed across Broadway and down Columbus until he saw the lower buildings which blocked out the base of the TransAmerica Pyramid. He followed the left side of the sloping tower up to the needle spire with his eyes.

His mind was pulp from alcohol and hormones. He mumbled his thoughts out loud, "I wonder how far up in the point of that thing a body can go."

A young woman on her way to the club just behind where he stood looked him up and down then went inside. A moment later, a Georgio clone came out and roughly shook Commander Blevins' shoulder. "Hey buddy, you gotta move along. The Condor don't allow no vagrants outside."

Commander Blevins turned on the fellow indignantly, started to dispute the matter, then reconsidered. The Condor bouncer was taller than Georgio and outweighed Commander Blevins by at least two hundred pounds.

Without saying a word, he stepped around the bouncer and walked up Columbus. The wind was cold off the bay, but Commander Blevins did not feel the chill. The vodka had numbed him and was playing havoc with his inner sensibilities.

A park appeared on his right after he had walked about three blocks. He wandered along its path until he found an empty bench underneath a huge cypress tree. He sat down. Although it was risky for him to be out in the cool breeze, sitting outside without shivering from the cold was a luxury. He indulged himself and smiled.

Pins had mellowed and was now playfully avoiding Greeny as It tried to do a Wrap. Ember bounced from one treetop to another. They all were happy with

Commander Blevins' relaxed mood. Had anyone who could see the unseen come along, that person would have marveled at the green, red, and shiny black light cords whipping around the park.

Commander Blevins tried to focus his mind. He was trembling, but not aware enough to notice. He knew something important loomed just ahead of him. A cane knocked at his foot. Startled, he looked up and said, "Hello," realizing the man was blind.

"Please excuse me. I'm still not too good at this," the man said.

"Oh, that's all right. Sorry I didn't notice you first."

"Do you happen to know what time it is?" the blind man asked.

"No, I don't carry a watch." Commander Blevins hesitated a moment, then said, "But I'll find out for you."

"I don't want to trouble you, sir." Before the man could finish his sentence, Commander Blevins was across the path and talking to a woman with two kids running around her.

In a moment, he was back. He sat down on the bench and said, "It's 1:40." Then he added, "In the afternoon."

"Yes, I can feel the sun on my face. It's a nice balmy day, don't you think? Thank you so much for your kindness." The blind man walked on down the path, swinging his cane back on forth.

Commander Blevins was lifted by the exchange. A little of the clinging gloom leftover from Club Paradise fell away. He also became aware of a distinct discomfort.

His appendage of the moment, which Estel—one of the Estels—had locked onto earlier, was still threaded through both flys of his two pairs of longjohns. Compounding this uncomfortable state of affairs was the position of his inner set of trousers. Both pairs of trousers had fallen down around his knees when he stood up after realizing there was vodka in his drink. In her haste to cut losses, Estel had pulled up his outer pants, buckled and zipped them enough to be legal, and then sent him briskly on his way. He now felt an immediate need to find a restroom.

Washington Square did not offer the relief facilities required by Commander Blevins. He stood up, grunted a little as he took a step, and wondered how he had been able to walk at all a moment earlier. The vodka had hit him hard, and he was far too fuzzy to answer his own question.

The neighborhood was thick with restaurants and coffee houses. Directly across Columbus and Union's broad intersection, where Powell Street, heading due north, crossed both Union and Columbus in triangular patterns that maddened tourists, Commander Blevins spotted a corner shop that held the promise of a restroom. The store was not the closest, but it was the first one he saw.

He walked quickly and as normally as possible to the western edge of the park, waited until there was a lull in traffic, then set off across the three-way intersection, not bothering with crosswalks or traffic lights.

In a day beset with misadventure, Commander Blevins was blessed with the absence of policemen or speeding motorists. He made it to the other side of the intersection without creating much of a stir, other than providing comic relief to several witnesses.

A man past his prime does not sprint gracefully. The body remembers how it ran as a child, the man remembers pulled muscles from simple chores, and a compromise develops, a usually non-synergistic comprise. Commander Blevins executed an unintentional parody of a grounded Gooney Bird in motion.

The three MEs followed in their own time, allowing light cords to reel out longer or not as suited them individually. Greeny led the way, keeping a close eye on Commander Blevins, hoping for new threats that would warrant more unseen fireworks. Pins came next, followed eventually by Ember, who was in no hurry. It knew Commander Blevins was cold and would not be going far. It was also a little sluggish from the low level of energy flowing to It.

Breathing heavily and just beginning to perspire, Commander Blevins made it to Green and Powell's far corner and leaned on the mailbox. The door was open across the sidewalk. After regaining his composure, he entered the little shop.

A long wooden bar ended just inside the front door. It was piled high with glass cases of food and goods for sale and obscured anyone behind the bar. The odor of pungent cheese smacked Commander Blevins in the face. An old couple was getting up from a small table near the far end of the bar. There were coffee cups on the table. Blevins leaned against the bar rail for support as casually as possible and moved past all the clutter.

"Hello, hello. What can I get you, my friend?" A short man with a white apron startled Blevins, popping up just beyond a pile of old newspapers. "The best coffee in the neighborhood. We got Expresso. We got Double Expresso. We even got Extra Double Expresso. What kind you want?"

Commander Blevins coughed once, then said, "I would like to use your restroom."

The little man changed his attitude instantly, "What, you some kind of bum? How come you come to my shop here? Don't you see that you'll drive away my good customers?" An old couple waved cheerfully as they left.

"See," the little man continued, "My best customers. Tommy Provoloni, he been coming here for twenty years. Today, for the first time in twenty years, he brings his beautiful wife Sophie in to see the shop. And what happens…"

Commander Blevins shifted uncomfortably.

"I'll tell you what happens," the little man said, "some bum comes in and asks to use the john, and there goes Tommy and Sophie. And this her first time here."

Commander Blevins cleared his throat. The little man stopped talking and looked at him. "I would like a coffee, please," Commander Blevins said.

"Of course, you would." The little man smiled, brushed away some invisible crumbs on the counter, and, with a flourish, laid a small paper napkin in front of Commander Blevins.

"What would you like, sir? Espresso?"

Commander Blevins nodded.

"Double or Extra, perhaps?"

Commander Blevins nodded, shifted uncomfortably again, and made a face. "Could I use the restroom, please?" he asked.

"Of course. It's in the back to the left." The little man pointed. Commander Blevins shuffled off, caring only about getting strategically readjusted. "We have just the one can, so put the lid down," the little man yelled at his back.

Over the whir of the espresso machine, the little man soon heard loud grunts and groans coming from the bathroom. He was glad there was no one else in the store. Still, a customer was a customer. He made the man an Extra. He liked to start new customers off with a bang.

The lid of the toilet clattered. Water ran. The door swung open too hard and hit the wall behind it. A picture rattled. It was a picture of a man standing in front of five other men, surrounded by an old wooden olive press. The little man cringed.

Looking a little less rumpled, Commander Blevins shuffled up to the tiny cup waiting on the bar. Looking at it dubiously, for he had not had any coffee for more than four years, he said, "How much do I owe you?"

"Let's no talk of money so soon, my friend," the little man said. "Sit down. Savor the atmosphere of the establishment. This is your first time here, no?" Commander Blevins nodded, yes. "Well, then, we must have a toast. My name is Solly," Solly said and extended his hand.

Commander Blevins shook hands with Solly. Both men had wet hands, but neither noticed. Blevins sat down on the high stool at the bar and made himself comfortable. Solly poured himself an equally small cup of coffee from a decanter under the bar and raised it before him. Commander Blevins stared at Solly for a moment, then gripped the small saucer underneath the tiny cup with one hand and picked up his cup with the other. In response to Solly's gesture, he raised his little cup.

"To new customers, old friends, and my mother, God rest her soul," Solly said and downed his cup in one swallow. Commander Blevins watched him. "Come on now. Don't be bashful. All in one swallow now, that's the way to drink Solly's Extra Double."

Commander Blevins brought the small cup to his lips, felt the warmth leap into his mouth ahead of the coffee, and drank it in one gulp. Halfway through the swallow, he knew he was in trouble. Coffee and alcohol do not counteract each other. In people like Commander Blevins, who get buzzed, not numbed, on booze, coffee stretches the peaks into sharp points like the top of the TransAmerica Pyramid.

The coffee rolled into Commander Blevins' mouth, and a sharp spike raced toward his brain, then shot back down and continued to do laps up and down his legs and arms at thousands of miles per second. Soon, small crawling things moved under his skin. Everywhere. His eyes glassed over, and he hung onto the rail for his safety.

"Glad to see you are enjoying my Expresso," Solly said. "Another one will take the bite out of the wind for your journey." Solly turned to make another cup for his new customer. He quickly went through the routine and looked back over his shoulder while filling a fresh little cup with Extra Double. His shop was empty except for himself. Crumpled and half-tucked under the edge of the saucer was a five-dollar bill.

By the time Solly had smoothed out the five and tucked it into his register, Commander Blevins was two blocks down Columbus Avenue and traveling fast. His legs had struck a rhythm of their own. His eyes fixed first on a traffic light that changed, next on a car door that slammed, then on a phone ringing in a second-floor apartment overhead. His physical senses were acutely aware of everything, his reactions sharp and immediate to the sensory stimulus that poured through his overloaded synapses.

Traveling down Columbus Avenue, he crossed Broadway and entered Grant Street, staring open-mouthed at the vast murals he passed on his right. Horns honked, someone yelled, and then he found himself in the thick of Chinatown, which smelled of fish markets. Suddenly he was the object of wrath from a middle-aged Chinese woman. Overwhelmed with distractions, he had inadvertently knocked over a large straw basket of slippers. Commander Blevins kept walking, glanced back over his shoulder once, and then adjusted his hats. The woman scooped the black cloth slippers back into the basket and reviled his ancestry. Blevins looked around just in time to steer clear of an ornate lamp post standing directly in his path.

The three MEs were merrily in tow. Pins looked like seventeen coats of hand-rubbed, pin-striped black lacquer and was doing barrel rolls over Grant Street. Greeny was trying to follow.

Commander Blevins abruptly turned right on Jackson Street, scattered a group of people visiting from Iowa, crossed the street at an angle, walked another quarter block, and turn sharply into Ross Alley. Jewelry Stores passed by on his left, and a twinkle from the window sparked a memory. Looking into windows and doorways, he saw women sewing, two men making fortune cookies, and a small child being sternly lectured by an elderly person of indeterminate gender.

He went straight across the street at the next corner, turned around completely, and crossed the road again exactly as he had come. He stopped in front of a window that held many open jewelry cases displaying watches, rings, and bracelets. At the back of the window display, near a man working on a setting, lay a small opened bag. Spilling out of the bag was a small pile of diamonds. The man was engrossed in his work. Bells and whistles roared through Commanders Blevins' head. He knew he should remember something...more than one thing. Agitated and driven, he turned and crossed the street for the third time and swiveled left when he reached the sidewalk. Just beyond an incredibly narrow restaurant, he stopped in his tracks again. The window of this shop was full of hanging barbecued ducks.

His mind raced through old patterns in unfamiliar ways: no, he was not hungry, and he did not like duck. The sight of them repulsed him. He could find no reason to be standing where he was, so he quickly counted the hanging ducks by threes. There were thirty-nine. Congratulating himself on picking an even divider to count by, and not questioning his accuracy, he turned and marched down Washington Street.

Commander Blevins crossed Grant again, looked to the other side of Washington, and momentarily peered down the narrow entrance to Wentworth Alley. The alley was lined with plain facades and little tourist activity, despite its colorful past. The building that he was hugging on his right suddenly ended, and he veered right and down into a park, feeling like he was falling. He noticed a statue of some man up a slope on his right, weaved through the rows of trees and around people playing cards and chess and zipped by three solitary book readers and an old man feeding pigeons, all the while negotiating the downhill terrain. Blevins exited on a wide street and turned left.

He continued up the street for a couple blocks until he ran into Columbus Avenue. A funny triangular building sat in the middle of the intersection like an ornate and over-built traffic island.

Turning the forty-five-degree angle up Columbus, he walked on. The energy rush was beginning to waver, and he could feel the distant vodka haze return. Adler Street was announced by a street sign, and bells went off again. He crossed Adler and turned left and found himself standing in front of a faded blue door with initials painted underneath a silver window.

"The Society!" he thought to himself. "Of course, I have an appointment at three o'clock. And it's now..." He realized he did not know what time it was. Panic struck quickly. The three MEs clustered above him, as though watching a dramatic scene unfold. Blevins adjusted his hats.

TWENTY-ONE
REPRIMANDS, ILLUSIONS,

And Awareness

The streets were devoid of life. Commander Blevins decided that if he was late, nothing could be done about it now. He took a deep breath, put his hand on the handle, tried it, felt it turn, and the latch click. He pushed the door back and stepped silently into the foyer. Suddenly the door closed back upon him. He jumped out of the way. Behind the door, Blevins saw three coats hanging on a coat rack, swinging. His mind boggled for a moment, then he realized the door must have swung against the coats, which then pushed the door back toward him.

He turned to the long flight of stairs, which led up to the Society's Offices. He walked gingerly up the steps. His senses were on such high alert that his body's normally fluid motion was broken down into hundreds of momentary stops and starts. He did not know if the erratic movement was only a feeling inside himself, or if someone would notice he was moving like a computerized robot with every third program command a "stop." Hoping for the best, Blevins topped the stairs and entered the waiting room.

As soon as he left the last step, he abruptly turned around and looked back down the stairwell, realizing he'd seen a shimmer of light behind him as he came through the door. A familiar presence filtered through his confusion.

"Commander Blevins!" a man exclaimed. The voice did not belong to the familiar presence, which faded, washed away by the shock of the greeting. Blevins jumped off the carpet and twirled around. "How good to see you!" a large round man said, extending his hand from behind a secretarial desk.

"Hello, McDervish. Nice to see you," Commander Blevins said, twitching. McDervish raised his left eyebrow and looked at Blevins closely. He then sat down and motioned Commander Blevins to do the same.

"I can see that you are a little tense about all this," McDervish said. "Don't let it get you down. I'm sure it's not as bad as all that. Stiff upper lip and all, old boy."

Commander Blevins' mind raced and darted. He was not sure if he was early or late, and he did not have the slightest idea what McDervish was talking about.

Another man walked into the room, through a doorway behind McDervish. The man looked at Commander Blevins and then back to McDervish. With veiled hand signals, he asked McDervish if Blevins was the man for whom they were waiting. McDervish nodded. An awkward moment passed as they both looked at Commander Blevins. Blevins looked at them, wondering why they were staring at him. He had never seen the other man before.

The other man cleared his throat, and McDervish jumped to his feet. "Oh, surely, excuse me, Sir," McDervish said to the man. This is Commander Blevins, Sir. And Commander Blevins, this is Sir Bilton Dweed. He'll be presiding over the, ah...discussion today."

"Thank you, Mac. It is sometime before the appointed hour, Blevins, but I think we can go ahead and start now. Tickle's already here." Turning to McDervish, he said, "Would you show Blevins inside, Mac." Sir Bilton Dweed turned stiffly and disappeared into the room. McDervish walked around in front of his desk and assumed the role of escort.

Commander Blevins was bewildered. Totally bewildered. A dim awareness pulled at him, but he could not pierce his veil of caffeine, vodka, and hormonal rampage. He followed McDervish's motioning arm, stood up suddenly, and lurched toward the open door. Hesitating for a moment, and unsure why, he then stepped quickly into the room, walked two paces, and stopped abruptly. Softly he heard the click of the door behind him and sensed that McDervish had settled into a chair just inside the room. A glittering shadow moved to one corner of the room. No one saw it.

Sir Bilton Dweed and Vice-Counsel Tickle sat at opposite ends of a long, dark mahogany table, which sat lengthwise against the far wall. The carpet in the room was a short, firm weave, and deep blue. Books lined the end wall to Commander Blevins' left, and three other chairs were grouped around a circular table on his right. Blevins was aware of several paintings hanging on teak paneled walls but did not examine them.

He locked his eyes onto a curious low wide stool that sat in the middle of the room. The stool had a short back and was richly upholstered. Commander Blevins felt a lightness being in the place and whipped his head back to inspect the ceiling, which was a light blue that seemed to fade lighter toward the room's edges. There were no lights visible in the room. The edges of the ceiling glowed with a gentle blue light that bathed the room and everyone in it.

Vice-Counsel Tickle looked at Sir Bilton Dweed with both of his eyebrows raised nearly to his hairline, looked back toward Commander Blevins, and then said, "Please be seated, Commander Blevins. We are convening early, but what are both time and space for, if not to be manipulated." Commander Blevins felt he should smile, tried, but could only make a strange face: his facial muscles were not his own at the moment. He stepped around quickly to the front of the stool, tested it for support, and then fell, rather than sat, down. A phrummphh of air escaped from the cushion as his weight struck it.

Sir Bilton Dweed stood up, clasped both hands over his heart as though he were a corpse, then opened his mouth and produced a long even sound in a well-trained tenor voice. Commander Blevins' raised *his* eyebrows. Sir Bilton Dweed ended his tone with a little flourish, said, "The Inner Leads, the Outer follows," and sat down.

"Thank you, Sir Bilton," Vice-Counsel Earl Roy Tickle said. "Commander Blevins, we are gathered here today to Review the Complaint filed with this Society scarcely less than twenty-four hours ago by a fellow Viewer whose identity must remain anonymous at this time. If this Review Committee deems that charges are warranted, then we will set an appropriate time and place for the Complaining Viewer to step forth.

Commander Blevins felt a crack ran through the glaze in his mind. A second crack soon followed.

Vice-Counsel Tickle continued. "On or about this time yesterday, note the date, Bill, you, Blevins, were carrying on with traditional Viewing activities. That being the Viewing of a particular set of Akashic Records. Give me the name and ID information, Bill." Bill handed the Vice-Counsel Tickle a small tablet.

Commander Blevins felt his neck spasm. His head snapped back. He blinked and then saw that indirect lighting poured out of an enclosed strip, which ran all the way around the edge of the ceiling, and reflected downward into the rest of the room, solving one small mystery. Another large mystery remained. More cracks zig-zagged across the glaze in his mind.

Vice-Counsel Tickle cleared his throat. Commander Blevins forced his head back upright. Tickle read from the tablet, "The tray you extracted was labeled 'Gladys Periwinkle Frumpwooler.' It was from a mixed active/inactive sector, but apparently, this individual is...or at least was yesterday...active. I think." Vice-Counsel Earl Roy Tickle squinted at the tablet, then handed it back to Sir Bilton Dweed. "Can you read that, Bill?"

"Yes, it says active, pending possible revision. Since the reading, something must have happened with this person, which is yet to be evaluated or recorded, ET." Bill handed the tablet back to Tickle.

"All right," Tickle said, "though that is not pertinent at the moment. The Complaint, Commander Blevins, is that your exit from the Causal Worlds caused undue disruption to another Viewer's Journey. This Viewer was, therefore, unable to retrieve the Records of their Client. Sufficient reputation and remuneration were lost by the Viewer in question to warrant this action. What do you have to say regarding this matter, Blevins?"

Commander Blevins had no idea what to say. He felt his mind collapsing and shattering like a plate glass window dropped from great heights. He opened his mouth, moved it, but nothing came out.

"Is this man well, Mac?" Vice-Counsel Tickle asked McDervish.

"Yes, Sir. I mean, well, Commander Blevins does have some ongoing physical challenges, Sir. But he doesn't seem to be succumbing to any of them, in general, Sir. I must admit that he seems a bit tense today. Must be the stress of...."

Commander Blevins chose that moment to rise through his personal quagmire, pierce his mind's shattered glaze, remembering his experience with Mrs. Frumpwooler vividly, and stand suddenly, ramrod straight. He said, "Mrs. Frumpwooler! Of course, that's what happened. She bounded back ahead of me to get the diamonds. She didn't wait for my instructions. She must have collided, or nearly so, with our fellow Viewer. Oh, please do accept my most profound apologies. It can be devastating when a Client is not sufficiently pleased with the service provided." Like a high-speed Dictaphone set to playback and then automatically shutting-off, Commander Blevins sat, abruptly silent. His words hung in the air, pregnant.

Vice-Counsel Tickle looked at Sir Bilton Dweed, who looked at McDervish, who looked at Commander Blevins. Finally, Vice-Counsel Tickle spoke. If I understand you correctly, your *client*, this 'Mrs. Frumpwooler' came *back* from the Records *without* your *instructions?*"

"Yes. Yes, that's what happened. I'm sure of it," Commander Blevins said.

"Blevins. Commander...ah," Tickle looked at the tablet again, "Z. P. Blevins, that is preposterous. Clients are not only not allowed in the Records, but they also *cannot go*! No one except fully trained and Verified Viewers can Journey to the Records."

"They can't?" Commander Blevins asked.

"No, they cannot." Vice-Counsel Tickle said, but then seemed uncomfortable as the contradiction to accepted doctrine slowly settled upon him. "Well, at least they have not, until now." After more silence, he continued, "Just how is it that you were able to take this...Client...along with you to the Records."

"Uh, by holding her hand."

"Holding her hand! Did you have a romantic liaison with this woman also?"

"No, I did.—"

"Ye Gods, Blevins, just how many Society Codes did you break on this Journey?" yelled Vice-Counsel Tickle, staring hard at Commander Blevins.

"I did not, do not have a romantic interest in Mrs. Frumpwooler," Commander Blevins said. "I only met her yesterday. If I broke any Society Codes, I apologize. It was not intentional."

"Do you mean to say that you were never told that it was impossible to take Clients to the Records?"

"I was told it was not allowed because it could not be done. I found a way to do it. I didn't think any more about it."

Vice-Counsel Earl Roy Tickle looked at Sir Bilton Dweed, shook his head, then turned back to Commander Blevins. "Well, just how did you manage to do this?"

"It involves the creative imagination, Sir. With

certain Clients, and Mrs. Frumpwooler was an excellent subject until she got out of hand a bit, I have been able to establish a link in the Inner 'Anteroom,' so to speak, and then step out of the physical and into the Inner Worlds."

"I see," said the Vice-Counsel Tickle. "Does this make any sense to you, Bill?"

"No, not much, ET."

"How about you, Mac."

"Well, to a certain extent, I'm following Commander Blevins," McDervish said. "I'd like to know what he did next." There was a twinkle in his eye.

"All right," Vice-Counsel Tickle said. "Continue with this tale, Blevins."

"Well, once out of the physical, we practiced focusing. She caught on quite fast. Then I started looking for a Blipspule. Actually, she found a bevy up near the ceiling and..."

"Wait a minute. Did I hear you right? Did you say 'Blipspule' Commander Blevins? " Sir Bilton Dweed interrupted.

"Yes, I did, Sir."

"What the devil is a Blipspule, Bill," Vice-Counsel Tickle said, turning to Dweed.

"They are reported to be windows, ET. Until now, though, no one had been able to master their use. This is beginning to make a bit of sense. Go on Commander Blevins," Sir Bilton Dweed said.

"Well, like I was saying, Mrs. Frumpwooler found this bevy...er, group...of Blipspules up near the ceiling.

With her in a state of sufficient fluidity from the linkage of our creative imaginations, it was easy to take her by the hand and scoot through the Blue Tunnel."

"The Blue Tunnel, of course!" McDervish snapped his fingers. "Oh, please pardon me, gentlemen."

"That's all right, Mac. This is an extraordinary Review," Sir Bilton Dweed said, adding, "Please continue, Commander Blevins."

Well, once through the Blue Tunnel, we crossed the Moondog World, did the Jump to the Astral, took the Bridge over to the Causal, found the Sand Lake Express, and soon were at the Records. The problems began, I believe, when the tray wasn't in order. In fact, there weren't even any codes on her cards."

"No codes?"

"Out of Order?"

"Impossible!"

"Amazing!"

"Do you think this could be a Hidden Agenda Plot, one that we haven't run across yet, Bill?" Vice-Counsel Tickle said.

"No, I don't think so, ET. I think this may be revolutionary," Dweed said and then addressed Blevins. "Commander Blevins, before discovering the tray out of order, did you have any indications that all was not well on this Journey?"

"Well, Mrs. Frumpwooler was a precocious student. She picked up focalshifting with ease, except for a couple small misadventures. She did generally handle the Agitation well as we neared the Records, but now that you have asked, I can look back and see that her behavior was perhaps a little more pronounced than that of other Clients.

"Agitation? Please explain that Commander Blevins," Sir Bilton Dweed said.

"Others! Please explain *that* Blevins," Vice-Counsel Tickle said.

McDervish sat quietly by the door, absorbing what Commander Blevins was saying with keen interest.

"Well, it is my experience that all of Akash is highly charged," Blevins said. "The Gardens, and especially the Records are even more highly charged,"

"Umm humm," Vice-Counsel Tickle said.

"Yes, of course," Sir Bilton Dweed said.

McDervish nodded silently, his eyes glowing.

Commander Blevins continued, "I've noticed that the closer to Akash and the Records that I bring a Client, often they exhibit an exaggeration of some portion or other of their personality. I call this the Agitation. It usually requires some effort to guide them safely on to the appropriate level of the Records. Curiously enough, this Agitation often disappears once the Client and I actually enter the Viewing Room with the Tray of Record Cards."

Sir Bilton Dweed exchanged glances with Vice-Counsel Tickle, who said, "I think that should be quite enough reason to stop this practice immediately. It is obviously hazardous to the Client. It also runs the risk of educating some unauthorized person to the point of visiting the Inner Worlds—and even the Records—by themselves. Where would we as Viewers be then! Where would the Society be then! I think..."

"Please, ET. Let's give this notion some air," Sir Bilton Dweed said. "Commander Blevins has shared with us today some potentially ground-breaking experiences and abilities. They cannot be..."

"Bill, this is rubbish. The man is trying to cover up his own disregard for Society Codes and other Viewers, and our Complainant in particular. I say we disbar him post-haste and be done with this concoction of his."

"No, ET. I don't think that is appropriate," Sir Bilton Dweed said.

"Then I will take this up with the Membership Committee, Sir Bill," Vice-Counsel Tickle said.

Sir Bilton Dweed looked thoughtfully at Earl Roy Tickle and said, while revising his opinion of Tickle, "I believe this has gone quite far enough, ET. The Membership Committee shall review the Review if you choose. You are the Chairman of it for the remainder of this term."

"I am glad you see things my way, Bill. It is most..."

"...Unless the board decides your attitude displayed here today, in the light of Commander Blevins' revelations, is no longer appropriate for a member of the Membership Committee, let alone for its Chairman," added Dweed.

"The Board? It is not scheduled to meet until January," Vice-Counsel Tickle said.

"There are ways to call emergency meetings, ET. I, for one, do not see things your way," said Dweed.

"Well, we shall see. You will have a devil of a time holding an emergency meeting without the Chairman. And no one that I know of has ever seen him or even knows what old Whirling looks like." Tickle was incensed.

"There are three people I know of who have seen him today, ET." Sir Bilton Dweed said.

Vice-Counsel Tickle gasped and said, "Not you, Bill, you couldn't be the...you are a member of the board, not its chairman!"

"You are quite right, ET," another voice in the room said. Vice-Counsel Tickle gasped again, for McDervish stood up and walked toward the middle of the room, near where Commander Blevins sat with his mouth hanging open. "I am the Chairman. And I have assumed the role of Secretary here because I have been disturbed for some time at the underlying attitudes of some influential, but intractable members. I have been able to observe several instances of resolute resistance that need to change. Today has been the capper." Turning to Sir Bilton Dweed, McDervish—Chairman Whirling— ordered, "Bill, schedule a meeting for November 7th. Check with Dooter and Lawrence to make sure they can attend. And I think we have taken far too much of Commander Blevins' time for today," said Whirling, extending his hand.

Commander Blevins grasped the Chairman's offered hand gratefully. Thoroughly awed by the past few minutes, Commander Blevins stared at Chairman Whirling until Blevins realized he was supposed to stand up. Whirling helped him to his feet, took him by the shoulder, led him toward the door, and said, "Commander, if I may be so presumptuous, please get some rest. It is apparent that you are and have been for some time, under some unique pressures. Your physical body needs to recover its vitality. As long as we do live in the Physical, we must be mindful of its limits. I would like you to refrain from taking any more Clients to the Records until we can review this Review. This is not an order, just a personal wish from me to you. I have an inkling that there is a new role for you to play with the Society that will require a fit and well-rested Commander Blevins."

They had walked to the waiting room by then, and Chairman Whirling shook Commander Blevins' hand again. "I will be in touch shortly. Good day, and thank you, Commander."

"You're welcome, McDervish...I mean, Chairman Whirling."

"Call me McDervish, Commander. It's my old Satsang nickname." He then winked at Blevins, who was forcefully struck by a deep blue glint in Chairman Whirling's eyes. Whirling turned and walked back into the room where the Review had been held. Commander Blevins heard the Review Room's door shut with a firm click. He walked down the stairs and pushed open the blue door leading to the street and the world outside.

The blue door stayed open after Blevins passed through it. He felt an urge to turn around, did so, and watched the door bounce a little, as though someone was holding it open as they left the building. Finally, the door closed, and Blevins felt a familiar presence. Tickling energy shot up and down his spine. A shadow of light formed briefly to the side of the door. Commander Blevins watched the light for a moment and thought he saw the outline of a man appear in the shimmering light. Then the light was gone. A long minute passed as Blevins waited for it to return. Suddenly he felt foolish standing in front of the Society's door looking at the blank brick wall, and he turned away.

The three MEs sat on the edge of the four-story building housing the Society for Verified Viewers' Offices, bored and nearly comatose. Little energy had been available from their host for the past hour or more since Blevins had entered the building. They followed him now, floating along lazily as he walked around the corner and up Columbus Avenue.

TWENTY-TWO
A TIME FOR REAPPRAISAL

Later that evening, Commander Blevins knew that he had managed to find his way home from the Society's office because he was home. How he had gotten there, he had no idea. After eating several garlic cloves, he sat in his overstuffed chair, sipping his second cup of dark-brewed Mugi- Cha, staring at the tall pine tree next door as it swayed in the breeze. Fog completely covered the Peaks. Slowly he was sliding into shock and trauma from the vodka, hormones, and caffeine. His body felt like a large tuning fork, which has been struck against a bulldozer blade, producing reverberations of gradually increasing tempo and disharmony.

This would have been a nice time for introspection, but his brain felt numb, the old viral feeling returning. He was never sure how low he would go before feeling better at this point in a downturn. The phone rang.

After a few rings, it stopped. Commander Blevins did not get up to answer it, only vaguely aware it was ringing. He felt cold, a deep low throb began in his body, and he decided to turn up the heaters. A little while later, he still had not done so.

Struggling against the effects of booze and caffeine, Blevins mulled over what had gone on at the Society. Was it possible that no one else knew how to take Clients to the Records? Were there inherent problems in doing this that he had not considered? And what to make of the power struggle he had witnessed that had spilled out into the open? Commander Blevins usually avoided groups and group functions because he could not handle the politics that accompanied them. He hoped he would not be pulled into this one to save his accreditation.

Finally, he decided to take a bath. The three light cords followed him solemnly. On his way down the hall to the bathroom, the phone rang again. It was still ringing when he turned the hot water on full blast in the tub.

TWENTY-THREE
BOY, THIS IS BORING

The next day was sunny. Commander Blevins became aware of a dream hovering close by when he awoke. His head felt like there were icepicks stuck into his temples and the slightest draft chilled him. Everything else ached, too.

Much of the day was spent moving slowly, cleaning and pairing adding machine parts. By dark, he felt better and had prepared forty-three pairs and twelve single earrings. He made a large pot of lentil soup but had failed to remember the dream. The phone had rung often, rung until it stopped ringing each time, unanswered.

"Boy, this is boring," Greeny said. "When is that old Crustacean going to do something?" The three MEs sat on their usual perch above Filmore Street.

Pins looked at Ember in disgust. New ones were always a pain and the brief comradery of the day before was history. They, too, were bored. So bored that there had been virtually no bickering since they all had returned from the extraordinary trip to North Beach. And they were losing their luster. Pins was greying noticeably. Ember was a dull red, and probably the least affected of the three by not receiving Its usual juice load. Greeny was obnoxious.

Commander Blevins spent much of the evening drinking his Japanese barley tea, sitting in the over-stuffed chair, and thinking. He had not put his futon away that morning, so he had to walk over it to get to the chair. He did not mind. His mind was still quite crisp around the edges from the events of the day before, numbing him to everything.

After his bath, Blevins found himself in bed, toasty warm, and unable to sleep. The dream of the night before still lingered and nagged at him, an indistinct memory behind a flimsy veil that whispered teasing bits he could hear but not understand. He tried deep breathing. He tried counting earrings. He tried planning his next project, which was not helpful because he did not know what his next project would be. He reviewed the Journey with Mrs. Frumpwooler. He wondered if he would ever hear from her again. He reviewed the Review at the Society. Was he missing something? McDervish was Chairman Whirling, the legendary figure behind the scenes at the Society. Old McDervish whom everyone respectfully acknowledged, but patently ignored: amazing.

Blevins had heard a rumor in Viewers Training that

the mysterious Chairman Whirling was the reincarnation of the Society's founder, Johann Fredrick Eck. Eck was a seventeenth-century violinist, instructed in the Inner Worlds' ways by an unknown Master. J. F. Eck was also a contemporary of Mozart, reportedly even a close friend. Mozart's Violin Concerto Number Six was thought to have been finished by Eck after Mozart had given him the sketch of it, with solo and vitranelli rounded-out, but with much of the rest incomplete. The original manuscript was dated, but was unsigned and could have been Eck's. Eck had shared his Inner World awareness and abilities with several close associates. Before his death, he had established the Society to ensure a continuation of high standards of conduct by members.

Commander Blevins then moved on to the disagreement between Tickle, Dweed, and McDervish at the Review. This promptly put him to sleep. Power plays bored him.

In the middle of the night, the moon rose, full and shining directly into Commander Blevins' face. The road rolled out before him as he sped down a narrow two-lane blacktop. He both watched himself from above and looked out through the windshield as the scene unfolded. He drove a white, mid-sixties Ford GT, the same cars that raced at Sebring and LeMans. Slowly he pressed the accelerator to the floor. The car flew down the road and went around turns as though it were on rails. Dark images of houses and trees flitted by. The car began to pick up speed, going faster than he felt was safe. He eased off the pedal, but it continued to accelerate. He pressed the brake gingerly, not wanting the car to spin out of control. It went even faster.

Then the car slowed. A left-hand turn was coming up. As he rounded the bend in the car, he saw a young boy run out into the road. The boy stopped in the path of the vehicle. He wore a grey sock cap and looked straight into Commander Blevins' eyes. The car headed straight for the boy, not slowing down. To Commander Blevins' horror, he felt the impact as the boy went down beneath the car's low nose, staring into his eyes all the way. Commander Blevins was then flattened against the back of the seat as the car accelerated harder. It went faster and faster and then began pointing up. The cockpit started getting warm. Soon it was hot. His grip on the wheel became his hold on life. Commander Blevins felt his skin being pulled back from his hands and face. He and the car burst through a cloud layer and exploded.

Soon Blevins was falling backward, down toward the ground, still locked in a driving position. He gripped a steering wheel he could still feel, but could not see.

Instead of hitting the ground, he awoke to an early gray morning. Wide-eyed, he rolled over and hid under the covers. Finally, stiff from being in bed too long and still aching from the adventures of the last two days, he got up. It took him a while to shake off the dream.

This day went by a little more quickly. His body and mind were functioning better, and he was able to focus on work. After a late morning breakfast of buckwheat grouts and carrot juice, he finished cleaning every adding machine part he could find. The phone rang twice. The second time he was turning over the Mozart tape near the phone and almost answered it.

He bundled up in the mid-afternoon and walked down to the health food store on Haight Street. He bought some broccoli, sprouted rye-berry bread, a large bottle of apple juice, and, as a treat, a quart of dairy-free ice cream.

Once home, he went to the walk-in closet and pulled out a collapsed cardboard box, a small computer fan, and a clip-on light. He reassembled a spray hood he had made with some wire and duct tape when he first experienced the downside of spraying lacquer indoors then dragged the hood to the bathroom. He had tried going up to the roof to keep the spray out of his apartment, but that often proved too cold, too hard to control dust, and the building manager generally frowned on people being on the roof. So he improvised and built the collapsible spray hood.

He attached the hood to several hooks mounted in the window frame above the bathtub, plugged the fan and light into the extension cord that ran to the heater under the sink, and reminded himself not to turn on all of them at once.

Back in the kitchen, he pulled out several coat hangers that had been bent to form little notches along their bottoms. In each of these notches, he carefully hung a small bent wire that had been threaded through a hole in a cleaned adding machine part. These fully loaded hangers were then hung on a wooden dowel that fit neatly across the tops of the two chest-high china cabinets by the kitchen.

When two dowels were full of loaded hangers with about two hundred parts, he carried them carefully into the bathroom.

"Rats." He had forgotten to bring in the small stool from the walk-in closet. He took the dowels and hangers back to the kitchen, metal parts tinkling all the way. After digging the little stool out of the closet, he took it back to the bathroom and firmly placed the stool on top of the toilet seat. Then he moved the two loaded dowels to the bathroom again and put them neatly in the place he had created for them: one end of each dowel resting securely on the stool on the toilet, the other end on the towel rack on the wall.

That finished, he pulled his old pea coat and older grey sock cap out of the front closet. He got a can of clear spray lacquer and respirator from the kitchen china cabinet, which housed his earring materials, and set off for the bathroom. He closed the door behind him as the phone rang again. Ignoring it, he opened the window behind the spray booth, shivered in the chill wind, turned on the light and fan, shook the can of clear lacquer twenty times, put the first hanger on the hook inside the top of the cardboard booth, and started spraying. He rotated the whole hanger horizontally with a large round wooden handle set up pulley-style, much like an old dentist's drill.

By dark, he had finished the second coat of lacquer on all of the pieces. He was cold and hungry, but confident the adding machine's parts would not tarnish anytime soon. He did not want the kids in the City to have rusted earrings. They might have liked them to rust, but he did not consider that. Commander Blevins was thorough, to the best of his ability, with most of his projects.

He could not warm up with a bath that night. The lacquer would set harder if allowed to cure overnight, so he went to bed with the heaters set a little higher than usual.

TWENTY-FOUR

SUNDAY MORNING ARRIVED LATE

Sunday morning arrived late, but sunny. Commander Blevins awoke, feeling more rested than he had in a long time. He spent the morning unhooking adding machine parts from hangers, attaching them to surgical steel earring wires with small "o" rings, and slipping each pair or single into a tiny zip-lock baggy.

By one o'clock, he had a mound of earrings on the kitchen table the size of a watermelon. The phone had rung several times, but he had moved the tape player into the kitchen, turned Mozart up as loud as he could stand, and closed the doors leading from the dining room into the hall and telephone.

He pulled the spray booth into the hallway, next to the pile of clean clothes, disassembling it as little as possible. He felt unspeakably grubby and went to the bathroom to draw a bath. Over the blast of the hot water, he heard the phone ring. This time he decided to answer it. As he picked up the receiver, he heard a 'click.' Replacing it, he reviewed the click's timing and decided that since the person on the other end had hung up while he was picking up, there was no malice intended.

After a long soak, a quick run to the corner store, a belly-stuffing lunch eaten as he enjoyed the paper—the World Series had opened on Saturday, the first one in history matching two Bay Area teams called the BART Series— he dressed for a trip outside that would last more than the brief jaunt needed to get the paper. He pulled on his heavy corduroy pants over his house pants and his fleeced lined boots. Then he slipped into a heavy gray wool sweater and opened the kitchen windows since he could not be inside too long once dressed for outside without breaking into a sweat, which made it hazardous for him to go out. Next, he piled on his short leather jacket and the wool coat with the deep side pockets. Grabbing wallet, change, and handkerchief, stuffing his pockets with handfuls of earrings-in-tiny-baggies, he grabbed his two sock caps with plastic liner, a long burgundy cape, and his scarf, then bolted for the door.

"Hey, Lookeyloo," Pins said.

"Where," said Ember.

"Where," said Greeny.

"Down there, Door Knobs." Pins pointed to the front door of 600 Page Street.

Commander Blevins was trying to fasten his cape

with one hand and adjust his sock caps with the other. Finally, he secured the cape and devoted both hands to the caps. When a plastic layer separates two stocking caps, the outer one was very slippery.

"Ain't he a stitch," Pins said.

"Yeah," Greeny said.

"I wonder where he's going," Ember said.

"Yeah, I want action, action, action," Greeny began chanting. "Let's Wrap someone." Soon It was hopping on the wire and bouncing both of his companions nearly off their perch. Pins was hanging by one little arm when Ember stood up on the wire, wavered a bit, and hopped over the short distance to where Greeny was jumping up and down and yelling, "Action, action, action..."

Ember manifested a large foot, just one, raised it, and whapped Greeny across the back. Both the Pins & Ember watched as Greeny fell like a rock, It being too occupied to rebalance itself, landing on top of and falling through a yellow Mercedes lumbering up Filmore, trailing black diesel smoke.

By this time, Commander Blevins was across Page and walking down Fillmore near where he had almost been mugged four days earlier. Greeny popped up for a moment, cleared the Mercedes, and landed on top of the 22 Fillmore bus. It thumbed Its nose at the two MEs ignoring It up on the wire. The bus labored up the hill and stopped at Oak street.

Ember and Pins watched Commander Blevins intently, their light cords shortening as he drew nearer to them. Blevins was hunched against the wind and wishing Mrs. Frumpwooler had paid him. He was on the floor of a cash flow valley. Most of the money he had at the moment was in his pocket, and the amount had been noticeably reduced since his trip to Club Paradise.

Greeny was hot to trot with nowhere to run. It bounced on top of the bus a few times as several passengers got off.

Then It saw a large opening in the back of someone's aura. The unwitting person walked down Filmore toward Page across the street from Commander Blevins' apartment building. Greeny mulled over the procedure for unplugging from one host and reattaching to another. Basically, It didn't know how to do so. The person who so held Greeny's attention reached the corner of Page Street. Across Page, the door of a little corner store stood open. The market was like so many other corner stores in San Francisco: similar yet unique. This shop was run by Turkish looking people who sold liquor, old canned goods, and newspapers. Half of its shelves were empty. Commander Blevins was a steady customer here, though not a big spender.

The person in Greeny's sights seemed to hesitate for a moment, a white scarf around their head, gazing toward Haight Street. The hole in their aura oozed a sticky substance.

"Maybe they're Hindu," thought Greeny. The person turned toward 600 Page Street and crossed Filmore. Greeny panicked, knowing the other MEs would also see the gaping hole in the person's aura. Greeny did what It knew how to do. It flexed Its little bellows around Its yahooney, sprouted a second light cord, and speared the person square in the back with a smushing sound, just as they reached the curb.

"What was that," Pins said.

"What was what," Ember said. It had just watched their host reach the corner at Haight Street and stop at the bus stop.

"I heard a...Holy Fragmentation...see what I see..." Pins said, "...and lookey what the kid has done now."

"Why that's her! Old Futz's last Client. The one that went with him when he brought back Greeny. What has that idiot done?"

"Don't remind me. But it may have solved our problem."

"Well, tie my cord in knots." Ember's mouth was wide open. "I have never seen anything so stupid in..."

"Anytime. Right as rain, though. This should be quite a show."

Greeny had done the inadvisable. Inadvisable, at least, to eons of MEs before It. It had produced and sustained a second light cord, had planted the cord squarely in the back of Mrs. Frumpwooler, and now was juicing for all Its life.

Mrs. Frumpwooler had been relatively placid until that moment. Her injuries beneath the Muni Bus had been amazingly minimal. She had been jolted hard enough to briefly leave her body, but the parting was only temporary. The driver was a Tai Chi devote and had exhibited reflexes of remarkable speed. Though his superintendent could not publicly praise him for only injuring a pedestrian, he had been reassured that his actions had been noted and encouraged to continue with his fine work. And to, "Look out for the kooks."

Mrs. Frumpwooler had been taken the few short blocks to St. Mary's Hospital Emergency Room. She spent two nights on the fifth floor. She almost spent several more in the locked ward, while her candid statements of the activities that led up to her attempt to embrace a Muni Bus were reviewed. A battery of X-Rays, probing and examining had determined her only injuries to be were scrapes and contusions, and she was eventually released on Saturday, the day before.

While in the hospital, she remembered that she had not paid Commander Blevins. Repeatedly during that day and the next, she had tried to call him but got no answer. Soon after she had returned home, Mrs. Frumpwooler realized she did not have her purple hat. She continued to call him that night and the next morning. Finally, about noontime, with the image of her purple hat leading her, she set out for his apartment to settle her debt and retrieve the hat. She was only a little stiff now as she waited to cross the street.

TWENTY-FIVE
FREE EARRINGS: TWENTY BUCKS

The 7 Haight pulled to a stop alongside the curb, just past Fillmore. Commander Blevins stepped up on the matted rubber steps, showed his pass to the driver, and walked back, out of habit, to the seats that faced in toward the aisle around the rear door. There was a clear center space at this point in the bus where people could stand two or three abreast. It was also an easy escape out of the back door. His guard was down, and he could feel the curiosity and the "hope- this-guy-doesn't-sit-near-me" vibes from some of the passengers. The driver had remained neutral as Commander Blevins had boarded. San Francisco Bus drivers were used to a wide array of characters.

Mrs. Frumpwooler found the front door of Commander Blevins' apartment building locked. It had been wide open the last and only time she had been there. Mildly disconcerted, she discovered the mailboxes. She buzzed the buzzer under number 307 five times. "C. Blevins" was printed neatly over the button. Finally, in disgust and with agitation rising, she decided to walk down to Haight and get a cup of coffee. She was not going to leave the area without getting her purple hat back.

Commander Blevins jostled with the bus as it rode up the gentle slope to Divisadero. It stopped, then steamed up and over the steeper slope on Haight Street and approached the north side of Buena Vista Park. In San Francisco, "hill" ends, and "steep" begins when an incline is too sharp to walk up or down, without steps cut into the sidewalk. Another deciding factor was whether anything could be seen in front of you as you drove over the crest. If something could be seen, then it wasn't steep. Commander Blevins had not experienced this particular thrill since he sold his last car, a 1974 Saab with an affinity for blowing head gaskets.

The Ember and Pins followed the bus easily, their light cords whipping around in the unseen breeze that affected them. Greeny's plight was an entirely different affair. Its second light cord was playing havoc with Its own internal guidance system. MEs move around in reference to their cords. If one wants to move left, It will whip out a section of Its light cord out to the right, thus giving It momentum in the other direction. This all happens with very subtle movements and is barely discernible to anyone watching...anyone who can see unseen things, that is.

Movement, therefore, now presented Greeny with a

whole new set of issues. Mrs. Frumpwooler had remained in the immediate vicinity, unlike Commander Blevins. She was providing Greeny with an overflow of juice, so It stayed near her. Once It finally found Its way back to the wire above Filmore, It duck-walked sideways as Mrs. Frumpwooler made her way down toward Haight Street.

"Boy, Greeny is a card. Did you see that triple barrel roll and the dive into the street? I wondered if we were going to be one fewer for a moment, there," Pins said, bouncing along behind Commander Blevins and the bus.

"Yeah, well, there is still time for that," the Ember said. It was better at riding unseen air currents and bounced little.

The bus didn't have to stop at Masonic, so Commander Blevins pulled the cord that ran along the top of the windows. The driver crossed Ashbury and rolled to a stop next to the curb at the next corner, covering the yellow rectangle painted on the street. Commander Blevins got off, tightened his cape against the wind, and looked for a moment at the storefront across the street that gave life to the three-story Edwardian building.

The building was painted in several different tones of yellow with raspberry pinstriping. The yellows were softer and gentler than the traffic department selected for its street markings. This tasteful use of muted colors was, at one time, a rarity in the Haight during the wild and wooly days of the late sixties. The used clothing store on the first floor had a green and purple window display, which saved the building from being ordinary. "Ordinary" is defined as only San Francisco can explain it.

A woman on roller skates shot by Commander Blevins and juked around two cars waiting to turn left onto Haight Street. Turning, he reached into the large coat pocket underneath his cape and pulled out a wad of adding machine earrings in tiny ziplock plastic bags. It had been a hobby of his for months to hand out his earrings to the kids in different parts of San Francisco. Since the Haight was the closest and probably the best spot for Commander Blevins' mission, he came here the least, not wanting to ruin a good thing so close to home.

He walked up Haight toward Golden Gate Park. In front of a record store-coffee shop, he found a group of three girls and a guy: WAURTZ, he had heard a store owner call the more affluent street kids: White Adolescent Urban RaTZ.

"Uh, excuse me," Commander Blevins said, "Anyone interested in earrings? Heavy metal earrings?"

"Heavy metal earrings? What are they?"

"Metal went out years ago."

"Like not music, Frankie, earrrrrings." The girl who set Frankie straight had jet black hair on one side and a shaved scalp. Her fingernails and one nostril were pierced and sported a variety of studs and rings. "Let me see." Her voice had a cutting whine. Commander Blevins winced and handed her three plastic envelopes.

"Awesome."

"Totally excellent."

"Nasty."

"Let me see."

"Like Punchy'd love these." The girl held up one that looked like a small meat tenderizer and asked, "Like how much?" Commander Blevins had already given away a few hundred of his unique brand of earrings, so he was as startled as the four young people around him when he said, "Twenty dollars."

"Too awesome."

"Like no way, old man."

"Off the plant."

"How much?"

The girl handed the earrings back to him in a handful and said, "Like no sale." The four moved on down the block.

Commander Blevins overheard their conversation for a few steps. The WAURTZ boy said, "Wonder why he wears so many clothes?"

"Like he's just a Four Roses Junkie. They're always like freezing."

"Yeah, but he was clean. Too weird."

"I heard some old Hippie gave out earrings after the Platonic Sluts concert."

Commander Blevins stood immobile. His mind pulled apart and snapped shut.

"The earrings are too good to just give away," he said to himself. "Yes, but I like to give them to the kids. You have to pay your rent. McDervish said no Journeys for awhile. Of, course if you could find Mrs. Frumpwooler, she owes you money. That's right, she does. Well, don't just stand there...find her. Right."

He stood in the middle of the sidewalk, waving a handful of earrings in the air during his self-contained debate. Suddenly, he decided he must find Mrs. Frumpwooler and bolted straight head, without looking. The woman ahead of him didn't have a chance. She had just been detouring around the caped, gesticulating figure, and stopped, herself, in the middle of the sidewalk. She had left her car door was unlocked, she remembered.

"Or did I?" she said out loud.

Commander Blevins heard her words but didn't know where they came from or what they meant. He heard her observations because he was almost on top of her. Then he was on top of her, or at least smack against her.

"Ohh, ugh," he stammered. He caught himself with his right hand on a newspaper machine, preventing the full weight of his body from crashing into her.

"Watch it. Hey!" she yelled as she stumbled against the street light pole behind her. She looked around at him and was about to yell at him, or for the police. His face stopped her. His eyes, really. They were kind and, at that moment, looking both sad and driven. He reminded her of a puppy who just knocked over something on its way to the door to go out—a large, over-dressed puppy, needing to pee.

He regained his voice first, "I am so sorry. Please let me help you." He reached for her arm to steady her but stopped. Her eyes were black and deep. Her face was a lovely burnt sienna, and she was dressed for downtown. She smiled. Her smile opened his heart, and he said, "I was giving my earrings to these kids who could not afford them and then realized Mrs. Frumpwooler still owed me money. If only I knew where she was."

The woman's smile sagged at the corners. "That's all right. I'm okay. Why are you so warmly dressed? If you don't mind my asking."

Commander Blevins opened his mouth to answer. At that moment, however, he had just received another strong pulse from Greeny, which he experienced, but did not understand, and said, "Toxic chemicals and lust. Here, you take these." Taking the woman's gloved hand, he pushed the wad of earring bags into it. "Have a nice day," he said as he sprinted away from the woman, away from Golden Gate Park, toward the Lower Lower Haight and his pursuit of the elusive Mrs. Frumpwooler.

He didn't stop running until he hit Divisadero. He was breathing very heavily and was so sweaty he wished he had waited for the bus.

The woman kept the earrings and later showed them to her friends, two of whom thought they were too outrageous to pass up.

TWENTY-SIX
LIKE DOES ATTRACT ITSELF

Greeny was in Hog Heaven, juicing both Commander Blevins and Mrs. Frumpwooler. Mrs. Frumpwooler was sitting in the window of a small shop on Haight Street called, "Beans To You," sipping her third cappuccino. The store sold only coffee, coffee beans, and coffee paraphernalia. Three tables sat near the window. Two had dual chrome chairs around them, and the third had a trio. This third table was the first immediately inside the door, and it was at this table Mrs. Frumpwooler was ensconced at. She faced the street. The area below the window was built-out, providing storage and an advertising ledge, which was underutilized. It held only two medium-sized cardboard promo signs, flanking the window. They each were a full-figured image of a wired looking character in an Uncle Sam, finger-pointing pose, announcing to all who passed in either direction, "Beans To You."

It was between these two guardians of the store that Mrs. Frumpwooler had propped her feet. Her right foot was tapping. She had a direct view of Haight and Filmore's intersection and was sure Commander Blevins would pass through her line of vision on his way home. Her diligence and keen eyesight increased with each cup of cappuccino, as did the tempo of her right foot.

Commander Blevins, unable to easily cross Divisadero at Haight, had ambled north almost to Page before the traffic had thinned. The breeze had increased, and he'd caught his breath but was sweating profusely, from exertion and panic at being caught outside in the wet cold.

Pins and Ember followed. They were in a state of suspense, waiting for calamity to befall Greeny. Meanwhile, Greeny was on tiptoes of Its stumpy little feet on the wire over the corner at Haight and Filmore. It was slowly turning one way then the next. It had a light cord in each little hand and was handling them like reins. Ripples of movement came back to him along each light cord. The pull from the light cord leading to Commander Blevins was much more pronounced, for it was longer.

As Commander Blevins moved about, the unseen wind blew his light cords in alternating directions, Greeny did a lopsided, swaying waltz, high up on the overhead wire for anyone to see who could.

Commander Blevins made it home, thoughts of Mrs. Frumpwooler pushed aside by the need to survive.

He rushed in the building, passing Mr. Fedulity, who was sanding the front door. Mr. Fedulity looked up; he could not ignore the swirl that followed Commander Blevins and wondered why he had not said anything. The man who lived in apartment 307 was strange, indeed, but always spoke in passing. Shaking his head at the general state of mankind, Mr. Fedulity went back to work. His wife would be calling him for lunch soon, and he wanted to finish sanding the door before then. He disliked cleaning up a mess twice and disliked more the prospect of leaving the front door to 600 Pages Street open for any vagrant or junkie to wander in and set up camp. The owners had entrusted the building's care to him, and he had shown their trust was well placed for the past thirteen years.

Commander Blevins crossed the wide carpeted foyer and hit the stairs two at a time. Three light cords followed him, cutting through the apartments overhead. By the time he had made it to the third-floor landing, his chest was heaving again, and he was dripping sweat. Ahead of him, standing at the top of the last flight of steps to the third-floor hall, was Mrs. Fedulity. She was just starting on her way down. She stopped.

"Oh, hello Mr. Blevins, how are you feeling today?" she asked.

"Murmph," he said. He was too tired to articulate.

They stood in a silent standoff for a moment, then longer. Mrs. Fedulity was waiting for Commander Blevins to step back, Commander Blevins was concentrating on standing up. Finally, Mrs. Fedulity saw that he was in a bad way and backed up. Commander Blevins lumbered up the last few steps.

"Thank you." His voice was hoarse.

"Why you poor dear," she said as she watched him make his way down the hall to his apartment. As he put the key into the first lock, she said, "Oh, Mr. Blevins, have you seen Abdul?"

Commander Blevins stopped with the key in the lock, took a deep breath, looked up at the ceiling, then turned toward her and said with a large exhalation of breath, "Yes, he is sanding the front door in the lobby."

"Thank you so much, " she said with a warble in her voice. Both Mrs. Fedulity and Commander Blevins vanished from the third-floor hallway.

Mrs. Frumpwooler was getting antsy as the caffeine charged through her veins. She downed the last half of her cup and broke through the front door at full gallop.

Greeny was juicing harder. The flow to It was reduced as Commander Blevins weakened himself. Consequently, Mrs. Frumpwooler received more attention, and Greeny received a good jolt of the caffeine, much more than It had received three days earlier from Commander Blevins.

"Lookeyloo, Lookeyloo," said the Ember. The two other MEs had settled in their usual spot when Commander Blevins entered his apartment building. They were only a half a block up the hill toward Page Street, but Greeny didn't notice them.

Mrs. Frumpwooler crossed Haight, dodged a speeding bicyclist, and rounded the corner directly underneath Greeny. It was dancing frantically above her. She had her head down and churned away at top speed up Fillmore.

"That's quite a deal," Pins said as she passed underneath them.

"This is a deal's deal, coming up next," Ember said, looking in the direction Mrs. Frumpwooler had come.

Pins followed Ember's gaze, and then said, "Yep, sure is." They both watched Greeny. It was utterly tangled in both light cords and was hanging from the triple set of wires intersecting at the corner.

"Think we ought to help?" Ember asked.

"And ruin the show...nah," Pins said.

Commander Blevins closed the door behind him. He dropped his cape on the laundry and cardboard spray booth inside the entrance. He took off his wool coat, added it to the pile, then walked into the bathroom and turned on the hot water in the tub. He flipped the toilet lid down and sat on it as the steam began to rise from the water. He was hungry, wet, tired, and confused.

Mrs. Frumpwooler crossed Filmore before getting to Page. A car honked at her, but she ignored it. She spotted the open front door to 600 Page and increased her pace.

"Oh, there you are, sweetheart," Mrs. Fedulity said as she came down the half flight on stairs into the foyer. Dark red carpet covered the lobby, and an old chandelier hung from the middle of the ceiling. The two side walls were covered in panels of mirrors with gold trim.

The room gave the feeling of once having been dressed up, and, having nowhere to go, was fading into oblivion, forgotten. "Time for lunch."

"Any time now, this will be done," Mr. Fedulity said. Mrs. Fedulity came over to where her husband was sanding the top corner of the door. He stood on a small ladder.

She walked around to the front side of the door, ran her hands over the smooth surface, and said, "This will look so nice when you are done, dear. Your work is always so well done." She looked up through the beveled glass near the top of the door and smiled at the distorted image up her husband, his face set in concentration.

"Coming through."

Mrs. Fedulity turned her head toward the street in time to see a figure marching straight for her. A long coat, unbuttoned, Unfurled behind the figure. Looking from the dimly lit foyer out into the sunny street, Mrs. Fedulity could only see a very wide person about to bowl her over.

"Ooohhh," she said, moving quickly out of the way.

"Now see here, see here," Mr. Fedulity said.

"Commander Blevins," said the person who hit the stairway two steps at a time.

"Ah, yes, now. That would explain that, explain that," Mr. Fedulity said. "Like does attract itself," and went back to his sanding.

"Now, now dear," Mrs. Fedulity said, smoothing her blouse, which had not been wrinkled.

Greeny hung upside down over the intersection of Haight and Filmore, drinking in the energy that flowed to It, unwilling to slacken Its juicing to untangle Itself.

Commander Blevins remembered the Bath Therapy as he watched the tub filling. He picked up the jar of bath salts that sat on the little wicker cabinet next to the door and poured about half of it into the tub. When the tub was three-quarters full of water, he turned the water off, walked down the hallway, past the front door and hall closet, and began shedding clothing.

He pulled off his short leather jacket and neatly hung it up. Oblivious to walking on his cape and wool coat piled on the floor, he sat down on the stool in the foyer and pulled off his boots and socks. Wiggling his toes in mid-air, and looking at them with a dull ache in the back of his head, he spotted his yellow and black Goofy slippers sitting just inside the walk-in closet, beyond his bare feet. He stood up slowly and walked over to the slippers. As he was chasing the second one around the wood floor of the foyer—his foot wouldn't quite slip into it— a loud knock at the door startled him. It was so authoritative that he did not think of looking through the peephole. He went to the door, opened it, and his mouth dropped open.

"You have my purple hat!" Mrs. Frumpwooler said.

"Mrs. Frumpwooler!" Commander Blevins said.

"Well, of course. Who else's purple hat have you absconded with?"

His mind cleared, and a bolt of energy hit him. "You owe me money!"

"You have my purple hat." They glared at each other for a long minute. Then, Mrs. Frumpwooler could no longer stand in one spot. "Perhaps you could invite me in," she said.

"Of course," Commander Blevins said. "Would you like to come in, Mrs. Frumpwooler?" He backed away from the door and bent low in a mock welcoming bow.

"Why, thank you, sir. I will if you will be nice." He straightened up as she passed. She looked him in the eye and added, "And if you give me back my purple hat."

"Happy to," he said. "Follow me." He led her into the main room, thankful that he had put the futon away that morning. "Please be seated. Would you care for some tea?"

Mrs. Frumpwooler sat down on the loveseat, saw the purple hat on his desk, and remembered his tea. "Just the hat, please."

"Of course," he said, handing it to her and sitting down in his overstuffed chair. "That's one matter taken care of. Now you owe me some money."

Mrs. Frumpwooler was occupied by refitting the purple hat over her white scarf. When she finished, she looked at him and said, "You said that was not necessary."

"You said you would pay."

"You said you were happy to help me free of charge."

"You said you would pay handsomely."

"I thought you were a gentleman."

Commander Blevins took a deep breath and said, "I expect to be paid for my services. I have returned your property to you in good faith, which was only here because you forgot it, and now I expect you to likewise follow through in good faith with your promise of payment. *Which,* if I may add, was the opening line that got you into this room in the first place, many days ago. 'I will gladly pay for your help, Commander Blevins.' Surely, you are not such a person that goes back on her word, Mrs. Frumpwooler."

Mrs. Frumpwooler saw that she had pushed the issue as far as she could and that he was not going to budge. "Since I did say that first, I see that I must abide by it. In the future, I will understand that you are no gentleman, Commander Blevins."

"Future?"

Mrs. Frumpwooler opened her purse, then stopped and paused. "Just how much do I owe you?"

"Whatever you feel is appropriate, Mrs. Frump-wooler. Let's not forget that we are civilized people."

Mrs. Frumpwooler rolled the angles through her mind. She extracted a wad of bills and counted out seven and handed them to him. "Here, I think this should be sufficient for civilized people, Commander Blevins."

Commander Blevins looked at the pile of one hundred dollar bills in his hand and agreed, silently. To her, he nodded his head.

"Now, there is another matter to discuss,' Mrs. Frumpwooler said.

"Another matter?"

"Yes, indeed, another matter." Mrs. Frumpwooler sat

on the loveseat, staring at her lap while Commander Blevins shuffled his hundred dollars bills. Finally, she looked at him with a glint in her eyes and said, "Diamonds."

He looked at her, nodded his head blankly, and said, "Diamonds."

"Yes, Diamonds." There was another pregnant silence that was broken by Mrs. Frumpwooler. "*The* Diamonds."

"Oh. *The* Diamonds." Commander Blevins sat, looking at her. "What Diamonds?"

"The Diamonds I—Gwenny—hid in the carriage house wall, of course. Don't you remember, Ito-san, you romantic little devil, you?"

"Oh, of course, *those* Diamonds." Commander Blevins remembered. "That was seventy, no eighty-plus years ago. You don't think those diamonds are still there, do you?"

"Well, we surely won't know without checking it out, now will we?"

"I see. I see." Commander Blevins nodded his head repeatedly.

"I want you to get them," Mrs. Frumpwooler said.

"Me?"

"Yes, you."

"How do you know I'll give them to you when I get them."

"Because I'll be with you, of course," she said.

"Perhaps I'll only give you part of them," he said. "After all, we both had a hand in the affair."

"*Your* hand, Commander Blevins. Ito-san was concerned with *other* affairs. I took the diamonds, and I hid them."

"Do you know where they are?" he asked. "Exactly?"

"Yes, of course, they're...I'll tell you what. I'll pay you three times what I just gave you. Whether or not we find the diamonds. What you have to do is help me find the exact house with that carriage house behind it, and then you will excavate the portion of the wall where I hid the diamonds. If you find any diamonds, you will give them all to me. If you don't find any, you will still have the money." Mrs. Frumpwooler was quiet for a moment, then said, "Deal?"

Greeny was still juicing hard on Mrs. Frumpwooler, and Commander Blevins did not think the Diamonds would still be there. He needed the cash. "In advance," he said.

"Half now, half when either I have the diamonds or you have excavated the wall, and there are no diamonds," she said.

"Cash."

"Cash."

"Deal." Commander Blevins held out his empty hand for the money. Mrs. Frumpwooler shook it.

"Now, when do we begin," she said.

"We begin after you pay me the first half," he said and held his hand out again for a second time.

"All right," Mrs. Frumpwooler said. She opened her purse once again, produced the same roll of bills, counted out ten of them, and handed them to Commander Blevins.

He remained motionless, his hand still extended, the ten one hundred dollar bills laying softly upon it. "You said half," he said.

"Well, isn't that close enough? I don't have any change with me." He did not say a word but continued holding his hand out and staring at her.

"What do you expect me to do, walk down to the corner store and ask them to change a hundred?"

"The deal is half now. How you accomplish that is your business." Commander Blevins withdrew his hand, which closed instinctively around the bills and rested it in his lap. He now had hundred dollar bills in both hands and was delighted with the feeling.

Mrs. Frumpwooler scrunched up her face and glared at Commander Blevins. "Well, if you insist," she said and took one more hundred from the roll, and let the rest fall into her open purse. Holding the bill by the fingers of both hands, she dangled in front of her. Commander Blevins piled the bills from one hand into the other and offered the empty hand to receive the full payment. There was a twinkle in his eye at calling her bluff. Faced with the choice of a silly errand or giving him more than half now, she was bending to his will.

In a flash, Mrs. Frumpwooler neatly tore the hundred dollar bill in half and placed Commander Blevins' share in his outstretched hand. His twinkle faded. Seeing that his bluff had been called, he quickly changed tactics to save face, "Well, now that's that. When shall we begin?"

"Now," Mrs. Frumpwooler said.

"No, not this moment. We must plan carefully," Commander Blevins said. The stimulation of negotiating with Mrs. Frumpwooler was gone. His exhausted body made its condition know to him again. "I need to rest this afternoon, and think this through. Come back at eleven o'clock tomorrow morning with walking shoes on, and we will proceed."

"But..." Mrs. Frumpwooler squirmed.

"I'm sorry, that is the best I can do, Mrs. Frumpwooler," Commander Blevins said.

"Oh, all right," she said. " I suppose another day won't matter after this long." She stood up and waited for him to stand. He did, and she marched out of the room. He stuffed the money in a stone jar sitting on his desk and followed her out of the room. She had opened the front door by the time he reached the hallway. She looked back at him, shuffling up behind her, and said, "Tomorrow, eleven o'clock."

"Right," he said and caught the door as she was closing it. He leaned out into the hall and called after her, "Oh, Mrs. Frumpwooler..."

"Yes?" She paused, almost to the stairs, and turned back toward him.

"Between now and then, please try to remember as much as possible about the neighborhood we watched you running through in 1906."

A woman materialized between them. To Mrs.

Frumpwooler, it seemed that a formless print dress had walked out of the middle of the wall and stood between them. After rapid blinking, Mrs. Frumpwooler saw that there was a woman in the dress. She held an empty wastebasket, wore an inquisitive expression on her face, and looked back and forth from Commander Blevins to Mrs. Frumpwooler.

"Oh, hello, Mrs. Todeyappee," Commander Blevins said. "Dumping trash down the shoot again, I see. Did you remember to use a plastic bag?" Mrs. Todeyappee hunched her shoulders and looked guilty. She continued to swivel her head.

Commander Blevins ran an uphill campaign to limit the gossip about himself in the building. He recognized that, at the moment, a good offense was the best defense. "You know that Mr. Fedulity gets very upset when he has to clean out the shoot."

Mrs. Todeyappee put a finger to her lips and mimed, "Shhhhh." Feeling a bit under fire, she tiptoed past Mrs. Frumpwooler toward the other end of the hall. "Say hello to Mrs. Frumpwooler, Mrs. Todeyappee."

"Hello, Mrs. Frummpph," Mrs. Todeyappee squeaked in a high pitch voice. Once excited, she did not regain her composure well these days.

"Hello," Mrs. Frumpwooler said.

Mrs. Todeyappee stopped at the next to last door down the hall. Commander Blevins was about to breathe a sigh of relief. Then, the door beyond Mrs. Todeyappee's opened, and Mrs. Fedulity appeared.

"Why hello, Mrs. Todeyappee," she said and then

noticed the empty wastebasket with a slice of tomato stuck to it. She quietly closed the door behind herself. "Ooohhh, have we been emptying our garbage down the trash shoot without putting it in a plastic bag again, Mrs. Todeyappee?" she asked in a loud whisper. "You know that Abdul gets very upset when he has to clean out the shoot. Please try to do better, Mrs. Todeyappee."

Hot with some new gossip and desperate to divert attention away from her abuse of the trash shoot, Mrs. Todeyappee hunched over still farther, pointed behind her so only Mrs. Fedulity could see her gesture, and said, "*H*im again," in a hoarse squeak. "Inside." She disappeared from Mrs. Frumpwooler and Commander Blevins' view, who still stood in their respective positions in the hall, watching the scene unfold.

"Why, hello, Commander Blevins. And?" Mrs. Fedulity let her question hang in mid-air, determined to learn Commander Blevins' guest's identity.

"Oh, yes. Please pardon me, Mrs. Fedulity. This is Mrs. Frumpwooler. And Mrs. Frumpwooler, this is Mrs. Fedulity. She and her husband manage the building. And do a fine job of keeping this place respectable." There was an uncomfortable silence, and Commander Blevins sensed that he needed to add more. "Uh...Mrs. Frumpwooler is a Client of mine...who was just leaving, weren't you Mrs. Frumpwooler?"

"Why yes, I was," Mrs. Frumpwooler said. She waved politely to Mrs. Fedulity and started down the stairs.

Commander Blevins then ran to the top of the

stairs, leaned over, and said, "Do think about what we were talking about, Mrs. Frumpwooler."

Mrs. Fedulity heard a fading, "Of course, Commander Blevins, see you to...." That was all Mrs. Fedulity caught because Mrs. Todeyappee was pulling at her arm.

When Commander Blevins looked up from calling over the stair railing, the door to Mrs. Fedulity's apartment was closing. He sighed, relieved to have the hall to himself once again. Shuffling stiffly, he made his way back to his door, closed it behind him, and walked into the bathroom. The water in the tub was cold.

TWENTY-SEVEN
TOO SICK TO KNOW

Greeny was sick and did not know it. It still hung upside down over the intersection of Haight and Filmore. There were red and black bumps on Its little face, and the area around his yahooney was fluttering with spasms. It had over juiced.

Mrs. Frumpwooler opened the front door of 600 Page, walked out to the middle of the sidewalk, and stopped. She looked to her right toward Golden Gate Park and the Pacific Ocean. Instead, though, she saw Page Street laid out straight west, edged on either side with apartment buildings built right up to the sidewalk. Lines were running everywhere: from pole to pole, from pole to building and from building to building. Most of the buildings were three stories, like Commander Blevins's, and were either white or brown, some both.

Across the street, a dark-haired fellow worked on the generator of a white 1969 Rover 2000. He had bought the car for one hundred dollars from his ex-girlfriend's ex-boyfriend, who had moved to Hawaii four months earlier. The vehicle had been driven almost every day by his ex's ex but had not run for him since the day after the previous owner had left the City.

Mrs. Frumpwooler did not know any of this. All she saw was a scruffy looking man in dirty jeans bent over a strange little white car in front of an open, narrow garage. The garage was dark inside, and Mrs. Frumpwooler could not see any details of its interior. None of this tableau interested her, so she turned toward Filmore to go home.

The Diamonds tugged at her consciousness, as did the amount of money she had given Commander Blevins. The pull was not as strong as it had been earlier. She pushed it aside to think clearly about how she would like to spend the rest of the afternoon.

It was too early to go home, and there was too much energy coursing through her. She felt like walking, and she wanted to get out of the Lower Haight. She made a sensible compromise with herself.

She saw a bus waiting for the light to change a block down at Haight Street. It was on Filmore and headed her way. She quickly crossed the street and began pumping up the hill toward the bus stop at Oak Street, one block north. She reached the corner ahead of the bus and turned around. It was still at Haight Street, having only crossed the intersection while Mrs.

Frumpwooler was dashing madly. A car was double-parked in front of the bus. There was a lot of honking and yelling going on. She was quite winded and took large gulps of air while waiting for the bus to break free, thinking how grateful she was that the air was clean here in the City, not like the awful stuff she had to breath when visiting her sister in Orange County.

The 22 Filmore arrived in a couple minutes. Mrs. Frumpwooler boarded it, fished in her purse for her Fast Pass, berated herself for not having dug it out while she was waiting, found it, showed it to the driver, and plopped down even more gratefully in the unoccupied front seat. She had a clear view up ahead, which thrilled her. Mrs. Frumpwooler always liked to know where she was going.

If Greeny had any sense, It would have taken a deep juice, popped off Its two light cords, fallen down on top of the 22 Filmore as it passed underneath him, and ridden up to where Mrs. Frumpwooler stood patiently. It then could have rested and reattached to her whenever she disembarked.

Greeny did not have any sense, though, and It was nearly comatose. Mrs. Frumpwooler, and the bus, crossed Oak and headed into the Western Addition. Pacific Heights, the Marina, home to Mrs. Frumpwooler, and the Marina Green that lay beyond. Greeny was still hanging over the uphill Bayside corner of Fillmore and Haight. As Mrs. Frumpwooler reached Fulton in her municipal carriage, Greeny became dimly aware that he was being stretched in some way. When

Mrs. Frumpwooler was carried across Geary Street, frantic warning lights went off in some instinctive region of Greeny's brain.

MEs do have brains. Everything that currently exists in or below the Mental Worlds has one. ME brains can not be dissected by knives or saws. Lasers can have an effect, but that is not widely known. Aiming is also tricky, even for those who can see the unseen. MEs have a disconcerting ability to fuzz-up and mush through space when under attack. This lets them occupy space only partially. Zapping something with a laser requires a pinpoint coincidence of mutual occupation in the time-space continuum. There was only one ME hunter who had shown any real promise to date. He had not yet visited San Francisco.

Greeny panicked. It felt one light cord being drawn out far past the normal limits. In the state Greeny was in, which dramatically affected its ability to control extension, contraction, and movement of Its light cords, Greeny felt the cord ripping from Its yahooney. This was not an enjoyable experience. In a blind grab for survival, Greeny contracted hard on the light cord running out to Mrs. Frumpwooler.

The result was swift and immediate. MEs use both the subtle manipulation of lights cords and the unseen winds to navigate. Greeny was not aware of the winds just now, and Its efforts to pull the light cord and the respective attache back to Itself misfired. Greeny flew to the anchored end of the cord, to Mrs. Frumpwooler as she made her way toward the Marina. Flew hard and fast, straining just about everything, including the other light cord's attachment to Commander Blevins, now blocks behind and receding rapidly. Panic begat more panic. Greeny lunged back toward Commander Blevins. Zigging and zagging, the two light cords tangled with each other, ripping one out of Greeny's yahooney. The freed cord would have pulled from the back of Commander Blevins, but Greeny was a negligent asset manager, so it instead was torn from Greeny.

Greeny landed with an unheard thud, yowling at the top of Its unheard voice. It was in real pain. As real as any ME can get. Just as quickly, It disappeared in the direction of the Marina.

"Lookeyloo, Lookeyloo," Pins said.

"A reeeal shew," the Ember said. Greeny had just passed underneath them at breathtaking speed, still tangled in a convulsing mass of light cords. "Never quite seen anything to match."

They both heard the pop as Greeny parted company from the light cord that ran to Commander Blevins. "I think we is now two," the Ember said.

"Goody, goody."

"Now, now, don't get impolite." They both winced when they heard Greeny's yowl pierce the air. "Heard about that happening once," the Ember said.

"A two-timer?"

"No, losing a connection. Heard it hurt real bad."

"Ow-owie." Pins scrunched up into a little ball.

"Well, as long as he doesn't venture back here, I'm sure it will turn out for the better. Hey, looky there," the

Ember said, pointing up the hill with Its stubby little arm. A smoldering green stripe ran down the street, then turned and wound its way into the side of 600 Page. "Look at that cord burn."

"Burnt Ovaries."

TWENTY-EIGHT
HAPPY SPIRITUAL NEW YEAR

"Ow!" Commander Blevins had just lowered himself into the new tub of boiling water. He had stirred in a double dose of Bath Therapy, a full container, shed his sweaty clothes, and congratulated himself on getting the water just the right temperature. When he slid down into the tub, a place in the middle of his back stung sharply. Sitting up straight so that the sore spot was out of the water, he found it still stung.

Puzzled, he got out of the water, rummaged through the wicker cabinet, and found a handheld mirror. He then climbed on top of the toilet seat, open the mirrored door above the lavatory, and bent down, so the middle of his back was in the mirror. The first shot he got was a clear view of his sagging buttocks. He had not seen them so clearly in quite a while and was shocked. Adjusting the mirror, he scanned as much of his back as possible, seeing nothing unusual.

Back in the tub, he lowered himself the last few inches into the water, gingerly. His back still stung, but not quite as badly. He wanted to mull over his new assignment: finding the house from 1906 and then, if the carriage house was still standing, finding access to it in a manner that allowed him to extract a few bricks from the back wall.

He was too tired, however, to think clearly.

Two light cords ran out of Blevins' back, into the back of the tub, reappeared coming out of the wall behind the tub, and then disappeared through the bathroom ceiling. The ceiling was spotted with quarter-sized brown spots and needed cleaning. Commander Blevins sighed deeply and let the water soak away his aches and chills. A small unseen greenish spot remained just to the right of where the two light cords entered his back.

Twenty minutes later, the phone rang. Commander Blevins groaned. He was nearly asleep, and the water had cooled. Slowly, he hauled himself out of the tub, slipped on his heavy robe and slippers, and shuffled into the hall and toward the phone. It was ringing for the sixth time. Most people who called him hung up before five rings, he had learned, so he wondered who was calling.

"Hello, Blevins here."

There was a pause and a small click, then a recorded voice said, "Happy Spiritual New Year! In celebration of the New Spiritual Year on October 22nd, the Society will be holding its quarterly meeting Saturday evening, the 22nd, at 6:30 pm. The event will be held at the California Historical Society's Whittier Mansion Museum located at 2090 Jackson Street at Laguna. The evening will begin with a reception in the lower level. At 7:30, a full course banquet will be served in the upper chambers. Following dinner, there will be the Society Yearly Summation, the presentation of the annual Viewer of the Year award, and a featured talk by Mr. Trudgewater Bryce III, a noted Viewer, and Inner World Explorer par excellence! RSVP to 362-1777, if you haven't already. Please remember that this is the only function of the year in which the Society allows--and encourages!--members to bring spouses and Significant Others. This is the final reminder of this event. Dinner reservations need to be finalized by Thursday the 20th at 5:00 pm. The Inner Leads, The Outer Follows."

Commander Blevins hung up the phone. He had received his invitation late in September and had RSVPed the next day. He now hoped he would be allowed to attend. A smile crossed his lips. Perhaps he should take Mrs. Frumpwooler. She certainly qualified as a "Significant Other" in the overall scheme of his status with the Society. "She might be a hit! Or at the very least, a sensation," he thought.

Blevins went back to the bathroom, smiling and feeling surprisingly good. After letting the water out of the tub and sorting through the pile of clean clothes in the hall, he dressed: heavy sweat pants over lightweight long johns, a single pair of thick socks, his Goofy slippers, long sleeve thermal shirt with a wool peasant shirt over that. He shuffled into the kitchen, warmed up the remaining cup of Mugi Cha, put on another pot of the Japanese roasted barley tea, and then retired to the main room and his favorite chair to watch the afternoon slip away.

Commander Blevins liked color. Perhaps it was an acquired taste from his many trips to the Inner Worlds with their beyond-the-physical rainbow of colors. It was more probably a trait he brought with him into this life that had laid partially dormant for many years. Whatever the reason, the clothes he chose to wear around the house were various purples, deep reds, blue-greens, and an occasional white, fuchsia, or yellow. He did own one pair of charcoal grey sweat pants that were now old and tearing at the crotch. He had tried to replace them, but the clothing buyer at Rainbow General Store said the color was discontinued. When he found he could no longer buy the dark pants he liked, he wondered if it was a waking dream, and if so, was the meaning only tied to which colors now were harmonious for him to wear, or was there another, more elusive meaning.

Sitting in the chair, with the fog just beginning to roll over the Peaks, he let himself drift. Relaxation did not usually come easily for Commander Blevins. Today, however, he was able to fully let go. Gentle energy and lightness swept over him. He heard a distant flute playing a wonderful melody. He began to smile and softly sing a single tone that he had heard in the Inner Worlds. This song felt like a spring shower of light floating down upon him. He heard a familiar voice speaking. Before he could hear any of the words, the voice faded.

Thoughts formed, passed through his consciousnesses, then melted away. His problem of the moment came into view, then moved on. A few minutes later, the puzzle surfaced again, and Commander Blevins found himself watching the scene of Gwenny fleeing the house that early morning long ago after the earthquake. There was an eerie pre-dawn light over the city. Some street lights were still on, some were not. He watched as Gwenny ran past a street sign. The sign was about as tall as her and looked like it was made of cast iron with ornate scrollwork on the top. Inset into this ironwork was a clear, flat space that read "CLAY STREET" in raised letters.

"Clay Street!" Commander Blevins sat straight up. He was wide awake. The flute was gone. "Clay Street!" he said again. "That's great! Now, how many streets did she cross before she got to Clay?" He thought about that for a while, but could not clearly reconstruct it. And the cross street: he was not sure of that, either. The houses looked like Pacific Heights, just west of Van Ness, around Lafayette Park, which made sense. Clay was interrupted by the park, as it ran west.

Evening approached, and Commander Blevins became hungry. He got up, shuffled off to the kitchen, and opened the refrigerator. Lentil soup, sprouted bread, and cashew butter stared back at him. He decided to indulge, pulling the large cast iron pot of soup out of the refrigerator and lugging it over to the stove. The flame would not light, so he had to use a match. He picked up a wooden spoon from the dish drainer, opened the pot's lid, and stirred the lentils, carrots, and green beans. A large piece of Kombu floated to the surface, stringy and gelatinous. "That should finish dissolving soon," he said to himself and made a mental note to put a small spoon of miso in his bowl before dishing up the soup. "Oh, jungle rot!" He remembered he had not gone to Rainbow the day before. He was out of miso and still needed Kombu, Hijiki, and a few other things.

He went back to the refrigerator and got out the sprouted bread and almond butter. The bread had raisins and cinnamon in it, and the naturally sweet taste of the cashew butter made it almost like dessert. He took the bread to the sink, cut three slices on the cutting board while holding it over the sink, and then sat down at the table. "Apple juice." He stood up, got the juice out of the refrigerator, the glass out of the cupboard, sat down to spread a slice. "Knife. Rats." He stood up, got the knife, and thought to turn on the radio. There was a sports show on KNBR, talking about the Series.

He was interested but did not really listen. As he ate the bread and cashew butter, he began looking at possible approaches to removing the bricks in the carriage house, once they found it. A midnight skulk was risky. He could pose as a tuck-pointer in need of work, but the homeowners probably would have their own workers they already knew. Besides, he would have a hard time looking the part of a laborer, even in San Francisco, a city noted for its tolerance of the unique and original.

He mulled over images of various professions that might have reason to inspect the carriage house, especially at enough length to bore whoever might be accompanying him so that he would be left alone.

"Eureka! I got it!" He pounded the table, and his apple juice sloshed over the edge of the glass. He caught the glass before all of the liquid spilled. Forgetting dinner, he went over to the china cabinet, where he kept all his earring parts and equipment and rummaged around in the back corner of the bottom shelf. "Ahah!" he said, pulling out a small custom printer. He took the printer over to the table, pushed his bread aside, opened the top, and pulled back the inker. Set in neat little rows were all the letters that had been required to print his business card. Congratulating himself on his foresight, he pulled out all but the top row and spread them out on the table. He soon realized that he would need more letters and went back to the cabinet to find them. When he had everything laid out to his satisfaction, he inserted the new letters into the groves in the top of the printer.

"Zounds!" he said, "I bet I'm out of card stock." Back to the cabinet, but this time he could not find what he needed. Next, he tried his desk. The closest to what he needed were blank 3x5 cards in yellow and blue. He picked the blue and grabbed a ruler and his good Xacto knife. Cutting several 3x5 cards into business card size, he inserted one into the printer, closed the inker, fastened the top, grasped the crank on one side, and gave it a steady turn. He loosened the top, opened it, and there lying in the bottom section of the custom printer was a new business card. It read:

COMMANDER Z. P. BLEVINS
Surveyor of Histeric Carriage Houses
San Francisco 415-626-1950

"Rats!" He made the spelling corrections and added a new line. The next edition read:

COMMANDER Z. P. BLEVINS
Surveyor of Historic Carriage Houses
San Francisco 415-626-1950
Do You Know The Heritage Of Your Carriage House?

Very satisfied, he cut and ran off about twenty more cards before he remembered this was a one-shot job. He also realized he was smelling burnt lentils. "Rickshaw droppings!" he cursed as he rushed to the stove to turn off the flame. The lentils on the bottom were charring nicely. He scooped some off the top and tasted them. "Yowie!" The lentils were hot but did not taste burnt. Careful not to stir up the bottom, he ladled a large bowl full and took it back to the table.

"If I only had a paper," he said. Scooting the printer and extra letters to one side of the table, he put the bowl down and went into the main room. In a moment, he returned with a map of the City and opened it to the Pacific Heights area.

As Commander Blevins finished his dinner and settled in for the evening, Pins and Ember relished their solitude. "That was a world-class Lookeyloo, what Greeny did," Ember said.

"Yeah, a real beaut. Wonder what the long-term effects are of pulling a stunt like that?" Pins then sat quietly, lost in thought. It was slowly losing Its luster and pinstripes and was returning to Its now-normal dull grey. It did not care. Life was very entertaining at the moment.

Ember was equally content, and gently juicing as Commander Blevins went through his nightly routine, staying as toasty as possible.

TWENTY-NINE

RIDING THE 22 FILLMORE

The 22 Fillmore bus lumbered up Fillmore, passing Pine and Bush. The street narrowed and jogged slightly, crossing Sacramento Street. Mrs. Frumpwooler had little business in the Lower, Lower Haight, so she rarely returned home this way. She was not returning directly home now, but the Marina Green was just beyond where she lived, and that was where the 22 Fillmore line ended. The old, grand houses that lined the street were thrilling. A large bay window looked back at her, outlined in black and green trim. A yellow brick three-story caught her eye. The house had two Greek statues framing the elegant steps which curved down from a small porch and entrance way set at a forty-five-degree angle to the house. Part of the delicate iron grill-work on the front door was visible. Mrs. Frumpwooler's heart leaped.

She watched more grand houses and stately apartment buildings pass by, then the bus came over the crest of the hill, and for a moment, all she could see was sky through a narrow vista before her. The Bay's grey-green water then replaced the blue sky at Filmore's far end as the bus started downhill. Stopping once to let a passenger off— "Probably hired help," Mrs. Frump-wooler thought—the bus continued down Fillmore to Broadway. Someone was kind enough to have torn down whatever had occupied the northwest corner of Fillmore and Broadway. Mrs. Frumpwooler hoped the demolished building had not been one of the really nice homes. She stopped trying to remember, though, as she was treated to a true panorama. The red-orange Golden Gate Bridge, in profile, glowed in the afternoon sun to her left. Marin County's green and brown hills were directly across the Bay from her. A multitude of white sails dotted the Bay and surrounded a large cutter coming through the Golden Gate. Alcatraz and Angel Island stood alone farther into the Bay, and the varied greens and purpled shadows of the East Bay framed her view on the right. Down below, tidal marshes curved in an uneven arc. Stunted trees and patches of tall growth peppered the area as Bay water rippled among them. Mrs. Frumpwooler blinked hard, then saw, in place of the marshes, the Marina stretched out flat and white, with mostly pastel colors punctu-ating it. The dome of the Palace of Fine Arts capped the western end of the neighborhood. Beyond the dome, the green forests of the Army Presidio rolled toward the ocean. Mrs. Frumpwooler wondered about her momentary vision. She did not fret long, though, as the scene below filled her with ecstasy...

...much unlike her unseen companion one floor up. Greeny had rolled and lurched around the roof of the 22 Fillmore as the bus made its way up Fillmore Street. When the bus turned sharply at Broadway, Greeny had been thrown off the roof and bumped along through the construction site until It had bounced up and managed to keep Itself aloft for a while. Its yahooney was dripping unseen greenish-grey goo. Greeny was not well.

The bus detoured for three blocks on Steiner to avoid an especially steep grade on Fillmore, returned to Fillmore, eased its way down the hill, and glided into the busy area below. Mrs. Frumpwooler felt as if she were coming down from the mountain and joining the urban circus. The vision of the marshes lingered, just beyond her comprehension. Van Ness Street was choked with traffic, but the Marina District's quiet was welcoming once past Chestnut. Five blocks later, the bus pulled into its turn-around point on the near side of Marina Blvd. She stepped down off of it onto the sidewalk. Across the street, happy bedlam reigned.

Hundreds of people crammed onto the Marina Green, flying kites, laying in the sun, playing with their dogs, roller skating, break dancing, playing Frisbee, talking quietly, kissing, hugging, laughing: enjoying a sunny Sunday in San Francisco.

Mrs. Frumpwooler joined the crowd. Greeny joined the crowd. Mrs. Frumpwooler took many deep breaths and exuded happiness. Greeny worked hard to remain conscious. Mrs. Frumpwooler moved easily between the many people, occasionally stopping to pet a dog or toss back a frisbee. Greeny had not enough energy to look for other MEs, nor did he even notice when he was sniffed by a large, raspberry, and blue fellow parasite.

THIRTY

IN SEARCH OF DIAMONDS

E leven O'clock on Monday came quickly for Commander Blevins. The buzzer buzzed, and he walked over to the front door and pushed the button in the bottom corner of a brass plate on the wall. It had been painted over several times and was peeling in places. A 1920s style telephone receiver hung from the middle of the plate on a hook above the remains of switches and labels across the bottom. At one time, the intercom had allowed an apartment dweller a reasonable degree of security and selection in who entered and who did not. Today it offered a basic set of options: buzz someone in blindly, ignore it, or go downstairs to see who was there. Commander Blevins usually trotted downstairs when he was not expecting anyone. Mrs. Frumpwooler was on time today, though, so he pushed the button firmly for several seconds and opened the front door a fraction.

On schedule, bright-eyed and bushy-tailed, Mrs. Frumpwooler knocked sharply on the door three minutes later. Commander Blevins opened the door and said, "Good Morning, Mrs. Frumpwooler. How nice you look today." Rested, back in control, and with a project at hand, Commander Blevins was the embodiment of charm and good humor toward his Client. "Won't you please come in?"

Mrs. Frumpwooler smiled, nodded, and walked in.

"Can I get you some tea?" he asked.

"I think we should get straight to work, Commander Blevins."

"That's exactly what I had in mind," he said. There was a pause as their two wills met. "Please, bear with me." Commander Blevins showed Mrs. Frumpwooler into the room, and she took her usual spot on the love seat. "Tea?" He shook his head in response to her shaking hers. "No. All right then, let's begin. First of all, have you given any thought to what approach we should take?"

"That's what I'm paying you for."

"Quite right. However, I find that my Clients are often just as capable of finding inspiration as am I. Two heads, you know. So please don't hesitate to chime in whenever something strikes you. Deal?"

"Deal."

"I've searched my memory of watching Gwenny flee the area, and I've studied a map of the City. I feel sure that the house is, or perhaps was, no more than three blocks west of Van Ness and a block or two from Clay...north, I think, but I'm not positive. Do you happen to remember seeing any other street signs as Gwenny fled?

"Franklin."

"Pardon?"

"Franklin. Franklin Street. I—Gwenny— was running down Franklin Street when she passed Clay, and several more streets beyond that." Mrs. Frumpwooler was not in an entirely benevolent mood. She meant business. Diamond Business.

"Franklin. Splendid! Good work, Mrs. Frumpwooler. Well, then our next move should be to reconnoiter the area in person. Is that agreeable to you?"

"I was ready to do that when I knocked at your door a few minutes ago. But now I have a question for you, Commander Blevins," Mrs. Frumpwooler said. "By what method do you propose that we gain access to the carriage house wall, once we find it?"

"I have given that extensive thought, Mrs. Frumpwooler. And I am prepared. I assure you that I have spent most of my waking hours since we last parted company on precisely that problem. My solution will require some acting on my part. You do not need to concern yourself. I will explain your presence in such a way that you will be free to be exactly who you are, without mentioning the Diamonds, of course."

"I'm intrigued. Please tell me more."

"I must beg off, Mrs. Frumpwooler. When I am

forced to present myself as someone other than myself, I lose the freshness, the natural qualities, if I rehearse, or even discuss it with someone. Please trust me on this one."

"It would appear that I don't have much choice. OK, Commander Blevins, show me your stuff. Let's get on the road and find my Diamonds." A slight chill went through Commander Blevins when he heard Mrs. Frumpwooler use the phrase, "My Diamonds."

Commander Blevins held the front door for Mrs. Frumpwooler, and they walked out of the building into the sunshine and a chill wind. Mrs. Frumpwooler breathed deeply and said, "What a nice day we have for our scavenger hunt, Commander."

Commander Blevins was busy buttoning his cape, pulling on his hat, and trying to not drop his scarf. He didn't notice Mrs. Frumpwooler's familiar address and certainly disagreed that it was a nice day.

"If you have such a hard time keeping warm here, why don't you move?" Mrs. Frumpwooler was eyeing Commander Blevins cape. It appeared to have been designed for a much larger person and was made of burgundy material used for backpacks. A heavy and rough white wool liner made it formidable protection from elements far harsher than San Francisco. Commander Blevins wore the hood back. He was adjusting an oversize green and turquoise stocking cap as she inspected him.

"You know, I get asked that often and I don't really have a good answer. Yes, the weather here does present a problem for me, but there are deeper pulls to stay. So I stay."

"Maybe you are a masochist," she said. They had crossed Fillmore and were walking up to Oak, toward the bus stop. Commander Blevins thought about what Mrs. Frumpwooler had said. He thought it about for so long that they both were wondering, silently, if he would answer her. Finally, he said, "No, I don't think so."

"Another Safari!" the Ember said. The two MEs were sitting on their usual perch watching Commander Blevins and Mrs. Frumpwooler cross the street. "And Lookeyloo what the cat drug in."

Greeny had been laying low all morning. Mostly recovered from Its misadventures the day before, It had been in control of Its actions and had perched on a wire around the corner on Oak Street when Mrs. Frump-wooler had gotten off the bus. Carefully, It had let Its light cord pass through the houses in the middle of the block as she had walked toward 600 Page. Ember and Pins had, therefore, not noticed Greeny's arrival on the scene.

"Do you think he'll try to horn in on our Man in Red again?" Pins asked.

"If that happens, we will blast him this time," Ember said. Greeny hovered cautiously on the far side of Oak Street, near Mrs. Frumpwooler and Commander Blevins.

"Right On!"

The 22 Filmore did not make Commander Blevins

wait long. It rolled up the hill in a few minutes. He and Mrs. Frumpwooler got on and found an empty double seat four rows back. The bus lurched forward just as Commander Blevins was sitting down. The sudden movement threw him into the seat, and he bounced against Mrs. Frumpwooler.

"Don't get fresh, now Commander," she said. Her mood was lightening. He missed the joke and mumbled an apology.

Ember and Pins floated smoothly up Fillmore as the bus moved north. The 'family' outing was underway.

"You know that you have my curiosity piqued, don't you, Commander?' Mrs. Frumpwooler was almost batting her eyelashes at him. "What exactly is it that you are going to do? Can't you give me a hint?"

"No. Just be patient. First, we need to find the house, and then the carriage house still has to BE there. Did you review any more the scene we watched as Gwenny ran from the house?"

"Yes, I did. I remembered her looking back and seeing the house for a moment as she was running. I also remembered the house across the street and the chimney that had fallen in the street from it."

"Good show! Mrs. Frumpwooler. I had remembered the house, but had not recalled the chimney and the house across the street."

"So all we have to do is look for a new chimney. That should be simple."

"Well, I don't know it will be that evident. The houses in that area are about a hundred years old. If the chimney fell during the quake, then it would be about eighty-three years old. Not a big enough difference, I'm afraid, to be noticeable from this point in time."

"Oh. I guess you are right." Mrs. Frumpwooler was disappointed and became quiet.

"Hey, Two Timer, how's it hanging?" Pins asked and raspberried Greeny.

"Hey, Jerk. That little Green dude could be all over your case in a flash. Want that?" Ember said.

"Uh...no, I guess not."

"That's a smart guess. He may have almost offed his little greedy self yesterday, but he had a whale load of juice and will be on the mend double-quick. And I might add that even as dumb as he appears to be, he's a strong new pup, not a faded old relic like an unnamed fellow wire-sitter I know of. Dig?"

"Yes, I dig," the Ember said.

"Wonderful. Makes my day. Now, stay smart." Pins was in no mood to have to tangle with Greeny because of stupidity if it could be helped. "Now, mellow out and enjoy the trip. Who knows what old Step 'N Fetch It is gonna fall into today. We need our wits up."

The 22 Fillmore pulled to a stop at Sacramento, and Mrs. Frumpwooler and Commander Blevins got off. Greeny hovered on one side of them, looking out toward the Bay. His two fellow MEs kept their distance. The 1 California jogged one block along Fillmore from California Street, turned the corner to Sacramento, and pulled to the curb's stop. Commander Blevins and Mrs. Frumpwooler climbed aboard the bus and sat down. A minute later, it lurched forward.

"Keep your eye peeled, just in case we are way off base or a house has been moved to a different lot," Commander Blevins said.

"Move a house? I've never heard of such a thing."

"Well, it does happen from time to time. The Spreckles Mansion--are you familiar with it?"

"Uh, no, I don't think so."

"It sits just above Lafayette Park." Commander Blevins paused for a moment and turned toward Mrs. Frumpwooler. "You DO know where Lafayette Park is..."

"Yes, of course, I do! It's right there!" Mrs. Frump-wooler pointed across the bus to the rolling green knoll, just coming up on their left. The bus topped the rise at the bottom of the park and stopped. Lafayette Park ran uphill from where they sat and covered four square blocks. At the top of the park, two blocks north from where Commander Blevins and Mrs. Frump-wooler sat, stood the Speckles Mansion. "What do you think I am anyway, a tourist from Iowa?"

"Now, now. Just having a little fun, Mrs. Frump-wooler. The Spreckles House sits right over the hill, beyond the park. It covers nearly half a block and--and this is the point of all this--when it was built about ten years after the quake, they moved six houses to make room for the mansion."

"If someone did move a house, surely they wouldn't

move a carriage house, too. Would they?" Mrs. Frump-wooler's voice rose a full octave.

"Not likely. Which means we could possibly find our carriage house behind an entirely different home than it stood ninety years ago."

"Oh, my."

"Not worth your fretting about. If someone was determined enough to move that house from the property, I doubt the carriage house would have survived the new construction."

"Oh, Oh." Mrs. Frumpwooler saw the bag of Diamonds disappear in front of her eyes. The bus jerked forward after two women climbed aboard. They walked passed Mrs. Frumpwooler and Commander Blevins and sat down somewhere in the back. It turned left, around the corner of the park at Gough Street, then back to the right one block later at Clay, and rolled down the hill.

"Here we are, Mrs. Frumpwooler," Commander Blevins said as he pulled the cord above the window. The driver eased over to the curb on the far side of Clay Street, and they got off. Both of them stood quietly facing north. As the 1 California moved on toward downtown, it unveiled Franklin Street in front of them, rising gently toward its last crest before heading down and running to its end at Bay Street and Fort Mason. They looked at each other, took deep breaths in unison, and crossed the street.

Greeny took the west side of the street. The Ember bobbed along over the cars parked by the curb on the east side, keeping an eye on Greeny. Pins floated a few meters behind Ember, keeping an eye on It.

"Can you imagine what this street looked like right after the quake," Commander Blevins said.

"Yes, I can," Mrs. Frumpwooler said. "We saw it, remember?"

"Yes...well...I...er...mean, we only got a glimpse of it." Commander Blevins hated to be made a fool of.

"We could always go back to that place and look at those little cards again, Commander. Maybe we could get a better view."

Commander Blevins didn't notice that Mrs. Frumpwooler was teasing. "I, well, yes, we could, but I don't think that's a very good idea." He snorted.

"Now, now. I was just having a little fun, to quote a certain someone who shall remain nameless." Mrs. Frumpwooler grinned at Commander Blevins.

He pretended to ignore the whole thing but was acutely aware that he had lost a round of repartee. He made a mental note to give Mrs. Frumpwooler a wider berth from now on. "This project is getting to me," he thought. "Craziness on the Journey, almost being censured by the Review Committee—or have I been by now and I don't know it—McDervish being Chairman Whirling and Chairman Whirling being at a Review and the scene that ended the review between Tickle, Dweed, and Chairman Whirling! It's enough to cause serious reconsideration."

They walked on in silence and crossed Washington. Suddenly he snapped out of his reverie. "We should be looking for the house. What's wrong with me!"

"I can't answer your last question, but as to your first comment: We don't need to." Mrs. Frumpwooler was glowing in the midday sun.

"We don't? What do you mean?"

"There it is." She pointed across the street and up the block. Three houses ahead of them, the Pacific Heights Victorian sat above the sidewalk, perched on the ground and held in place by an old concrete retainer wall, it reached high into the sky. Its four gables made it appear to have a pitched roof. A small front porch and convoluted front steps were a little incongruous to the rest of the house. The large corner turret on the top of the house dominated the facade, with its overly tall windows set high in the tower.

"Son of a." Commander Blevins caught himself. "Good work, Mrs. Frumpwooler!" He somehow thought he would never be faced with what now met him: approaching the owners of the home and working his way into their confidence, putting himself in a position to extract a few bricks from the carriage house. From the angle they viewed the home, they could not see behind it. Commander Blevins did notice a narrow drive running up to the yard on the near side of the house.

"Well, let's get going." Mrs. Frumpwooler said.

"Yes, let's do. No, now wait a moment." Commander Blevins stopped after he had taken a step. Holding his temple with one hand, and looking down at the sidewalk, he said, as though he were reading it from the back of his eyelids, "Please, follow my lead, and keep quiet. I must have the freedom to improvise if you get my drift."

"Oh, right. I forgot. This should be exciting. Lead on, Commander."

THIRTY-ONE
CONVERSATION WITH A DANCER

They crossed the street diagonally, Commander Blevins in the lead. He walked by the two houses separating them from their target and then said under his breath, "Eureka! There's the carriage house. Or at least a carriage house." He did not look back to see if Mrs. Frumpwooler had heard or noticed. He was on the scent now, and his excitement went beyond the bounds of anything material. Mrs. Frumpwooler was walking full-tilt behind him, on her tip-toes.

All three MEs knew something was afoot.

Commander Blevins turned off the sidewalk and took the steps leading up to the porch two at a time. He reached inside his cape, inside his coat, inside his jacket, and found the upper pocket of his outer wool shirt. As he was contorting in front of the door, Mrs. Frump-wooler paused by the bottom of the stairs. She was looking at a large rectangle in front of the shrubbery.

"Commander Blevins!" she hissed. He turned toward her and was about to motion her still, emphatically, when he saw her intent look. She was pointing furiously to something in front of the bushes. He walked back down the steps and looked at what Mrs. Frumpwooler was looking at. Tucked neatly in front of the wall that enclosed the porch's super-structure and nestled among the greenery, it was a rectangular wooden sign, finished, painted, and varnished to withstand San Francisco's fog, damp days, and proximity to the ocean. The sign was tasteful and designed to convey information quietly while not intruding upon the integrity of the house itself. It read:

The Foundation for San Francisco's

Architectural Heritage

2007 Franklin Street

"What the devil," Commander Blevins said.

"Some kind of Foundation it looks like," Mrs. Frumpwooler said.

"Hmmm, this may change the complexion of things." He picked his nose with a passion until he realized what he was doing and who he was with. "Well, now, let's take a look around back. No, first, I do want to peek inside the front door." He went back up the steps and discretely peered through the beveled glass of the front door. He whistled low and shaded his eyes from the outside light.

"What's there? What's there?" Mrs. Frumpwooler said.

Commander Blevins craned his head in several

directions trying to see as much as possible in the house. Finally, he motioned Mrs. Frumpwooler to join him on the front porch. She hurried to do so, her footsteps making a racket.

"Ssshhhh. Ssshhhh," he said. "Look at this."

Mrs. Frumpwooler did and said, "Oh my, Oh my. It hasn't changed a bit."

"I thought not," Commander Blevins said.

"It looks the same as it did when I—when Gwenny— was here."

Commander Blevins pulled out an ornate pocket watch from deep inside his many layers, looked at it, and said, "Well, it's still 1989. We haven't been caught in an errand time schism."

"How can you tell by looking at that thing?"

"Deduction. Time fractures are rarely laterally consistent." Mrs. Frumpwooler looked at him, doubtfully. He added, "In moving from one era to another, the time of day is rarely the same."

"Oh."

"Anyway, let's look around back. We may be in unimaginable luck."

"How's that?" Mrs. Frumpwooler came down the steps behind him, a little quieter this time.

Talking over his shoulder, he said, "I only saw a little light coming from the kitchen. Did you see any other sign of life?"

"No."

"Any papers or coats or toys or junk lying around?"

"None." They walked, crept really, around the

porch's corner and down the narrow walkway running along the Bay side of the house. It was enclosed by a ten-foot-high latticework fence covered with ivy.

"We may have stumbled onto a museum. Or the home of a very old person who never comes downstairs."

"Really!"

"I vote for the latter, I think."

"Why?"

"I don't know. Say what this?" Commander Blevins asked.

"It looks like a little buzzer box. Shall we ring it?" Mrs. Frumpwooler said. A small square brown box was attached to the wall of the house about shoulder height just before a side door. Three steps led up to the door. The box had a white button in one lower corner, a round grill in the center, and a nameplate above it. The nameplate said: "HERITAGE."

"No, not just yet. Let's see if you-know-what is in back." Commander Blevins led the way, and they padded back toward an arched trellis that seemed to herald something of promise beyond it.

Mrs. Frumpwooler gasped when they poked their heads through the arch. A small pond piled high with vines and trash sat in the middle of the backyard. There was no evidence of water in the pond or birdbath, which rose from the midst of the pond, vines, and trash.

"Amazing. Amaaazing. I think we've found it," Commander Blevins said. He saw the yard as it had been in 1906 when he had worked and played in it as

Ito. It had been from this vantage point that he had spied on Gwenny as she had hidden the bag of Diamonds. He shifted back to the present and turned around to Mrs. Frumpwooler, their faces nearly touching as she looked over her shoulder. The expression on her face stopped him. She was still staring into the yard, but as he followed her gaze, he realized she was looking not at the pond and birdbath, but at the...wall. The back wall of the carriage house. The carriage house was still standing. And pretty much unaltered, except for the back wall. It stood naked, freshly brushed, and fully exposed. Commander Blevins looked from it to the pond and back again.

Ember and Pins hovered over the front of the house, in growing expectation. Greeny floated immediately over Mrs. Frumpwooler, very alert.

"They've torn the vines off the wall. And they've tuck- pointed it," he said.

Mrs. Frumpwooler gasped again. "What does 'pucktointed' mean? Is it as bad as I think? Have they rebuilt the wall? Oh, tell me no, Commander. Please tell me no."

She was about to begin wailing.

Commander Blevins reached around and started to place his hand on her neck below her ear, and then remembered they were in the physical. The point of infinite peacefulness only worked in the Inner Worlds. He shifted his arm, so it wrapped around her shoulders. "Courage. Courage, Mrs. Frumpwooler. There was no guarantee we would find the Diamonds, you know."

"Yes, I know," she sniffed. "But I had so hoped." She turned into his shoulder and sobbed quietly.

"We still may."

"What?" She looked up into this face.

He nodded and said, "Yes, we still may. The term is 'tuck-pointing,' not 'puck-tointing,' and it means to scrape out the loose mortar between the bricks and replace it with fresh mortar."

"You mean they didn't take the bricks out, or down, or off. Whatever they do with bricks."

Commander Blevins smiled. "Not likely. Not unless a brick was very loose, and it needed to be refitted or replaced."

"Oh, I hope my...the bricks the Gwenny pulled out were in there tight enough."

"Well, if it's any consolation, this wall should have been tuck-pointed more than once in the past eighty-three years."

"Oh, yes, that makes me feel...wait a minute, that means more chances for the bricks to be pulled out. That doesn't make me feel better!"

"Not necessarily. If the wall has been properly maintained, then there is a good chance your bricks, er, the bricks that Gwenny put in, were properly secured before they had a chance to become so loose they needed refitting."

"Oh, thank you, Commander. You are so wonderful." She looked directly into his eyes.

The line between soothing a Client and becoming

uncomfortably close was about to be crossed. "Yes, well, I think we should inspect it, don't you," he said.

"Yes, of course!"

"Quietly."

"Right."

They walked gingerly into the yard. There were twigs scattered on the walkway, and they crunched underfoot.

"Hello there, can I help you?" The voice came from the back of the house. Commander Blevins and Mrs. Frumpwooler froze in their tracks. Commander Blevins flashed on Frau Swope. This voice was unaccented, however, and distinctly male, though not without female modulations. He recovered first, Mrs. Frumpwooler having gone all akimbo inside at the sound of another person, and turned to the voice.

"Yes," he said, straining to see who he was talking to. He tried to sound firm, clear, and happy to have finally found someone. "I certainly hope so. We weren't able to raise anybody at the front door."

"Oh, yes. That front door thing is impossible to keep in working order. Did you try the side door buzzer? It usually works, and more often than not, someone upstairs will answer."

The owner of the voice had been standing in the deep shadow of the back door. He now appeared outside on the low porch and began coming down the steps, which took him along the back of the house instead of out into the yard. He was still in partial shadow. The steps led to a curving walk cutting across the far corner of the yard and around the side of the carriage house. He turned off the walk and came across the yard toward Commander Blevins and Mrs. Frumpwooler, standing by the pond, vines, trash, and birdbath. They could now see him clearly.

"Oh, was that a buzzer back there? Wondered about that," Commander Blevins said.

"But you said..." Mrs. Frumpwooler whispered behind him a little too loudly. He took a small step backward and placed his foot squarely on hers. "Owwie, owwie, owwie, you are on my foot, Commander!"

He jumped away from her, turned around, feigned surprise, and said, "Oh, gracious, Mrs. Frumpwooler, please pardon me. I am so sorry." Leaning close to her ear, he whispered, "I *know* about the buzzer, *please* keep your cool!"

"Oh, sorry," she whimpered.

Commander Blevins turned back to the approaching man. The first thing he noticed was his legs. They were very visible and covered with a tight forest-green material. Commander Blevins' eyes traveled up and lingered on a pair of leather shorts: fuchsia and very short. A gloved hand lingered near the shorts, holding a pair of garden clippers.

"Hi, Ho." The man was upon him and extending his ungloved hand. Commander Blevins gripped it and looked at the man's face. It was finely boned and smooth. "My name is Niven," the man said. Greeny perked up even more.

"Oh, hello. I'm Blevins, and this is Mrs. Frumpwooler." Commander Blevins pointed back to his Client.

"Charmed," Niven said, stepped around Commander Blevins, and gently shook Mrs. Frumpwooler's hand.

"What brings two such delightful people to our little yard on a Monday afternoon?" Niven was taking in this unusual couple as he spoke. The woman, Mrs. Mompper, or something, was normal enough at first glance: middle-aged, wearing a purple hat and dressed uninterestingly. Her eyes, though, held a driven sort of gleam and had made Niven uncomfortable when he had looked into them. Her hands were sweaty, too.

The man. Blimpins. He was talking now, and Niven had no idea what he was saying. His appearance was truly extraordinary. He wore a burgundy cape that looked like it could withstand a Siberian blizzard, and he appeared to be a bulky looking fellow underneath the cloak. And his head. He had a sock cap on it—probably liked to stay warm—and it was somewhat oversized. Niven had a secret weakness for big heads. His knees were beginning to get weak when he forced himself to tune into what Blimpins was saying.

"...having spent these past many months in archive research, we, my assistant, Mrs. Frumpwooler, and I felt it was time to venture forth into the world of matter and document our hypotheses."

Niven faded again. He had never been able to follow scientific verbiage and was soon lost in Commander Blevins' diatribe.

Commander Blevins noticed a feverish look in

Niven's eye, then saw it glaze over. He couldn't imagine what had caused the first look but was relieved to find his monologue having the desired effect. While continuing to assail his opponent with words, Commander Blevins again began searching for his bogus business cards. He slid his hand inside his cape, inside his coat, inside his jacket, and finally into the top pocket of his heavy wool outer shirt. Pulling it out, he said, "A-hah!" which served as a convenient ending for a rambling non-sequitur that was slightly out of control. He produced the blue business card and handed it triumphantly to Niven. Niven took it and read:

COMMANDER Z. P. BLEVINS
Surveyor of Historic Carriage Houses
San Francisco 415-626-1950
"Do You Know The Heritage Of Your Carriage House?"

He had to read it three times. His head was still ringing with words that had nowhere to go, and the glimpse inside Blimpins' cape had raised more questions than it had answered. "Surveyor of Historic Carriage Houses. I don't think I have ever heard of anyone with such an occupation, Mr. Blimpin...Blevins," Niven said.

"No mister, just Blevins," Commander Blevins said.

"Well, all right, Blevins. I'm afraid that I'm still a teeny bit confused as to how I can be of service to you and Mrs. Mum...your assistant." Niven was not the least bit suspicious, just confused.

"Well, I guess what we would like is to be able to inspect your carriage house."

"Inspect...our *carriage* house." Niven was quiet for a moment. "Oh, you mean the *garage*."

"Yes, the garage, if that's what you call it."

"Well, what do you mean by inspect? Oh, I can't decide this. I haven't got time! I do hope you understand and come back." He flashed his eyes at Commander Blevins. Commander Blevins blinked, not sure what to make of this sudden shift. Mrs. Frumpwooler stood stoically at his side.

Greeny began hyper flexing the area around its yahooney.

"My God, he's going to do it again," the Pins said.

"Another show!" the Ember declared gleefully.

Niven was cranked up now, and he continued, "I have an obligation to get to, you see, and I was just on my way out and, oh I hope you don't think this is what I normally wear around here, I'm usually much more in control, if you know what I mean." He scrunched his nose at Commander Blevins. "Anyway, I was just on my way out when Marc asked me—that would be Marcus Upright, the Director of Heritage, I call him Markup behind his back; he would never get the joke." Niven twittered. "Anyway, Marc asked me to do the flowers for tonight's board meeting. I mean, I don't mind doing them, I'm actually quite good at it, but I had told him last week I would be leaving early today. We have a final dress for our opening, did I mention that to you?"

Both Mrs. Frumpwooler and Commander Blevins shook their heads.

Greeny took a deep breath, and his yahooney sprouted a stubby new light cord.

"Lookeyloo! Lookeyloo!" Pins said.

"Hush, Flem Breath," Ember replied. Ember stuck a tongue out at Pins and raspberried it.

"Oh, dear. Cecil, my roommate, who authored the comic dance, would just *skewer* me if I didn't invite you. It's opening tonight at 7:30 at our little third-floor studio on 17th, that's Street, not Avenue, just off Castro. You *do* know where Castro is, don't` you? Its the *only* place to be in the City."

Commander Blevins and Mrs. Frumpwooler found themselves paralyzed by Niven's stream of consciousness or lack thereof.

"Anyway. Oh, I do go on sometimes, Cecil is always telling me. The final dress is today at 2:00, so I decided to change into my costume here at home. I live here, you know, I'm the only one who does." Commander Blevins found that interesting. "Instead of having to change once I got there, I just knew I'd be late today. Anyway, the performance is at 7:30 tonight. It's called "The Enhanced Bulge: Does He Or Doesn't He." Oh, it's just going to be a scream. This is only the second thing our little troupe has done. We call ourselves the Rock Hard Players, and we do dance and some improv, and we are all so nervous. We are going to have shows all week, tomorrow we have a Happy Hour show and the evening show sort of back-to-back." Niven twittered again. "The Happy Hour show is an experiment. I really do have to finish the flowers and get out of here. Its been so nice meeting you." Niven reached out to shake hands.

Greeny hovered just over Niven, salivating.

Commander Blevins did not need to open his mouth to speak; it was already open, even if his mind was numb. He said, "Well, do have a good show. Break a leg and all that, I think they say." He ignored Niven's offered hand unconsciously.

"You are *too* kind," Niven said and turned to go. Commander Blevins and Mrs. Frumpwooler were rooted where they stood, watching him as he walked back to the porch, swishing ever so slightly. When Niven got to the steps, he turned and, seeing them still standing in the yard, said, "I'm afraid I can't let you do your surveying, or whatever, without Marc's OK."

Commander Blevins gulped and said, "Well, that's all right."

Niven flapped both hands in the air and came dancing back out to them.

Greeny was about to shoot Its cord through one of several wide gaps in Niven's aura when a dim memory returned. It hesitated. "Maybe this is not such a good idea," It said to Itself. "Maybe one or the other, isn't that the rule? Yeah." Slowly Greeny floated a little higher and withdrew the new light cord.

"Aw, shucks, he's not gonna do it," Pins said.

"Harrumph," said the Ember. It was interested only

in Greeny not trying to reattach to Commander Blevins.

To compensate Itself for Its self-imposed disappointment, Greeny juiced deeply on the cord leading to Mrs. Frumpwooler.

"Oh, what's the matter with me," Niven said. He should still be up there, let's go check. I knew I was going to be late anyway."

"Well, I don't think..." Commander Blevins started to say.

Niven grabbed him by the hand, "Here, I'll go buzz the buzzer for you and get you started on your way. He marched out through the trellis with Commander Blevins in tow. Mrs. Frumpwooler followed at a safe distance, looking back longingly at the barren brick wall.

"Here we are," Niven said, pushing the white button on the buzzer box.

A voice answered in a moment, "HERITAGE."

"Oh, *hi*! Connie. Is Marc busy right now? I have some people who would like to see him." Commander Blevins was sweating, wondering what he would say to a Director of a Foundation.

"Sorry, Niven, Marc left right after he talked to you. He's out for most of the afternoon with Mr. Hall. I think they are preparing for the board meeting tonight. Let me check his calendar."

There was silence on the secretary's end of the line, and Niven turned to Commander Blevins, shrugged his shoulders, and said, "Sorry, he's out, apparently."

Connie was back on the buzzer box speaker and said, "Niven?"

"Yes, Connie, we're still here."

"It appears that Marc won't be free until Wednesday, late morning. He's booked up all morning tomorrow, and he's leaving early to go to the Series game. Shall I write your people in for ten o'clock Wednesday morning?"

Niven looked at Commander Blevins and Mrs. Frumpwooler. Mrs. Frumpwooler had a very blank look on her face. Commander Blevins was smiling and nodding hard. Niven turned back to the speaker box and said, "Sounds good, Connie." He held up the bogus business card and read from it into the buzzer box, "Commander Z. P. Blevins and..." He lowered the card. "...his assistant, Mrs. Mumpper. Thanks, Connie, you're a jewel." Niven blew a kiss into the buzzer box and slid by Commander Blevins and Mrs. Frumpwooler, saying as he went, "Hope that's ok, dear-ries. Toodles for now." He waved backward over his shoulder.

After Niven had disappeared through the trellis, Commander Blevins looked at Mrs. Frumpwooler. Niven popped back around the trellis and shouted, "Promise me that you will come to a performance tonight or tomorrow." They both jumped at the surprise but managed to nod their heads. Niven vanished again. Slowly they walked down the narrow walkway, closed in by the house on one side and the tall grey fence on the other side.

When they got to the street, Mrs. Frumpwooler

broke the silence and said, ""Oh, I hate to leave here without knowing."

Commander Blevins looked at her, smiled broadly, and began whistling loudly and walking toward Sacramento Street and the bus stop.

"What's gotten into you?" she asked, moving quickly to catch up with him.

THIRTY-TWO

HATCHING A HAMMERING PLAN

They walked past Clay Street with Mrs. Frumpwooler's question hanging in mid-air, unanswered. Commander Blevins still whistled. One block later, at Sacramento, they stopped to wait for the 1 California bus, heading toward the ocean. Commander Blevins began singing. Mrs. Frumpwooler looked at him like he was crazy. He sang, "If I had a hammer, I'd hammer in the morning...I'd hammer in the evening...I'd hammer aaaall day long...."

Mrs. Frumpwooler was feeling out of sorts. They had left the wall behind, untouched, and she did not have the slightest idea why Commander Blevins seemed so happy. Meeting with Director what's-his-name didn't seem like a solution to her. And that was not until Wednesday! After several repetitions of the song by Commander Blevins, she finally said, "If I sang like that, I wouldn't sing in public."

He turned to her, grinning and still singing. "If I had a hammer, I'd *not* hammer in the morning...I'd hammer in the evening...I'd hammer all evening long...." He sang this three times and stopped cold. Turning to her, he said, "Well?"

"Well, what!" she snapped.

"'Hammering in the evening,' doesn't that give you some ideas?"

"You want to go back there tonight and pound away on that wall while they have their Board Meeting? You are crazy!"

"No, not tonight." The bus rolled up. They boarded it with silence hanging between them.

After taking seats near the front, Mrs. Frumpwooler said, "Well, *when*, then?" There was a slight hiss in her voice.

"Tomorrow night, of course, when the Director is at the game and Niven is at his dance thing and after everyone else has gone home. Kapish?"

Mrs. Frumpwooler nodded several times as the impact of his plan settled in. "Kapish! You are so wonderful! Now I'm really excited!" She squeezed his arm as Lafayette Park glided by on their right. Commander Blevins felt full of congratulations and did not object to Mrs. Frumpwooler keeping a firm hold on his less than firm biceps.

They rode on in happy silence.

When the bus reached Fillmore and began to turn right, Commander Blevins reached up and pulled the cord above the windows. His movement reminded Mrs.

Frumpwooler she still had a grip on him, and she let go with a small blush. He didn't notice. The driver let them off on the ocean side of Fillmore, just south of Sacramento. They walked down the sidewalk, looking into the store windows.

"It's getting warm, don't you think,' Mrs. Frumpwooler said.

"Uhmm, why yes, I guess you are right." Commander Blevins was surprised he had not been aware of the temperature change. He now remembered he had not been chilled all afternoon and was, in fact, close to too warm. He took off the great cape and, folding it twice, draped it over his arm. The long wool coat that he wore underneath it was once a fashionable Woolridge plaid hunting coat, though he bought it for its large side pockets, not to hunt. It now was long out of style and in need of repair in several places.

Mrs. Frumpwooler took one look at it and said, "What a charming coat. You must let me sew up those tears and holes."

"Well, that would be very kind of you, but not necessary."

"I've been wondering; oh this is a personal question, am I taking liberties?"

"I don't know without hearing your question." He looked at her and smiled. They were at the next corner, and he turned to cross Fillmore. The light was against them, though, so they waited.

"I have two questions, really."

"Ok, shoot."

"Well, why do you wear so many clothes and where on earth did you buy that cape? It is the most amazing and large thing I've ever seen."

Commander Blevins was silent. The light changed. They began walking. The three MEs were floating behind them like children in a zoo, relatively calm and not bickering.

"The last question is easy," he said, hoping to dodge the first. "A friend of a very dear friend made it for me a couple years ago when I first had such trouble keeping warm. My friend is a choreographer, and her friend is a costume designer for their dance company."

"Oh, you mean like the group Niven belongs to."

"Well, in a way, yes, but very different, I would imagine. Anyway, she offered to make this for me if I got the material. I found a company that sold yard goods for awnings and backpacks and bought the outer layer there."

Mrs. Frumpwooler's eyes widened. "You mean this would have been an awning," she said, pointing to the cape hanging over his other arm now. It was a cumbersome garment.

"Backpack. And the lining is two wool army blankets I found at a surplus store down on Mission Street." He looked at her and smiled. They had stopped in front of a hardware store window. "Now you have the story of the burgundy cape," he said in a dramatic, final way. "I suggest we now go in this conveniently located establishment and select our implements of attack for tomorrow's assault on the carriage house and history."

He made a flourish with his free arm, and Mrs. Frump-wooler laughed. They went into the hardware store.

Fifteen minutes later, they came out laughing. Commander Blevins held a large canvas bag. "Would you like for me to carry that, Commander?" Mrs. Frumpwooler said.

"Oh, thanks, I'd appreciate that. The day had gotten still warmer, and he was laboring as they walked to the corner. "Are you hungry?"

"Yes, a bit."

"Good, there's a great Macrobiotic restaurant just up this block, if you'd care to try it."

"Macro-what"

"Macrobiotic. Its a way of eating that is Japanese in roots but cuts across cultural boundaries. Very healthy."

"All right, I'll try it. Then I must be getting home after I help you to your apartment with these tools, of course. What time tomorrow should we get together?" she asked.

"Let's think about that over lunch."

THIRTY-THREE
CAPITALIZING ON A FAULT

Five o'clock Tuesday afternoon arrived at four o'clock. That's when Mrs. Frumpwooler buzzed Commander Blevins' buzzer. He was recording a dream in his dream journal and couldn't imagine who it could be. As he padded down the steps in his robe and goofy slippers, another dream came back to him. It often happened that way. When he put attention on one dream, another appeared. He usually wrote down his dreams when he awoke in the night, or first thing in the morning. They were much clearer then, and he could remember more. He had begun recording his dreams several years earlier when someone had shared with him how much more they remembered when they wrote down their dreams. He had said he didn't dream. They had said, sure you do. Try it. So his reawakening in the dream state had started with a dare. It had quickly opened his Inner Awareness and led directly to his involvement with the Society and Inner World travels.

This dream brought a smile to his face. In high school, and then in college, Zoider had been a close friend of his. Zoider's girlfriend Andi and Commander Blevins had shared an attraction and an irritation for each other. He cherished his friends, and Zoider was at the top of the list in those days. He fiercely resisted getting involved with any friend's girlfriend. After Zoider had gone on to graduate school, he and Andi kept bumping into each other and had dinner a couple times. Then his apartment flooded, and Andi offered to put him up for the night. He had slept on the sofa cushion in the middle of the living room, not far from Andi's open bedroom door. The evening was filled with a subtle tension, but no bickering.

In the middle of the night, he had awakened enormously aroused. Half asleep, he had walked, naked, to Andi's door. She slept just inside the room. He could hear her breathing, and though he didn't know for sure, he thought she might welcome him into her bed. He could not do it. His love for Zoider poured through him, and he returned to this bed and satisfied himself.

Years later, in hormonal rages, he would sometimes return to that scene in fantasy, wishing he had played it out. Of course, then he wouldn't have had it to fantasize about. He never fantasized about the women he had been with entirely.

In the dream, he and Andi were frolicking in the shower, without reservation. It had been memorable.

Her slim naked body was cavorting in his imagination when he turned the corner on the last landing and saw Mrs. Frumpwooler fussing with her purple hat outside the front door. He came down the few remaining steps to the foyer, hurried to the front door, opened it, and said, "You're early!"

"Yes, I know. I couldn't sit at home any longer. I hope I am not an inconvenience." She saw that he was struggling to be gracious, but she came prepared for that eventuality. "I had to go to the bank anyway before it closed, and I thought that it was risky to carry around so much money." Commander Blevins' objections dissolved. She continued, rushing into the gap, "You were so grand yesterday that it would be silly of me to wait until after we do our work tonight to complete our financial arrangements."

Commander Blevins suddenly found gallantry overflowing. "You are truly a lady, Mrs. Frumpwooler."

"Call me Gladys."

"Gladys. And you may call me Commander."

"Commander." They stood that way, for a long minute, overcome with their respective emotions.

"Hello, hello. Don't hold the door open too long, you'll let in all the strays in the neighborhood, neighborhood!"

Both Commander Blevins and Mrs. Frumpwooler turned to find Mr. Fedulity coming down the steps and laughing at his own joke.

"Good afternoon, Mr. Fedulity. How are you today?" Commander Blevins asked.

"Fine, fine. And how are you folks?"

"We are both just ducky, I would say, wouldn't you agree, Mrs. Frumpwooler? Gladys."

"Certainly, Commander."

"Delighted, delighted," Mr. Fedulity said and went through the door in the side of the foyer that led into the garage.

"Shall we?" Commander Blevins extended his arm to Mrs. Frumpwooler.

"We shall," she said and took it. "We must be off very soon!". They were unable to walk up the stairs side-by-side, however, so Commander Blevins graciously allowed Mrs. Frumpwooler to precede him.

The MEs were still in peaceful co-existence outside. Pins had not harassed Greeny when he arrived. Greeny had chosen to perch on the ocean side of Filmore, keeping Its distance from the other two, just in case.

Mr. Fedulity opened two of the garage doors and began cleaning his tools. It was a hot day, the second in what was probably one of the City's rare three-day heat waves. He wondered where Floyd and Semblance were. They almost always showed up to talk story in the afternoon. After he finished putting away the socket wrenches, screwdrivers, and big blue-handled channel locks, he swept the four car garage and set out three lawn chairs on the sidewalk in front of the garage door then sat down in the sunlight. He loved the sun and got far too little of it in the City.

"Isn't this too early to go there?" he heard a woman say.

"You're the one who got here early and has been hurrying me along," a man replied, chuckling. The voice sounded familiar, like...

"Well, that doesn't mean we..."

"Oh, hello, Mr. Fedulity," Commander Blevins said.

"So it was him," Mr. Fedulity thought. "Good day once again. Good Day," he said to his tenant and the woman in the purple hat who trailed along behind him, looking a little agitated. They were gone without another word. Mr. Fedulity shook his head slowly and brushed aside uncharitable thoughts. At least the man wasn't wearing his strange cape today. With determination, he pushed that out of his mind, too. He had found that thinking ill thoughts about other people had a way of coming home to roost. He did wonder what was in the bag Commander Blevins carried, though.

Commander Blevins and Mrs. Frumpwooler crossed Fillmore, got honked at, and walked up the hill to Oak Street to wait for the bus. There was a curious silence in the air and an unusually stifling feeling.

"The timing is OK, Mrs—Gladys, trust me," Commander Blevins said.

"Well, all right, but what if someone is there," she began.

"Then we will walk down to Union and get some coffee, or tea. And wait."

"How are we going to know if someone is there or not?"

The bus came, and they got on, both flashing their Fast Passes. It was mostly full, and they didn't find two empty seats together until they got near the back door. As they settled into their seats, Commander Blevins leaned over and whispered loudly into Mrs. Frump-wooler's ear, "I told you that I called twice today. The second time, just before you arrived, I got their machine. I think the boss took the afternoon off, and everyone else has left early, too."

"But..."

"Shhh." He put his finger to his mouth, and they rode on in silence, slicing through the Western Addition. When the bus crossed California, Commander Blevins pulled the cord above the window. The bus' brakes squealed as it pulled over to the curb at Sacramento. The doors opened, back and front and they stood up, Commander Blevins clutching the bag of tools, and walked the two rows back to the rear door. Mrs. Frumpwooler walked down the rubber matted steps.

Commander Blevins noticed people entering and leaving the stores strangely. It was a subtle feeling. He wondered what it was about the people that looked out of the ordinary.

"Maybe it's me," said out loud, shrugging his shoulders.

"What? I didn't hear you," Mrs. Frumpwooler said, yelling a little and half turning around to look at him. She took the last step down to the sidewalk with her head still turned. She put one foot on the sidewalk, shrieked, stumbled, and fell sprawling across the concrete. Commander Blevins heard her scream as though she were down a long tunnel from him. He was looking at the corner through the bus windows. Just before Mrs. Frumpwooler's outburst, he noticed the light pole running up from the sidewalk. No one was standing around it, but it was undulating like spaghetti at the end of a shaking stick. He thought it was an optical illusion caused by the heat and the glass. A car's tires screeched, and there was the crunch of metal and tinkle of breaking glass.

Then he saw Mrs. Frumpwooler lying on the ground. He hopped out of the bus with one leap and landed on shifting rubber. He, too, went down and felt the sidewalk bucking and skating underneath him. His bag crashed down beside him and rolled over twice, clanking. He managed to push himself over on his back and sit up on scraped hands. Mrs. Frumpwooler was still hugging the walk, but other people getting off the bus by the front door, and a few others at the corner, were standing up. They were hanging on to each other, but they were standing up. The ground shook for another few seconds, then stopped.

The silence ended. Car alarms were going off everywhere. A siren wailed in the distance, then two, then twenty. People began running and shouting. Someone almost stepped on Mrs. Frumpwooler. Commander Blevins struggled to his feet and looked around at a crazed world. There was no apparent major sign of damage to the buildings nearby. No storefronts were collapsed, no piles of bricks were in the streets. The theater marquee for the Clay was still intact, though swaying a bit. All around them, though, was disarray and budding chaos. The neighborhood looked like a lady of the evening awakened suddenly in the late afternoon without a chance to straighten her hair or put on make-up. The newspaper machines at the corner were on their sides. Brooms and rolls of carpet and racks of magazines and barrels with knickknacks on them—all the things that held doors open and greeted customers entering the shops on Fillmore— these various and sundry things lay askew and fallen in doorways. Several plate glass windows were cracked. Plants hanging outside a little cafe lay broken on the side- walk, and tables were scattered and turned over.

Commander Blevins bent over to help Mrs. Frumpwooler.

"Dear God, are you OK, Mrs. Frumpwooler?" he cried. "Speak to me, speak to me." She groaned and rolled over. Terror colored her face.

"What? What was that!" she said.

He knelt down beside her. "An earthquake, I think. Are you all right?"

"My heart, my heart, is racing. I can't believe we've had an earthquake."

"Breathe deeply," he said and steadied her back as she tried to sit up. There was another shock, and the whole street screamed. It was short and less severe. The sun beat down on her, hot and oppressive.

"I'm hot, and my hands hurt," she said. They were sitting on the streets, two doors from a small coffee shop.

"See if you can stand, we might be able to sit down

in that shop. Maybe they have something to drink." He helped her up and walked the twenty paces very slowly to the storefront. Mrs. Frumpwooler hung tightly onto Commander Blevins.

The three MEs on Fillmore Street, and a couple of others around the corner on California, zoomed around nearly out of control. They had received substantial jolts of fear from their respective hosts, absorbed the terror of all the people in the area, and had been bombarded by the astronomically high energy release of the quake. Normally, a ME would be aware of and protect Itself from energies that came Its way from sources other than Its own light cord. The shock of the intense bolt of terror—without warning or logic—had fried all three MEs' borders. They were now acting like mad, suicidal fighting kites, that, of course, no one else could see. If any special people in the immediate area could see the unseen, they were well occupied otherwise.

"Come in. Come in." A man in an apron stood looking into his kitchen, bewildered. He had turned around when Commander Blevins had called out to him. "Please come in and make yourself comfortable. My other customers ran out screaming when it first hit." He saw that Mrs. Frumpwooler looked dazed and was being helped by Commander Blevins.

"Please, let me help you." He took Mrs. Frumpwooler by her other arm, and they guided her, crunching on glass and silverware, to a seat near the back and in the middle of the room. It was somewhat dark in the restaurant.

"Oh, thank you," Mrs. Frumpwooler said, pressing one hand to her breast and breathing deeply. Commander Blevins sat down next to her.

"Can I get you anything? Oh, I'm not sure what I have to offer." The man went in the back and began rummaging around. He called out, "The lemonade jar is not broken, here are some Danish, and...son of a gun...the coffee pot is unbroken and not a drop spilled. What would you folks like?"

"Some lemonade, please," Mrs. Frumpwooler whispered.

"She'll have the lemonade, and I'll have some coffee and a Danish," Commander Blevins yelled back to the man. All dietary bets were off during earthquakes.

The man brought out the pot of coffee, the jar of lemonade, three cups, three glasses, and a plate heaped high with sweet croissants, what he called "Danish." He wiped the dust and plaster off of the table, poured coffee and lemonade for all, and spread napkins out in front of both Commander Blevins and Mrs. Frump- wooler, taking great care to be sure no wrinkles remained. Then he put two rolls in front of each, using his fingers. Mrs. Frumpwooler and Commander Blevins were oblivious to his eccentricities. She drank the lemonade desperately, and he ate the two rolls in four bites and gulped the coffee. Then they stopped and looked at the man and each other and burst out laugh- ing. It was not a time for middle-of-the-road behavior.

Greeny was in desperate shape. It was still attached to Mrs. Frumpwooler, but so little energy came through that It had lost Its purpose and direction in life. It was sniffing anyone that passed by and running out abbreviated light cords whenever It detected a broken aura, which was quite often. Ember and Pins had found a wire above the street and sat two doors down from the restaurant. They were a little numb themselves and watched Greeny.

"What a circus that Crustacean is," Pins said.

"Yep," Ember replied. It burped.

Commander Blevins slowly regained his perspective. Could they go on? Should they go on? It was getting darker. He mulled these concerns over as silence fell in the disheveled restaurant. It sounded like bedlam outside. The shouts, clamor, sirens, car alarms, dogs barking, honking all sounded like a cacophony from hell.

Mrs. Frumpwooler was staring at him, looking a little less lost. "What are you thinking about, Commander?" she asked. Her voice was still raspy. He hesitated, then asked the man across the table if there were any more rolls.

"Oh sure, I'll check in back," he said and left the table.

Watching him as he walked behind the counter, Commander Blevins said, "I was wondering if we should go on or put things off for another day."

"Of course, I had forgotten. I was wondering if my house is all right."

"Oh yeah. We could go check. I don't know if the busses are running, though. Are you up to walking to the Marina?"

"I might be able to walk there, but I don't think I would then want to walk back." Mrs. Frumpwooler thought it over briefly. "I suppose it might be prudent to wait, but I would really like to know. And what's happened has happened. These things are over once they happen, aren't they?"

"Don't know. Don't know if anyone knows. I think the 1906 Quake was over after about a minute. But aftershocks are common," Commander Blevins said. "I wonder if our carriage house is still standing?"

"Oh. Oh, my!" Mrs. Frumpwooler's face turned inside out: from quiet shock and reviewing options in a detached way to gripped by fear that something might be taken from her—something she valued far more than her home and belongings. "Somebody might find the Diamonds just laying in a pile of bricks. Oh, Commander, we can't just leave them there for anyone to get!" Mrs. Frumpwooler's eyes were wide open and gleaming.

Greeny felt a summons from home. It was wanted after all, and It was being called with the strongest of voices.

"You have a point, Commander Blevins said.

"I have more than a point. We must get to the carriage house as soon as possible."

A minute later, a voice sounded from the back room, "I'll be right out with some candles, and I found some mor..." The man came out into the front of the restaurant and found it empty.

Commander Blevins and Mrs. Frumpwooler walked up Fillmore past Sacramento as briskly as they could. The Bus they had come on was gone, and there was no sign of another. The atmosphere was incredible. People were huddled around radios, laughing, crying, drinking. Two men were arguing with each other across the street in front of a liquor store. The sirens and alarms still wailed in the distance. They walked on. Commander Blevins carried the bag tight under one arm, and Mrs. Frumpwooler held his other arm.

"Lookeyloo. Lookeyloo. We're on the road again," Pins said.

"Yeah, and lookit old Greeny. Straightened up and flying right," Pins said. Greeny was back on course and hovering not far above Mrs. Frumpwooler. Its little bellows were pumping hard. The other MEs followed, lazily, but not missing anything.

The group reached Clay and turned east. It was dark.

THIRTY-FOUR
ON THE ROAD AGAIN

They passed some people sitting on a front step of a large house. A boom box sat in their midst. Commander Blevins and Mrs. Frumpwooler heard a voice from the radio say, "...are still trying to get confirmation of earlier reports. In an effort to prevent misinformation from causing unnecessary alarm, we are withholding specific reports until confirmed by two sources. We can tell you that at 5:04 pm today, an earthquake of an unknown magnitude hit the San Francisco Bay Area."

"No shit!" someone said.

"Shhh!"

"...been confirmed that the Bay Bridge has been damaged. We are not sure the extent of that damage at this time, but we urge everyone to avoid using any and all bridges unless entirely necessary. If you are not already in your car, stay where you are. We will be hearing from KNBR's Tom Rority, who has contacted the local civil defense authorities, in a few minutes. Tom will be bringing us specific updates and what is happening to stabilize the region and what each and everyone one of us can best do to help protect our families and ourselves and the..."

Commander Blevins and Mrs. Frumpwooler walked on. The radio faded behind them. At the next corner, they found their way blocked by the back of a large white building.

"Oh, that's the Pacific Medical something," Commander Blevins said. "Let's go that way." He pointed north, and they walked up a block to Washington Street. It was much different than Clay. There was no one around, and the houses were all dark. No flashlights or candles flickered.

"Pretty eerie," Mrs. Frumpwooler said.

"Yes, let's go on." They turned to the right and continued up Washington. Two blocks later, they were on the northwestern edge of Lafayette Park, and the City was beginning to unfold to the south...or parts of it. They got to Octavia--in the middle of the northern edge of the park--and stopped to look out over the hills and valleys of San Francisco. Where there was usually a panorama of street lights, signs, lighted homes, cars moving throughout the City: now there was only a patchwork of mostly black. A few areas still had electricity. Even those isolated pockets, however, seemed dimmer than usual. The rest of the City— and they could have seen most of it from where they stood—

was dark with slow-moving snakes of traffic, flashing red lights, and sirens. And car alarms. They shrilled like a chorus of synthesized cats, all with their tails caught in a slammed door.

The Bay Bridge was not flowing normally. It, too, was dark except for a block of red tail lights. The whole time Commander Blevins and Mrs. Frumpwooler looked at it, no headlights came over the bridge. They remained silent. Finally, Commander Blevins said, "Let's go." Fear and greed gripped Mrs. Frumpwooler. She walked beside Commander Blevins, very numb.

Greeny was in about the same shape, but for different reasons. After the burst of energy from Mrs. Frumpwooler had gotten Its attention, It stopped sniffing every aura in the neighborhood and followed her. When Mrs. Frumpwooler lost her momentum again, however, It also lapsed back into a haze. As the party left the summit of Lafayette Park, Greeny was maintaining sporadic focus and aimlessly following the group. The other twos MEs watched It curiously, staying far out of the way and prepared to do whatever was necessary should It turn aggressive and shoot a light cord in Commander Blevins' direction.

"Let's walk past the house on the far side of the street first," Commander Blevins said. They had reached Franklin, only one block past the park, and crossed it. There was no traffic, no one in sight, and only a couple of houses on the south side of Washington showed the flicker of candles through drawn curtains. Commander Blevins took Mrs. Frumpwooler by the elbow and guided her left, to the north, and switched sides so he would be next to the curb. They began walking up Franklin Street. The house was only a half a block away, and they could already see its large corner turret outlined against the sky, black against near black.

"I don't see any lights, do you?" Mrs. Frumpwooler said.

"No, I don't." They walked up the hill, their heads turning slowly as they both kept their eyes glued on the house. As they pulled even with it, they stopped.

"Can you see anything down the walkway?" Commander Blevins asked.

"No. It's dark."

"Great!"

"It's creepy around here."

Commander Blevins turned to her, releasing his hold on her elbow. "Gladys." He waited until he was sure he had her attention. "Do you want to retrieve your Diamonds?"

She said, "Yes," and then was quiet.

"Are you sure? We don't have to do this, you know?"

A low light shone from her eyes, then it began building. "What do you mean, 'We don't have to do this;' are you daffy? *Of course*, we do! Let's get on with it." Greeny perked up, and Mrs. Frumpwooler began marching across the street.

"Whoa, slow down." He caught her by the arm again and said, smiling, "Shouldn't cross the street without looking."

"What? No cars are coming, idiot." Greeny was juicing hard.

Commander Blevins was experienced, by now, with this side of Mrs. Frumpwooler. "You're right, no cars are coming. But let's look around a little bit more before we plunge ahead. Follow me." They walked back down Franklin until they were directly across from the driveway, which led up the steep entryway to the back of the property, along the southern side, and to the open end of the carriage house.

"I think the door is open," she said.

"I think so too. And I don't see anyone around." They looked at each other. "Let's check it out." Taking Mrs. Frumpwooler's hand, Commander Blevins crossed the street with his Client close on his heels. They walked up the front of the driveway. There was a flicker of candlelight from the second floor of the house next door. A cornice near its front corner was hanging crooked, vaguely defined in the dim reflected light from the sky. Everything else was black.

THIRTY-FIVE

ANY ONE HOME TONIGHT?

"I can't see. Didn't you bring your flashlight? I saw you buy one yesterday."

"I have it," he said, "but it's too soon to turn it on. We'll just stay on the driveway. Walk carefully." They reached the front edge of the carriage house and heard a shrill, metallic squeal. They stopped. Then the squeal repeated and was followed by a furious scratching. Mrs. Frumpwooler grabbed Commander Blevins, who was frozen. The MEs felt the energy shift and held their collective unseen breaths. Greeny, especially, sensed something unusual was afoot.

Suddenly, right in front of their faces, a dark pole separated from the corner of the carriage house with a loud tear and hovered in the blackness above their heads. It had a lumpy top. Then it came straight at them. It was as though the carriage house was reaching out to bat them away.

They moved just before the pole struck them. It crashed onto the concrete driveway with a hollow thud and bounced a few times, making a scratching sound. As it hit, the lumps at the top screeched, divided into two, and ran off. They were black blurs, but unmistakable.

"Oh, my!" Mrs. Frumpwooler said, clutching her breast and breathing hard.

"Cats!" Commander Blevins said, and walked to the pole on the ground, now laying silent on the drive. "On the downspout. Must have torn loose in the quake. Wonder what those two were doing clinging to it?"

"I don't know, and I don't want to know. Let's find the Diamonds!"

"Well, it's pretty clear that no one is around." He looked back over his shoulder at the neighbor's house. The candlelight still flickered, but no shadow appeared in the window. "Let's go this way. And take my hand." She did so without comment, and they walked gingerly on the grass around the street side of the carriage house. Its back corner was its closest point to the home and they came to a walk that connected the back wall to the back porch of the house. All the windows were dark.

"Do you remember this walk?" Commander Blevins said.

"Yes, I noticed it yesterday. It leads to a doorway in the back wall of the carriage house that should be just around the corner. Will you *please* turn on your flashlight!"

"All right, but only for a moment." Here hold this. He plopped the canvas tool bag in her arms before she was quite prepared.

"Oouufff."

"Sorry." He tore the zipper open and then froze. "God, that made a lot of noise." They stood still for a full minute, then he rummaged around inside carefully but still made a racket.

"Can't you do that quietly?" she whispered.

"I'm trying. Here." He pulled out the flashlight and turned it on. The middle of the backyard sprang at them. The birdbath now stood stark and naked in the empty little pool. He turned the light toward the wall. It was much the same as the day before, though it was tidier around the bottom and sides. Then he shut the light off.

"Why'd you do that. Now I can't see anything," Mrs. Frumpledorf said.

"Our night vision will come back in a minute. Let's just wait here to see if anyone appears. In fact, let's move down to the end of the wall." Commander Blevins squatted as though someone was watching and duck-walked the width of the back wall, touching it with one hand as he went. Mrs. Frumpwooler followed behind him, standing straight up, carrying the canvas bag. He got to the end of the wall, turned around, and stood up.

"What were you looking for?" she said.

"Looking...? I was trying to avoid detection. You didn't...."

"Well, I couldn't walk all silly and scrunched down like you carrying this bag!"

"Oh, forget it. Let's just stand here for a while. Don't say anything. And I'll take that."

"You're the one that's talking."

"Shhh." He took the canvas bag from her and set it on the ground near the wall's back corner. It clanked.

They stood without moving for what seemed like forever. Then Commander Blevins heard a soft voice somewhere nearby. It was saying something over and over. It got louder, and he whispered to Mrs. Frumpwooler, "Do you hear that?" She did not respond, so he leaned closer to her and started to repeat it. But he stopped, for when he put his head near hers—she was facing away from him—he heard the voice clearly. It was saying, "Diamonds, Diamonds, Diamonds," and was coming from her.

Unknown to both Commander Blevins and Mrs. Frumpwooler, Greeny was juicing in rhythm to Mrs. Frumpwooler's chant.

Commander Blevins snapped his fingers loudly and said, "Gladys!"

"Oh, what. Hello. Must have been daydreaming. Say, when are we going to get started. I don't think anyone is around here. They are all out there, running around in ambulances or stealing cars." The car alarms and sirens still dominated the background noise of the City.

"Well, I think you are right, for the most part, though I believe the earthquake is responsible for all the car alarms going off, not thieves. There's something

I want to do first before we begin dissecting this wall. Stay here for a moment."

He walked a couple steps toward the pond, turned the flashlight on to avoid falling in it. She said, "I'm not staying here by myself, buster," and followed along behind him. They made their way quickly across the back yard to the arched trellis and passed underneath it. A moment later, they were at the side door next to the buzzer box. Commander Blevins pushed the white button. Mrs. Frumpwooler held her breath.

"Hear that?" he said.

"Ahhh...what?"

"This." He buzzed the buzzer again.

"Oh, yeah." They listened to a faint ringing somewhere upstairs in the house as Commander Blevins pushed the little white button over and over again. Then he stopped.

"No one home tonight," he said.

"Goody!" she said.

"Let's get to work."

"Goody, goody!"

THIRTY-SIX
LET'S GET TO WORK

They walked quickly back through the arched
trellis, around the empty pool and birdbath, and
to the newly tuckpointed rear wall of the carriage
house.

Commander Blevins stopped and shone the flashlight on the wall. Then he turned to Mrs. Frumpwooler.
"Do you remember which bricks you took out?"

Mrs. Frumpwooler thought for a moment. "Well,
there were two of them, and they were both a little
darker than the rest, and they were about shoulder
high."

"Which part of the wall?"

"The back part, about there," she said and pointed.

He went over to the area she was pointing to, turned
back, and said, "Here?"

"You don't need to yell. Yeah, about." She was
standing right next to him. "I don't see any bricks that

are darker than the others, though. I guess they all might have darkened with age, do you think Commander?"

"Either that or they have all gotten lighter with wire brushing. I kind of doubt that, though." They stood looking at the wall, so close to their goal, yet so perplexed.

"We could just tear the whole wall down," Mrs. Frumpwooler said. "Oh, I do want those Diamonds. Please, Commander!" She grabbed his arm and began whining. Greeny increased its rhythm.

"Calm down, Gladys." She whined louder. He shouted, "Gladys!" and snapped his fingers directly in her face."

"Oh, what? Hello. When are we going to get started, Commander?"

Shaking his head, he said, "As soon as we figure...Wait! I've got it. You said shoulder height, right?"

"Yes, I can even remember going up on my tip-toes a little to push in the bag of Diamonds. Oh, Diamonds, Diamonds."

"Well, that's it," he said and shook her shoulders hard.

Gwenny was taller than you are now, right?"

"Oh, well, I never thought about it, but I suppose you are right. I was—Gwenny was— a big girl. She was taller than anyone in the household except the nephew of..."

"Never mind who she was taller than. *How* tall was she?"

"I don't remember. Tall. And don't get uppity with me, Ito-san. Don't *you* remember how tall Gwenny was? You were the one caught groping her. And you saw where the Diamonds were put as well as I, Commander Ito-san. How about earning your pay now and *finding those diamonds?*

Commander Blevins could see the veins sticking out on Mrs. Frumpwooler's neck. Before he snapped back at her, he caught himself and thought, "This is not a well woman." He said to her, "You are quite right, Madam. I shall earn my keep. Please stand back."

"Oh, no. I'm standing right here."

"Gladys. I'm going to be banging away at this mortar and these bricks with a twenty-ounce mason's hammer. If I strike a corner of a brick, which is highly likely, pieces of it will fly out at high speed. If one of those hits you anywhere, it will hurt. If a piece of brick strikes you in the eye, at best, you will lose the eye. At worst, you would be dead."

"Oh!"

"Mind moving back now?" He smiled sweetly.

"No, I think not." She moved back several paces.

"Oh, would you hold the light?" He held it out toward her. She stepped in to take it and moved back out of range quickly. "Please shine it on this part of the wall." He pointed to a spot that was off to his left and a little higher than his shoulders. He bent down to the bag. "Drat."

"What? Is something wrong, Commander?" Mrs. Frumpwooler was standing on her tip-toes, trying to see into the bag at his feet, but still keeping the light on the wall.

"No, I just can't see." He picked up the bag and moved it out in the yard to a spot halfway between where she stood and where he would be working. "That's better."

"Shall I shine the light," she said, turning the light on the bag.

"No! Keep it one the wall, please. I can see enough here." She directed the light back to the wall and was silent. The chant of "Diamonds, Diamonds, Diamonds," though, kept echoing through her mind.

He pulled out a pair of goggles and set them on the ground. Next, he found the hammer, two small chisels, a large flat bar, and a pair of gloves. The flat bar was not a standard masonry tool, but it had been a favorite all-purpose weapon when he used to do renovation projects. "What a long time it's been," he thought. He put on the goggles, then took them off and rummaged through a back pocket. It was still unusually warm. He pulled out a handkerchief, wiped off his forehead and face, then cleaned the goggles. They were smudgy.

Goggles on, but pushed back on his forehead; flat bar tucked in his belt and sticking out from under his jacket and coat; gloves and one chisel in his side pocket; the other chisel in his left hand and the hammer in his right: he approached the middle of the wall. Mrs. Frumpwooler held her breath. He felt the wall with three fingers of one hand and muttered under his breath.

"What was that, Commander?" she asked and exhaled loudly.

"Nothing, nothing. Just talking to myself. "Hold that light still, now, right about here." He pointed to a spot a couple feet to his right. "I can't find your dark bricks, but I'm going to try here." He placed the end of the round pointed chisel against an intersection of horizontal and vertical mortared groves. He braced himself and held the hammer over the end of the chisel. Just as he was about to swing, he stopped and wiggled his goggles into place. Another stance, and as he took a short backswing...he stopped again.

"Good grief, Commander!"

"Sorry Gladys, I forgot my gloves." The new leather gloves were stiff, and he struggled to put them on. Finally, ready again, he nodded back to her, as a pitcher might to his not-so-patient catcher, took his stance, and struck the chisel hard. A sharp metallic clang pierced the night. They both winced.

"Rats," he said and turned back to the canvas bag once again. This time he pulled out a three-inch leather cylinder with a small cap on it and a loop that a belt could thread through.

"What on earth is that?" Mrs. Frumpwooler asked.

"It's a carpenter's wooden match holder."

"A what?"

"I hadn't seen one in years. They're usually made out of metal to keep water out. This one is leather, like the one the man I learned carpentry from had. He put his wooden matches in it and carried them on his belt. He liked to strike them with his thumbnail in mid-air and light his cigar with a whoosh." He mimed his former boss.

"But what does that have to..."

"Watch." He opened the top of the little cylinder and bent the lid back as far as he could. Then he slid the match holder over the top and partway down the shaft of the chisel. "See." He held it up. "It will dampen the noise."

"If you say so."

"I do." He assumed his position and struck three quick blows. There was no sharp metal twang. Only a dull thud as the hammer met the leather, and the chisel bit into the mortar. He stopped for a moment, then continued. He hammered quickly and moved the chisel along as he went. White dust hovered in the air, and bits of mortar bounced off his coat. Soon he had dug an outline in the mortar around two bricks as deep as the chisel would go and began attacking the bricks them-selves. Then he went back to the bag, mimed a tip of his hat to Mrs. Frumpwooler, who stood mute, rocking back and forth on her toes, and dug around for the second chisel. Then he remembered it was in his pocket. Acting as though it was his plan all along, he pulled a handkerchief out of the bag, wiped his fore-head, and put it in another pocket. He was beginning to sweat under all his clothes. Back to the wall with the second chisel, a sharp-pointed one, he positioned it strategically against a brick, made one fast swing, and visibly winced again. Mrs. Frumpwooler sighed. Commander Blevins retrieved the other chisel and switched the leather match holder to the pointed chisel in his hand.

He set to work with a passion, turning small round holes into cracks in the first brick. Finally, it became a pile of pieces still held in place by the other bricks around it. He tossed the pointed chisel to the ground and pulled the flat bar out of his belt. It was a blue, eight-sided steel bar, about eighteen inches long. One end was flat, tapered to a sharp edge, and was notched to pull nails. The other end had a similar notch, but was bent at right angles to the shaft and was short and stubby. Commander Blevins jabbed the flat end between the brick pieces and began prying them out. At first, nothing came, then most of it tumbled out at once at his feet. He stopped and peered into the hole.

"Wonderful!" he said.

"Did you find it?" Mrs. Frumpwooler came running up behind him.

"No, I did not."

"Oh. What was wonderful then."

"That I did not find them."

"How could that be? I don't understand you some-times, Commander."

"If the bag of Diamonds had been behind this first brick, they would have been scattered over half this yard. This way, I can carefully work my way out from this hole until I find them, or until the wall is down."

"I'm sure you'll find them. I just know it." There was an electric calmness about Mrs. Frumpwooler.

"Well, let's hope you're right." Over the next twenty minutes, he removed six more bricks. His only hold-up was in finding the pointed chisel. He rummaged through all his pockets and the canvas bag twice before he kicked it where he had thrown it on the ground.

As he removed the seventh brick, a shiny pebble dropped out from behind the brick above. He stopped it with his hammer and looked at it.

"Here's something. But I don't think it's one of your Diamonds. It looks soapy."

"Oh! Oh! Oh! Let me see!" Mrs. Frumpwooler flew across the few steps separating them. "Oh, that's it. That's one of them. I remember old man Von Blume saying they were uncut. Malvandian used to dabble in precious gems, too. Ouououuouweeeee!" She was dancing and squealing at the same time.

Greeny was doing half-ganers from the low peaked roof over the back porch, floating down, and then doing it again. The other two MEs were looking on dispassionately. This was Greeny's show. Their host wasn't doing anything but wearing himself out.

Commander Blevins watched Mrs. Frumpwooler, shook his head, and turned back to the wall. He couldn't see anything.

Mrs. Frumpwooler was dancing with the flashlight.

"Gladys! Gimme that, will you!"

"Oh, well sure. A girl can't have any fun around you."

He took the light and shined it up and under the

bricks which spanned the empty row he had excavated. There was a larger than a normal blob of
mortar at a back corner where one brick met the
next brick on its course. He poked at the mortar.
Nothing. He poked harder. It gave way suddenly, and
a stream of little soapy, slightly shiny pebbles
dropped out, bounced on the bricks below, and fell at
his feet.

"Jackpot."

"Whoopee. Goody. I'm rich! I'm rich! Oh, don't lose
any. Here, I'll get those. Where's a bag. Why did the bag
break? How much do you think they are worth. Oh, I'm
so happy. Thank you, thank you, thank you."
Commander Blevins was frozen in amazement that he
had actually found the Diamonds and in befuddled awe
at Mrs. Frumpwooler's stream of chatter.

She probably would have talked forever, but a siren
suddenly went by very near the house, and they both
froze. As it moved on down Franklin toward the
Marina, they relaxed and laughed.

Commander Blevins pulled a small canvas draw-
string bag and a plastic bag out of the large canvas bag
and said, "Here, put them in this."

Mrs. Frumpwooler took the small bag and began
pouring the Diamonds in her hand into the bag. She
mumbled, "Thanks."

He went back to the wall and, holding the plastic
bag underneath the brick and over his large pocket,
began digging around the hole. More Diamonds and
mortar fell and bounced into the bag. Then they

stopped. Finally, a rotten and shredded piece of cloth came floating down from the bricks.

"The bag." He said, holding it up for her to see.

"Screw the bag. Did you find any more Diamonds?"

"Just these," he said quietly.

"Great, you are a peach." She grabbed the plastic sack, stuck it, and the little draw-string purse in her bosom and head for the arched trellis.

"Where are you going?"

"Home." She was through the trellis and walking hard down the narrow walkway that ran beside the house.

He ran after her, but stopped at the trellis and called, "Don't you want me to come with you." He heard a distant, "No, I'll call you," then her voice faded out as she went down the front steps and across Franklin Street.

Greeny pranced over the high roof and did several barrel rolls off the high corner turret in the front of the house.

"Boy, there's one stoked dude," Pins said.

"Glad that's over," Ember said.

Commander Blevins shone his light around the little backyard and felt very alone. He began picking up tools and pulled out a small dustpan and brush. He swept all the fine mortar up into a little pile and then arranged the bricks in a ragged pile underneath the hole in the wall. It wasn't a full hole, just one layer deep. He sprinkled some of the mortar onto the pile and around the area. The rest he put into his bag. When he had everything loaded up, he turned off the flashlight and made his way out to the front of the house.

The air was charged with a wildness he had never felt. A great cloud of smoke hung in the sky north of him. He wondered what was burning. The shriek of sirens hit him like a visible slap. He realized he had heard only one since they had arrived. Car alarms whined in the distance.

THIRTY-SEVEN
DIAMONDS IN THE SKY

Mrs. Frumpwooler turned left when she crossed Franklin and walked to the corner at Jackson Street. Sirens of all types were shrill in her ears: some near, some far. She stopped for a moment and debated whether to walk or take the bus. Was the bus still running? She looked down Jackson toward Van Ness. It was choked with traffic. Franklin Street was nearly deserted. She wondered why. No cars had passed by earlier in the evening when she and Commander Blevins had staked out the house. She thought of the house. She looked back for a moment. The corner turret was outlined against the dark sky. Memories flooded her of Gwenny, leaving the house in disgrace. Her body shook for a moment, like a dog just in from the rain. She turned away from the house, away from the noise and blare of Van Ness, and walked briskly across Jackson and on down the long sloping hill of

Franklin Street as it ran toward Lombard and Fort Mason.

Two blocks later, she looked up and saw the sky filled with smoke. It looked bizarre against the night sky, like black ink billowing up across a charcoal back-drop. Where was it coming from?

Fear seeped in, fear for her home and all the precious things she kept there. She clutched her bosom and the Diamonds. They shifted, feeling like rough-edged marbles rubbing against each other. Precious little rough-edged marbles.

Something she had heard on a radio at the center of a knot of people they had passed during their walk from Fillmore to the house echoed through her mind—something about the Marina. Suddenly she missed Commander Blevins. Should she go back? Would he still be there? No, she decided to continue. He was the only one that knew about the Diamonds. She wanted to get them safely tucked away before anyone else knew she had them. The bus would be faster. No one would know on the bus. And she was tired. Abruptly tired. Energy drained out of her. She turned to her right and headed for Van Ness.

Greeny was not tired. Greeny was high as life itself and bounding from one roof peak to another, delirious.

Commander Blevins was not high. He did not look back at the house as he left it, nor did he flash on Ito, Gwenny, or Frau Swope. Something nagged at him. Feeling alone was not new for him and, although never fun, he had learned to manage his emotions rather well in the years he had been ill.

This alone was different, as though something was missing. Something he had not previously been aware of having, or of its absence. Light burst at him from the shadow of a doorway. It lingered for a moment, then vanished. Blinking, only the darkness remained.

He reached Van Ness about the same time Mrs. Frumpwooler did, but five blocks south of her. He had turned away from the smoky black-on-black sky to the north. Van Ness was a circus. He was shocked at the difference between it and Franklin. The electricity was off, of course, and only motor coaches were running. But the din! People were everywhere with flashlights, lanterns, spotlights. Many businesses were lit up with improvised light sources, keeping a vigil against possible looting. He saw a 42 Downtown go by, heading north. It was overflowing with people. Two buses were pulled over to the curb, empty and silent. He walked over, curious. They were trolleys that pulled their power down through spring-loaded arms that glided against the underside of the overhead wires running throughout much of the City.

These same overhead wires, strung in pairs over both traffic directions, were the bane of San Francisco Firemen. You had to be an exceptional Firefighter to dodge all the overhead utility wires in the City, bring the fires under control, and not fry yourself or a fellow Fighter. As Commander Blevins and Mrs. Frumpwooler planned to head in opposite directions on Van

Ness, the Firemen and women of San Francisco were tackling their most significant challenge in eighty-three and a half years.

Mrs. Frumpwooler squeezed on the bus. She wasn't sure which one it was: that didn't matter. All that mattered was that it was heading north, and there was a space for her. The first three buses to pass were so full the doors couldn't close.

"Would you like to sit down, dear?"

The voice startled Mrs. Frumpwooler, coming from her elbow. Or so it seemed. She peered around and moved her arm.

"You look all done in." A clean-cut young man stood up and made room for her to sit down.

"Oh, why, thank you. Yes, I am tired. It has been a day to remember, I'll say," she said, sitting down.

"I think we can all say that," the young man said. Mrs. Frumpwooler looked at him again. There was a strange glow in his eyes, they were wet, and he was half-smiling, almost a smirk, but not quite.

The bus lumbered along Van Ness. Mrs. Frump-wooler looked out the window on the downtown side and saw blackness just past Polk Street, one block east. It spread out forever.

Greeny dipped and sailed along behind, over and ahead of the bus. It stretched itself out into a flying wedge and cavorted in the unseen breeze blowing off the Bay.

A few blocks later, Lombard Street rolled past. This was the intersection where the residential Lombard ended suddenly. The commercialism of Highway 101 grew along Lombard like a fetid blight from Van Ness west, across the Marina. 101 then jogged, shaking off the stores and neon, and continued through the Presidio and over the Golden Gate Bridge to Marin County. Mrs. Frumpwooler looked at the calm, and now wholly dark, side of the street. She remembered how much Malvandian had enjoyed turning here, driving all around Russian Hill, always to end up at Lombard and Hyde. He would then, with glee, point the car down the hill and snake through the many switch-backs of what the tourist brochures called the "Crookedest Street in the World." It was a funny thing for a man who disdained almost all other visitor attractions to enjoy. Dimly, she realized she needed to get off the bus soon.

A block later, she pulled the cord above the window and was let out at Francisco Street. She waited behind the bus for it to leave and then gasped. The Marina was covered with black smoke. It was thick in the air. No buses ran on Francisco, and she did not think of checking on Chestnut, a block south. She began walking with her eyes on the column of smoke in the distance. It was about where the Palace of Fine Arts stood. "Oh, I hope its all right," she said to herself. She also said a prayer for her home, a third story stucco flat on Broderick near Beach, only a block from the grounds of the Palace of Fine Arts and right where the blackest of the smoke was coming from.

It was dark, and yet people were still loading up cars

as though they were all going on vacation at the same time.

"Ridiculous," she thought. "They ought to stay here and protecting their homes." Their homes looked fine to her, in the dark.

Then she ran into the Moscone Recreation Center and had to detour around it. Turning left meant Chestnut Street, and it seemed loud over there. She turned right. One block later, she turned left on Bay Street: another strangely quiet area. A corner of Fort Mason touched the Rec Center here, forming a narrow pass for her to cross, from one mini-neighborhood to another. The sounds of the City reeling from the earthquake faded a little. She walked along Bay Street, past the Rec Center, and was aware of noise and flashing lights coming from Lombard. She walked another block to Cervantes and turned onto it. It ran toward the Bay at an angle. There were more people around, but she hurried by them. She noticed a dark pile of something on the sidewalk across the street. A block later, she angled back to her left.

The smoke was getting closer. She could see some flames now and then. As she got still closer, she saw an outline of a rooftop sitting at an unusual angle against the sky, backlit by the fire. Another shape caught her eye off to the left. With it came a sound that she had never heard before. The way roots hang-on and then snap one by one when a stump is being ripped from the earth: that was the feeling of the sound. Only the sound was coming from above ground, too, and there were many awful squeaks and rips and crashes. She looked left and stopped immediately. Three houses up the street—what street? She had no idea. There was a short house sitting, no sliding into the middle of the road. It had a roof with the regular projections, but it also had a jumble of juts and protrusions underneath it. And it seemed to be riding on this mass of chaos...riding into the street, in slow motion. She couldn't watch it anymore.

Her fright finally punctured Greeny's euphoria. It sensed that Its host felt threatened and hovered closer to her, oblivious to the physical upheaval.

Mrs. Frumpwooler crossed Divisadaro and froze. A whole line of three-story flats were crumpled. They looked like little stick boxes that had been carelessly dumped by a small child. The fire was just beyond this block, and a group of Firemen was unrolling hoses. "Why aren't they over *there*, fighting the fire?" she thought.

"Hey, you, get out of here," one of the Firemen said.

Mrs. Frumpwooler hit full speed in one stride. She didn't run. Dignified middle-age women don't run, but she was going to be hard to catch.

Beyond the fire was the Palace of Fine Arts. She could not see it, but she knew it was there. Between it and the fire was her home, her home sweet home. She prayed the fire had not reached it yet.

Somewhere behind her, a man yelled, "You can't go in there! The whole block's going to blow!" Mrs. Frumpwooler broke into a run. Dignity had no place at that moment. At the next corner, a gas main was spewing mud and gas fifteen feet into the air. It smelled horrible. She veered away from it and turned left, heaving hard. The Diamonds banged her chest and hurt.

Greeny was almost still, directly above her.

Looking down and across the street, several houses away, she saw the little greenhouse jutting from her bay window. It was always a landmark to her and had been installed at considerable expense. She hoped her garden of herbs and orchids had not been traumatized by all the craziness. If she could just ride out this horror, all would be well.

She stopped in front of her door and was stunned. She had not thought of her purse since she had left Commander Blevins' apartment. Did she even bring it with her? Not having her keys, though, was academic. The front door to her home stood wide open. "Vandals," she thought. But peering inside the door, she saw that the wall had buckled and popped open the door. Plaster and dust covered the steps leading up to her apartment. She took one step, then another, then a third. It felt solid, and she turned the landing with her hopes mounting that all would be right.

It happened with a slow-motion quickness that is hard to comprehend and even harder to tell about later. To the people standing behind the barricades two blocks away and the Firefighters as close as half a block, the line of townhouses built wall-to-wall went up in one huge fireball. But it only seemed to happen that way. The house at the corner, down from Mrs. Frump-wooler's flat, was the first to go. It raised into the air several feet then flew apart in a mass of splinters. The flames followed the explosion. As it rose in the air, just before it disintegrated, the house next to it began to lift off its foundation. The force of the explosion rolled down the street, popping townhouse after townhouse like bubbles blown too big. It happened so quickly it seemed to happen all at once.

Mrs. Frumpwooler heard a sharp clap, then was swept away in a firestorm. In that briefest of moments, her Inner Vision opened up to a different view of the Marina, a view from the top of Divisadero looking down at the Bay. There was no Marina Green or arcing concrete finger enclosing Aquatic Park; there was no pastel patchwork of three story townhouses; there was no neon bustle of Lombard Street: only the tidal marshes. The tidal marshes that were later filled, paved over, and built upon becoming San Francisco's Marina District. Those same landfilled marshes had now shaken like unset jello, bringing the force of the earthquake to bear on the Marina residents in unforgettable fashion.

Somewhere in an area of several square blocks, someone surely found one of the soapy little stones. Perhaps more than one was found. If any of these Diamonds ever found their way to jewelers or gem merchants, though, it was discreetly done.

THIRTY-EIGHT

GUILT AND KARMA

Commander Blevins' homecoming was not as eventful as Mrs. Frumpwooler's. He reached his apartment tired, bewildered, soaked with sweat, and collapsed into his overstuffed chair without turning on a light or taking off more than his coat and second jacket. If he had turned on the lights, it would have been futile. There was no electricity.

600 Page Street was structurally unaffected by the earthquake. The contents did not fare so well. In apartment 307, the kitchen and dining room were covered with broken glass, mostly brown. Commander Blevins kept his small bottle collection on the top shelf of the high cabinets at the far end of the kitchen. During the first year and a half of his illness, he had taken large amounts of vitamin C. Later, he cut down to more normal levels. It was one of the first tools he had found to combat the ongoing

cycle of virus symptoms, and he had used it with his standard approach to life: taking it to an extreme. The vitamin C helped with the symptoms, for a while, but his body was knocked further out of whack by the heavy doses. The balance was still proving to be elusive.

The entire collection of little and medium-sized brown bottles, all with their labels soaked off and the black lids stored separately in a yogurt tub, flew out of the top shelf when the first jolt hit. Either the bottles knocked the cabinet doors open, or the doors were flung open themselves by the quake. Whichever way it happened, for the quarter minute the ground shook, the kitchen had become a war zone of shrapnel from flying and shattering little brown bottles.

All the adding machine parts from the kitchen table were scattered like sewn seeds. Earring supplies from the china cabinet were also spilled onto the floor. They had hung on for several jolts, before those doors finally opened, and then slopped onto the floor like someone had emptied a wastebasket in an unusual place. The containers of concentrated jewelry cleaner and grease solvents were on their sides and, thankfully, still sealed.

The main room was disheveled, but not dangerous. Commander Blevins was a sparse, functional decorator and had no breakable brick-a-brack in his apartment. There was a large pile of papers and magazines scattered around his desk, near the window. The walk-in closet was now a wade-in closet, and the little wicker cabinet in the bathroom next to the tub was on its face.

Bath Therapy was spilled across the floor, which he had yet to discover.

None of this, however, had made an impression on him. It was too dark to see, he was too tired to even go to the bathroom, which he needed to, and he was now sound asleep and heading toward morning and a backache.

It was a wild night on Page Street in the Lower Lower Haight. Few people wanted to go inside. Women were propositioned openly. Men were threatened. Drugs traded hands. Many people who lived there went somewhere else that night to be with friends, or just to be somewhere else. Some did not come home for two or three days. There was a feeling in the air that tonight was the last night. The big one had come, and now civilization was toppling.

Commander Blevins transferred himself from the chair to his bed a while later without waking. He tossed and turned. He snored, which he rarely did, and he dreamed. In the last dream before waking in the middle of the night he was with a black-haired young woman. They were about to get in the shower together. She had told him Zander was waiting outside. In the dream, it had been years since he had seen his old friend and yet only a day since he had showered with Andi, who was now Zander's wife. He knew why Zander was there.

"He will wait," he said to the black-haired girl in the dream. They got in the shower and started to soap each other. The phone rang in the distance. He stepped outside of the shower and found himself standing by a coffee table in his living room. Zander was lying on the floor at its end, propped up against the edge of the sofa, asleep. Commander Blevins prepared himself to face his old friend and the consequences of giving in to temptation. But he could not remember the prelude to getting into the shower with Andi. He only remembered being there with her. Zander opened his eyes. They were set farther apart than normal and were cat-like slits. Clear, light grey eyes stared out at him, shining with pain and murderous anger. Commander Blevins recoiled in fear.

His physical world phone rang loudly. Commander Blevins came out of his sleep and looked around him, caught between two realities. The phone was next to his bed, which seemed unusual, and on the hook. He answered it. It was a wrong number. He hung up and fell back into bed, staring into the darkness. He could hear voices and rap music from the street below. He drifted back into a not-here, not-there haze. His body was throbbing with a hard, jarring pulse.

Guilt, consequences, and apprehension flooded through Commander Blevins. He did not buy into the concept of guilt, but it thrashed around inside of him just the same. He had not slept with Andi in the physical world, but his long-standing desire for her nagged at him. Could intent trigger guilt?

*** some rewriting starting here

Consequences, on the other hand, were very real to him. The goes-around-comes-around shorthand for Karmic entanglements was evident in his life.

Reviewing his most recent set of choices, he felt he had really messed up. His ability to venture into the Inner Worlds had simply settled onto him a few years ago without his seeking it or having more than fragmentary preparation. It was an on-the-job-training he had eagerly jumped into and was only now beginning to see its destructive potential.

Half pondering his unfulfilled desire, he floated through his haze, unaware of either the three diamonds that had earlier fallen unseen into his coat pocket or the shadow of shimmering light forming in the center of his room. Had he a clearer Inner Vision at the moment, he would have seen the outline of a man appearing in the sparkly light.

In his state of half sleep, he did hear the man say in an inner voice, "Your choices, so far, have kept you in a circle of lower Karma. It really isn't as bad as all that. That's how Soul learns, how It matures. When you travel to the Inner Worlds with your Clients, you find yourself knowing things you didn't realize you knew. That's how it happens when awareness expands. It is a very natural process."

The man continued, "You have been using your gift for material gain, however, and traveling throughout the Psychic Circus. The effect on your Clients has been dubious and unpredictable at best. There are enough Charlatans around today without you wasting your gift, adding to the confusion. We pay for everything we do and get. Cause and effect are not negotiable.

"Balance is essential. The act of balancing is ongoing. When extremes are chosen, like a metronome set to full swing, balance is passed through only so often. When the swing to each polarity is shorter, balance is passed through more often. Contemplate your choices more wisely, and you will contribute more good and less turmoil."

After a period of silence, the man spoke again, this time in a fading whisper, "I am always with you. Like a Shadow. A Shadow of light." As quickly as he had appeared, the man was gone, leaving behind a gentle mist of sparkles.

Commander Blevins intuitively digested the man's message, which felt familiar and encouraging, as well as emphasizing that he had messed up. There was also a surprising amount of warmth and affection radiating from the man and his voice. As he lapsed back into full slumber, the feeling that he had a lot to answer for settled over him.

The City around him writhed in chaos. Mrs. Frumpwooler was on her way to her next lifetime, with a now scheduled layover in the Reflection Pool of Infinite Responsibility. Commander Blevins' immediate future was less well defined, though full of possibilities.

About the Author

BC embraces life's adventures by focusing more on what he is doing than what he has. Relying on spiritual awareness, often called intuition, helps him to see the hidden lessons behind everyday encounters. Learning (still!) that ignoring this inner guidance often makes the road rougher to travel, he accepts opportunities to unfold however they come.

When asked about his writing, he explains, *"Forty years ago, I found I had little to write about. Ten years later, I began to develop my writer's voice."* Today BC lives in Honolulu with his lovely wife Sweetie, delving into his personal experiences and imagination through his writing.

www.bccowling.com